LOVER FROM THE WAVES

THE KRAKEN #7

TIFFANY ROBERTS

LOVER FROM THE WAVES

A lonely widow. A determined kraken. An attraction they can't resist

Long ago, the sea took Kathryn's husband. She never thought it would give anything back. But now that her children are grown with little ones of their own, she finds her eyes drawn more and more to those restless waters—and she sees part of herself reflected in them. Something out there calls to her.

She yearns to discover what it is.

What she didn't expect was the attention of a kraken with golden eyes, sculpted muscles, and a heated stare that makes her melt. Ector reawakens a passion in Kathryn she'd thought long gone. When he accompanies her on her journey into the unknown, she can't help but wonder if what she wanted—and needed—is right in front of her.

Cover Illustration & Chapter art by Fadhila Inès (IF_Art)

Character Portrait by Marespinosa

❀ Formatted with Vellum

To our wonderful readers. Thank you for taking a chance on our kraken—and on us.

CHAPTER 1

365 Years After Landing

"And when the heroine found the missing youngling, she knew she could not wait for help—because there was a monster in those waters," Ector said, flashing his sharp teeth and raising his hands to brandish his claws.

The younglings—both human and kraken—gathered on the sand in front of Ector gasped, staring at him with awed, frightened eyes. Sarina and Jace, two of the half-kraken, half-human children, clasped each other's hands.

Ector rose on his tentacles, spread his arms, and drew in a deep breath, swelling himself as big as possible. He ignored the dull aches those simple movements produced in his joints. "The beast was immense, as long as the dock, and had teeth longer than a grown human stands tall. It was covered in spikes as sharp as harpoons, and its terrible eyes were red as blood." He changed his skin to crimson.

Several of the younglings recoiled, but they all remained transfixed. Ector was glad most of these children knew razorbacks as nothing more than monsters in stories. That was likely to change for many of them as they grew, but he wouldn't allow his thoughts to follow that path; this wasn't a tragic story.

"But worst of all," he continued, "that monster was hungry—and it had a taste for little kraken. Our heroine had never fought such a foe before, but she remembered its eyes—because this beast had chased her and her mate through the depths, its eyes glowing red with savage hunger, and they had only barely escaped."

"Did she grab the kraken youngling and run?" asked Emma, one of the human children.

"No. She knew she could not flee that monster. It had nearly caught the Wanderer already, who was one of the fastest kraken. But our heroine was brave, and she could not leave anyone to such a fate, especially a youngling." Ector flashed scintillating colors over his skin and curled his hands into loose fists, tucking his bent arms against his sides. "So she challenged the beast."

"What? No," said Eros, Sarina's younger brother. "She couldn't beat that thing. That's crazy, Elder Ector."

"She knew she could not beat it, but that was not her goal. The monster snapped its massive head toward her"—Ector turned his head aside and swung it forward, opening his mouth to display his pointed teeth again—"and gnashed its wicked teeth. Cold fear pooled in the heroine's belly as she looked into those ravenous, merciless eyes."

"But you said she was brave. How could she be afraid?" asked the little human girl, Megan.

Ector smiled. "She was very brave, little one. Are any of you ever afraid?"

A few of the younglings hesitantly raised their hands. Nearly all the children stared at Ector in shock when he lifted his hand, too.

"I have been afraid many times," he said.

"But...you're so *old*," said Jace incredulously.

Ector laughed. He wished his people had had more reason to laugh in the years before they'd connected with the humans of The Watch; it felt good. "I am old, but age does not stop fear. There is no shame in being afraid. Even big Dracchus is afraid, sometimes."

"Uncle Drak is the biggest and the strongest! No way he gets scared," declared Eros.

"He does, little one. Everyone does." Ector spread his tentacles and sank low, leaning closer to his audience. "But we all have it in us to be brave, regardless. *Brave* does not mean you have no fear. It means you do not let fear stop you. It means you still act no matter how scared you are."

"So, I can be brave, too?" asked little Megan.

"Absolutely, little one. Brave and strong, in your own way." Ector wrinkled his brow and moved his hand to his chin. "Now, where were we? Was it the part where the monster eats our heroine?"

The chorus of emphatic protests from the younglings made Ector chuckle. He lifted his hands, holding his palms toward the children. "You are right, that is not how our story goes."

When they quieted, he continued.

"She caught the beast's attention, and despite being so afraid, she did not freeze. She told the youngling to race home. Then the beast charged the heroine, opening wide its toothy jaws. She swam for shelter in the rocks on the sea floor, and just as she reached them"—he spread his arms, one high and one low, and slapped his hands together, making the younglings gasp and jump—"the monster caught her leg between its teeth."

Ector swung his arms in wide, exaggerated swimming motions. "She struggled to escape, but the beast was too strong. She kicked at the monster's face desperately. When her foot caught the monster in the eye, it let out a roar of pain that rippled across the entire sea. Those massive jaws opened"—he brought his hands together, fingers bent like hooked teeth, and drew them apart again—"and she was suddenly free. But the beast rounded on her, determined to finish what it had started.

"She drew her gun and fired, but the monster didn't slow. Yet even when her gun was empty, she didn't give up. She drew her knife"—he held up his left hand and straightened his little finger, stretching his webbing tight—"and fought the beast."

"That tiny little knife couldn't kill a monster that big," said Ben, one of the human younglings.

Sarina's eyes lit up. "But it did."

"No way," Ben replied.

"She is right, young one," Ector said, smiling. "Our heroine slayed the beast with that little knife and saved the youngling's life—because she was brave and protective and did not surrender. And it was our brave heroine who set into motion all the events that eventually brought kraken and humans together."

Eros's brow wrinkled. "Hey…that story's about my mom!"

"Your mommy fought a giant sea monster?" asked Megan.

Sarina nodded. "She even has a scar on her leg where it bit her."

The younglings erupted into enthusiastic chatter, and Ector couldn't help laughing again. These children played together freely, seemingly oblivious to the differences between them—or perhaps they were aware but indifferent. Either way, they served as an example to the adults of their respective species. Coexistence and cooperation were both possible and beneficial to everyone.

If only the few individuals of either species who still viewed this new society with mistrust could learn from these younglings.

"All right, little ones," Ector called over the din of conversation, "I believe Randall and Dracchus are nearly ready to begin the land and sea relay. You had best head over to him if you wish to participate."

The children climbed onto feet and tentacles and scurried across the sand, charging toward Randall, Dracchus, and the group of adults and younglings that had formed around them. Seeing them all laughing together warmed Ector's hearts and made his chest swell with pride. This new unity, this new joy, had become one of his favorite things about living in The Watch these last two years.

He let his gaze wander across the beach. There were dozens of people here today, humans and kraken together. Many adults were still sitting at the tables where everyone had shared in a huge meal less than an hour ago, and many more were scattered nearby, laughing, talking, and playing games alongside younglings like it was the most natural thing in the world. A few short years ago, Ector could never have imagined anything like this.

"The size of the dock, huh?" asked a familiar voice.

Ector turned his head to find Macy approaching him, a warm, amused smile on her lips, and her youngest daughter, little Amelia, in her arms.

"That thing gets bigger every time you tell the story," she said. "Next time, it'll be big enough to have swallowed the whole Facility in one gulp."

Chuckling, Ector shook his head. "That will take at least two or three more retellings, dear Macy. Such embellishment is a gradual process."

She laughed, and the sound coaxed a wide smile from Amelia, who stared up at her mother with wide green eyes like Macy was her entire world.

"I'm not a hero," Macy said. "I just did what I thought was right."

"Exactly. And everything you did—and Jax, Arkon, Aymee, all of you—brought us to here and now. Brought us to peace and prosperity. You deserve praise for all you have done."

Macy's cheeks reddened. "Like you said…it wasn't only me. You were part of it, too."

"A very small part, perhaps."

Farther down the beach, Randall called out instructions to the many younglings who'd gathered to participate in the race—including Sarina and Eros, the older two of Macy's younglings. Her mate, Jax, was there as well, making lines in the sand with his tentacles to help everyone assume their positions. The race would take place on land and sea in several phases, working from the youngest children up to full grown adults, alternating between kraken and humans.

"Do not let me keep you, Macy," Ector said. "They will be racing soon. I have been told Sarina is the favorite in her grouping."

"Yes, to Jace's annoyance," Macy said with a chuckle. "He always wants to be teamed up with her. It's adorable how disgruntled he gets when he doesn't have her full attention. He's very protective of her." She tilted her head. "You're going to come watch, aren't you?"

"I would not miss it. But I will catch up shortly." He rolled his shoulders. "I fear I require a bit of time to…catch my breath after story time."

Macy offered him a bright smile. "Okay. See you soon, Ector."

Giggling, Amelia waved a chubby little hand at Ector as Macy carried her away. Ector raised his own hand and wiggled his webbed fingers in response. He watched them go for a few seconds before he dragged himself toward the water, stopping only when the surf flowed, cool and refreshing, around his tentacles.

Ector filled his lungs with the sweet, briny air and stared out across the waves. The sun would set in a few hours, casting everything in brilliant reds and oranges as it sank, but for now its bright rays gleamed on the water's surface like countless sparkling stars. For some reason, a saying drifted through his thoughts—*reclaimed by the sea*. That was what his people said of the dead.

He frowned. Was anything as vast, beautiful, and ravenous as the ocean? According to Arkon, the sea, in its insatiable hunger, was even slowly devouring this beach, stripping it away a few grains of sand at a time.

"You do not have me yet," Ector muttered.

This change of demeanor was out of place after the fun and delight of a couple minutes before, but he thought he understood it—such introspective, sometimes grim moods had become increasingly common for him as of late.

Turning away from the sea, he looked at the people who'd come together today in celebration, at kraken and humans embracing both each other and a tradition that had existed in The Watch for many generations—Dryfall, which marked the end of the stormy season.

All the people gathered here had become neighbors, friends, *family* in the three years since the kraken first came to The Watch to make peace—and it was beyond the scope of even Ector's wildest imaginings. Living alongside humans went against everything his people had believed for hundreds of years. But the good that had come from it was apparent; the kraken were connected, happy, and thriving like never before.

This situation had been shaped by a group of males who were half Ector's age, males Ector had taught while they were younglings. And it was those younger males who would lead the kraken into a bright new future.

There was a small chance he'd sired one or more of those kraken—Jax, Arkon, Rhea, Dracchus, Kronus, Vasil, or at least a dozen others of their generation—but it didn't matter if he had. When he looked upon them, he was filled with pride of the same sort human parents sometimes displayed for their children. It was an oddly bittersweet sentiment.

For the first time in his life—which had spanned at least sixty years—Ector wasn't sure what role he was meant to fulfill. His purpose had always been to serve his people in whatever capacity would best benefit them. But looking at them now... What more could he offer? They had ample access to food and shelter thanks to their friendship with the humans, and old, advanced technologies were slowly beginning to reemerge thanks to the work of Arkon, Theodora, and the computer, Kane, who was implanted in the human woman. The kraken were prosperous. Their survival had become much less of a struggle.

What did that mean for Ector? He'd accepted so many drastic changes over the last few years, but this latest realization felt at once subtler and more powerful than all the rest. If his people didn't need him, what was he to do?

Those thoughts led to a question he'd never asked himself —*What do I* want *to do?*

That question was both liberating and terrifying.

Unbidden, his wandering gaze halted on one of the female humans in the crowd that had formed to spectate the race. Her name was Kathryn. She worked as a seamstress, though she often lent a hand in the fields. He'd spoken to her briefly on a few occasions—just as he'd spoken to most of the people in town—when she'd delivered food to the fishermen and dock-workers, many of whom she was very friendly with.

She was older—though Ector was sure he was still several years her senior—and her hair was an alluring silver; even now, his fingers itched with longing to comb through those shining strands. The few lines on her face only enhanced her beauty, and the joyful light in her bright blue eyes had always drawn his attention.

What do I want?

The question seemed heavier now.

Kathryn was standing with her daughters, smiling while the

younger women directed their children to their places for the relay race. The same sort of pride he felt for the kraken he'd taught was reflected in Kathryn's face as she watched her children and their younglings.

Without meaning to, Ector moved toward her. It had been a long while since he'd pursued a female, and longer still since he'd mated, but the old kraken concept of mating wasn't on his mind. What would it be like to have a mate the way the humans did? In the way Jax, Arkon, and all the others did? What would it be like to have lasting, meaningful companionship?

What would it be like to put an end to this nagging sense of loneliness, this deepening lack of purpose? For once in his life, he could do something not for his people but for himself.

Before he reached Kathryn, the relay began. The various legs were covered by children of increasing age, starting with a few of the smallest younglings, who endearingly stumbled and crawled across the sand at the encouragement of the onlookers. Ector took a place on the fringes of the crowd to observe.

The race wove from the sand into the water and back again, over and over, as teams of kraken and humans pushed themselves in friendly competition, working together toward victory. The lead position changed repeatedly, rousing a surge of cheers from the crowed each time. Smiling, Ector cheered along with them.

In the end, it came down to the final racers—Jax, Arkon, and Vasil. All three adult kraken hit the water within a second of each other and threw themselves into a frantic race back to the point where the race had started, well over a hundred meters by human reckoning. The spectators, including the other racers, moved closer to the water's edge to cheer on the swimmers.

Kronus awaited in the water, serving as a living marker for the finish line, with a tentacle stretched straight out to either side. Ector glanced at Kronus's mate, Eva. The human female was standing on the beach nearby, holding their little youngling,

Phoebe—who was giggling and smiling—in her arms. Ector's hearts warmed further. Kronus had begun the journey to become the kraken he was today on his own and had made great progress in that journey despite himself, but his relationship with Eva had triggered the final bit of growth he'd needed. Ector had never seen the ochre kraken so at peace.

The swimmers were head-to-head as they neared Kronus. The crowd's excitement only grew, as did the volume of their shouts and cheers. Ector's smile widened. This healthy, friendly competition was only further solidifying the bonds formed between kraken and humans over the last few years. There was more work to be done, and not everyone on either side had accepted this new reality, but this would all be normal within another generation or two, and memories of kraken and humans being separate would fade.

In the last few meters of the race—barely one kraken's body length—Vasil pulled ahead. Amidst delighted cheers, Kronus declared Vasil and his team the victors of the competition, having won by half a finger's length of distance.

The crowd broke into smaller groups of family and friends, and the beach was soon abuzz with laughter and conversation. Ector watched as Melaina, Rhea's youngling, rushed to Vasil— her sire—and congratulated him with a hug.

A few short years ago, Vasil and Melaina would never have known one another as father and daughter. Some of the kraken, even today, believed it was a violation of traditions that should've been adhered to. Though he would not deny the right of his people to keep to the old ways, Ector saw the relationship between Vasil and Melaina as nothing but a good thing. There was undeniable value in forging these bonds.

All the same, Ector couldn't suppress a pang of loneliness that made his chest feel hollow. Not long ago, Arkon had told him there were ways to determine an individual's parentage, but Ector had refused to pursue them. Knowing which, if any, kraken he'd sired couldn't change anything now. They were all grown, and he'd been as much of a father to them as he could've been under the old ways.

But he still longed for a deeper, more meaningful relationship—he longed for the companionship of a female, for a relationship of the sort so many of the younger kraken had found with human mates.

The crowd had already largely dispersed. Many of the younglings were back at play along the beach, and most of the adults had returned to the tables. As Ector turned his head, his gaze once again fell on Kathryn. She knelt to give three of her grandchildren, Ben, Megan, and Emma, hugs before they hurried off to join their peers.

Kathryn's daughters offered her waves and walked toward the tables. She watched them for a few moments, her lips curved into a smile, before turning to face the sea.

Ector's gaze lingered upon her. He wasn't blind to the appeal of humans, as alien as they looked, and there was something about Kathryn that was even more appealing than the rest. Perhaps it was that long, wavy hair of hers with its shimmering silver strands. Or maybe it was her smile, which always seemed to sparkle in her eyes. Every time he'd seen her, she'd radiated such warmth and happiness. Such kindness.

Yet he could not deny that there was something more there now, something subtle. Her stare—still directed at the sea—was wistful, bearing a hint of longing. A hint of...loneliness. It called out to him like nothing else could.

For some weeks, he'd wanted to speak to her beyond the usual pleasantries he often exchanged with the other denizens of The Watch. Why hadn't he? What had held him back? He knew Kathryn didn't have a mate, that she'd been without a male for even longer than Ector had been without a female, so there were no claims to be disputed. And she was *beautiful*. He could only assume the human males were either blind or foolish for failing to court her.

He'd sought the attention of so many females in his younger days, had danced many dances and fought many challenges, and never once had he hesitated before now.

But this wasn't a dance, it wasn't a challenge that would result in a physical confrontation with another male. All it needed to be—at least in that moment—was a conversation. Simple. Easy. Ector knew how to talk; he usually did far too much of it. And anyway…he wanted to know her better. Part of him already yearned to find a way to chase that lonely gleam out of her eyes forever.

Nothing to lose, you old kraken.

He drew in a deep breath that he didn't fully release—telling himself it *wasn't* just to swell his chest a bit more—and started toward the silver-haired female.

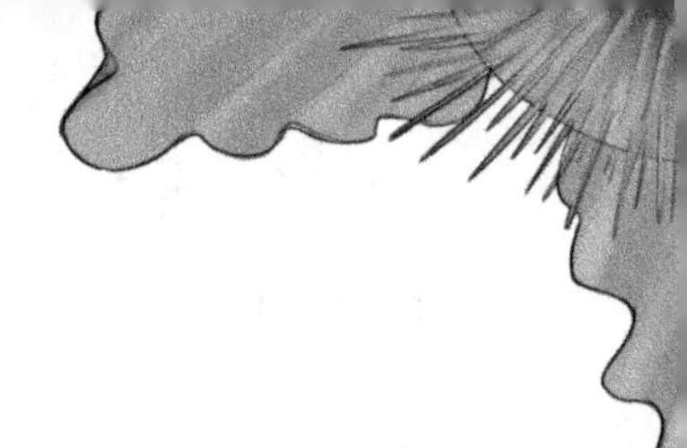

CHAPTER 2

With a gentle smile, Kathryn watched her daughters walk away. She could almost imagine them as they'd been years ago—two little girls walking hand-in-hand on this very beach. She recalled the way they'd laugh and sing, the way they'd peer over their shoulders to make sure Kat was watching, recalled the wide, mischievous smiles they'd gifted her. Those were the days when they'd never stray far from Kathryn's side. Now, they walked away without a backward glance.

Kat knew time moved at its own steady, unchanging pace, but the years seemed to pass faster and faster as they stacked up behind her.

Allison and Charlotte were grown up now, with families of their own. They didn't need her like they once had.

Sighing, Kathryn turned and stared out at the sea to watch the waves roll ashore. The wind tousled her hair and tugged at her blouse and skirt, molding the fabric to her body. Foamy water swept over the sand and around her feet. By midnight, the entire beach would be under water. There'd be no evidence of today's festivities when the tide receded tomorrow morning.

The sea continually washed away any marks left in the sand,

offering the beach a fresh start each day. The beach didn't have to carry its scars and blemishes for long—they could all be forgotten thanks to those tireless waves. Even if the land was slowly being worn down over thousands of years, what difference did it make? It had been here since long before Kathryn's ancestors had come to this planet and it would still be here long after she was gone.

But the sea couldn't wash away the marks—both visible and hidden—that Kathryn carried. Every scar, every wrinkle, was a record of the life she'd lived, hers to bear forever. That life hadn't always been easy, but it had been fulfilling. Rewarding. She'd raised two beautiful daughters, had gained two wonderful sons when her daughters joined, and had five grandchildren she loved and adored. And yet...

Something was missing.

Her eyebrows fell as she swept her gaze along the nearby cliffs that jutted into the sea, forming the promontory atop which the town's iconic lighthouse was perched. Fishermen sailed out of this little bay almost every morning and returned each evening. How long had it been since Kathryn had been on a boat? How long since her stomach had fluttered with exhilaration as she rode those rolling waves, since she felt ocean spray on her skin and briny wind through her hair, since she'd looked out over the water and been excited by the limitless possibility offered by the endless blue?

It's been eighteen years since Colin...

"You look to be lost in thoughts as deep as the sea," said a rumbling voice to her right.

Kathryn gasped and took a reflexive step back—except her feet didn't budge. They'd sunk into the loose, wet sand. Her eyes widened as she lost her balance and tipped backward.

A strong arm banded around her from behind, and her back struck a solid chest, which halted her fall and kept her upright.

Heart pounding, she curled her fingers tightly around the

arm holding her but kept otherwise still for a few moments. Water continued to flow around her ankles. She wiggled her toes, loosening the sand that had locked her feet in place. It caused her to sway slightly; only then did she register the hand firmly cupping her left breast. Despite the barrier provided by her clothing, she felt that hand as clearly as though it were pressed against her bare flesh—felt its strength, its heat, its roughness.

Unbidden, her nipple hardened beneath that palm, and sudden, unexpected desire jolted through her, piercing straight to her core. Her heart quickened.

"Oh," she breathed, and looked down. Her wildly beating heart leapt. A large, *green* hand with webbed fingers and black claws was over her breast. The pale skin of her fingers stood out in stark contrast to that drab green flesh. "Oh!"

The one who'd startled her—and who'd saved her from tumbling into the sand—was a kraken.

"My apologies," the kraken said in that deep, familiar voice. "I did not mean to frighten you. Are you all right?"

Kathryn cleared her throat, eased her grip, and gently— though awkwardly—patted his arm. *Such a strong arm...* "I'm fine, thank you. I was just...letting my thoughts wander."

She didn't know how it was possible, but her nipples tightened further, so much so that it was painful. The slightest shift sent another pulse of arousal to her core, followed by a rush of heat between her thighs.

What is wrong with me?

It'd been years since she'd felt this sort of attraction, this sort of lust. Why did she feel it now? Why...with him?

With surprising care, the kraken righted her, allowing her weight to settle on her feet again before letting his arm fall away. "I understand the dangers of that all too well these days."

She tried not to think about the absence of his touch, tried to ignore how heavy her breast suddenly felt, how *cold* it was now that it wasn't cradled by his heat.

Kathryn turned, carefully pulled her feet out of the loose sand, and faced her rescuer. She recognized him immediately—Ector. She'd seen him around town most days since his kind had come to The Watch, talking to people in the town center—including the members of the town council—or helping the fishermen and other kraken down at the dock.

Like most of his kind, he was big, towering over her on those thick, powerful tentacles. Despite the few wrinkles on his face—none of which were much deeper than her own—his green skin was taut over the sculpted muscles of his arms and chest. She knew he was referred to as an elder by his people, but she'd never thought it possible to maintain that kind of physique in one's twilight years.

Her eyes trailed over his broad shoulders and thick neck to stop on his face. Unlike some humans, she'd never found the kraken unsettling. They were just...different. Though Ector's nose was flatter and less pronounced, and he lacked hair and ears—there were tube-like protrusions on the sides of his head instead, called siphons—he was remarkably humanlike. And with that well-defined jawline and those arresting golden eyes... well, this kraken was rather handsome.

She met his gaze. His alien, oblong pupils expanded, and she could have sworn his skin shifted toward maroon for an instant while he studied her as intently as she had him.

"I have not disturbed you, have I?" he asked.

Kathryn smiled. "No, not at all. I was just reminiscing." She turned her head toward the others, seeking out her daughters and grandchildren amongst the crowd.

Austin and Ben were playing tag with a group of children around the place where the relay had begun, and little Megan was sitting at one of the tables with her mother and father, Charlotte and Taylor. Allison was standing with a group of women from town, chatting near the leftover food. Kathryn wasn't sure where the other two little ones, Emma and Logan, had run off to, but she knew they were just like the others—laughing, smiling, enjoying themselves.

Once again, that insistent sense of loss and displacement struck Kathryn. She felt like she was watching her family move on from the outside. Her smile wavered. "They grow so fast, don't they?"

Ector hummed. "They do. Hard to believe how small they all were, though sometimes it seems like no time has passed at all. At least in my head. My bones certainly feel those years."

She chuckled, turning back toward Ector. "Mine too. If not for those aches—and what I see when I look in the mirror—I'd still believe I was in my twenties."

His answering smile was warm and disarming despite the flash of sharp teeth it offered her. "You are beautiful, Kathryn."

"Oh." Heat flooded her cheeks, and she glanced away, bringing a hand up to cover the side of her face. No one—no *man*—had complimented her like that in a long time. "That's kind of you to say. Thank you."

At the bottom edge of her vision, one of his tentacles slid toward Kathryn over the sand. Her heart fluttered. How could she go so suddenly from feeling every one of her fifty years to feeling like a giddy teenager again?

Before he made contact, he withdrew the tentacle. Kathryn couldn't hold back a pang of disappointment at that—not that she understood her disappointment, or the desire thrumming through her body.

What is *wrong with me?*

Had she gone so long without an intimate touch that she now craved the tiniest caress from Ector's *tentacle?* They'd only spoken with one another perhaps half a dozen times in a couple years, and it had never been anything more than innocent small talk.

"I know the customs of our respective peoples are different," Ector said, easing a little closer, "and that humans tend to take a somewhat subtler approach, but... I have lived long enough to have lost some patience for subtlety. I find my eyes drawn to you more and more often as of late, Kathryn, and I would like to know you better."

Kathryn's eyes widened and again locked with his as a huff of laughter escaped her. This was...unexpected. She hadn't been in a relationship with anyone since her husband's death all those years ago. At first, the pain of loss had kept her from seeking companionship, but even when that ache had eased, she'd been so focused on her children and her work. It wasn't that she hadn't had opportunities over the years, it was just... she'd never felt the spark. And as the years passed, Kathryn had set aside any thoughts of finding a new relationship. She'd had her routine, her work, her daughters who needed her...

But she didn't have to worry about the girls anymore, did she? They had husbands and families of their own, while Kathryn went home to an empty house every evening.

It'd been so long since she'd been intimate with anyone, she wasn't sure how to even go about it anymore. Colin had been the only man she'd ever been with, and he'd passed away eighteen years ago.

Keeping the corners of her mouth tilted upward, Kathryn shook her head. "You really aren't subtle, are you?" She reached out and placed her hand on Ector's striped shoulder, meaning to let him down gently, to tell him she wasn't looking for a relationship, but the moment she touched him, something overcame her. She couldn't *stop* touching him. She slid her palm down to his chest, relishing in the feel of him. His skin was so different from a human's. It was soft, like velvet, but everything beneath it was solid muscle. Enticing heat radiated from him.

Ector's smile stretched a little wider. "I am normally, but today... I wanted to try something different."

"Something...different?" she absently asked as she stared at her hand, which had dipped a little farther down his chest so her fingertips could trail over his abs. Something within her warmed, and her breath shallowed.

So many muscles...

This time, his skin definitely changed, going from drab green to a deep maroon right before her eyes. One of his tentacles brushed the top of her bare foot and curled loosely around her ankle. His suction cups pressed against her flesh like small lips, offering gentle, soothing kisses.

"Am I appealing to you, Kathryn?" he asked in a rough whisper.

It was only then, hearing those husky words, that Kat realized what she was doing.

I'm feeling up a kraken! In public!

She yanked her hand away and snapped her gaze back up to his. Heat flooded her face. "I'm so sorry! I...I don't know what came over me."

"No need to apologize." He extended his arm, hooked a strand of her hair with one of his claws, and lifted it slightly, rubbing it between his fingers. "This has intrigued me since the first time I saw you. So lovely."

Kathryn's breath hitched, and her sex clenched, flooding with liquid heat, but she did not pull away.

Oh, fuck me.

The new color on Ector's skin only darkened. "Now who is not being subtle?"

Kat's brows angled down in confusion.

What is he talking abo—

She gasped and clamped a hand over her mouth. "Did I just...?"

Oh God, she had! She'd spoken those words—*oh, fuck me*—out loud. Kathryn's skin burned even hotter in mortification; this was worse than any hot flash she'd ever experienced. What was *wrong* with her? She'd never, ever lost her senses in such a way before.

Removing her hand from her face, she reclaimed her hair from his loose hold and took a step back. The tentacle around her ankle clung briefly before releasing her.

"It was…lovely speaking with you, Ector, but I should really go."

He let his hand drop slowly, smile diminishing. "I did not mean to spoil your enjoyment of the festival."

"Oh no, no. You didn't. I'm just…not feeling quite like myself right now." She reached out as though to comfort him, but thought better of it a moment later and jerked her hand back, tucking it into the folds of her skirt. No. Touching was bad right now. Really bad.

Then why does it feel so damn good?

His skin had reverted to its normal green. Why did that make her feel like garbage?

She cleared her throat and offered him a smile. "Please, enjoy the rest of the festival, Ector."

He dipped his head in a nod. "I will. I hope you feel better soon, Kathryn."

Glancing down, she carefully stepped over his tentacle and walked toward her daughters. Sand clung to her wet feet and ankles. Though she didn't look back, she knew Ector was watching her; she could feel his eyes moving over her body like their gaze was a physical touch.

Why was she acting this way? It was like she was a teenager all over again, unfamiliar with her own feelings and unsure of how to handle them. Unsure of how to talk to the person she desired…even a bit afraid. It wasn't that he was a kraken—well, perhaps it was a little, but not *really*. She just didn't know how to respond to his attentions.

As Kathryn approached Charlotte's table, Megan spun to look at her, big brown eyes sparkling. The girl's smile was huge, made even more adorable than usual by the icing smeared on her face—and the little bit that had found its way into her shoulder length brown hair.

"Gramma!" Megan pushed away from the table and darted toward Kathryn.

Crouching, Kat spread her arms. The little girl barreled into her, knocking Kathryn onto her backside, the fall cushioned by soft sand. Laughing, Kat embraced Megan—who had already locked her in a crushing hug—and pecked a kiss atop that sun warmed brown hair.

"You'd think you hadn't seen me for a month," Kathryn said, still laughing. "I thought you were playing with your friends?"

"She was until she realized she was *starving*," said Charlotte, Megan's mother and Kat's younger daughter. "Megan, be gentle with Grandma."

"Oops." Megan loosened her hold and eased back. "Sorry."

"It's okay, love. I'm stronger than your mommy thinks." Kathryn brushed a glob of icing off Megan's cheek with her thumb. "I see you've been enjoying the cakes, even after you ate *so* much dinner. Where is that all fitting in your little tummy?"

Megan giggled. "The race made me hungry, Gramma! My tummy was really empty, so I had to eat. But now Mama says I can't have more."

"Well, your mama is right. You'll get sick if you eat too many."

"Daddy had *five*." Megan thrust her hand up with all her fingers spread wide.

Her father, Taylor, laughed and twisted in his seat to look down at his daughter. "Daddy is also an adult."

Megan folded her arms and tilted her chin down in the ultimate pout. "Not fair."

Kathryn smiled, brushed her fingers through Megan's hair, and stood, dusting the sand off her backside. She looked at Charlotte. "I'm going to head home."

Charlotte frowned. "Why so early? Everything okay, Mom?"

"Everything's fine. I'm just tired and thought I'd get some rest." Kathryn hated lying to her daughter, but in this case, Kat thought it was warranted. In all honestly, she was anything *but* tired. She was…she was *aroused*. She just needed to get away, needed a place that was quiet, a place to think.

Charlotte leaned closer and hugged Kathryn. "Sure. Do you want me to come check on you later? To make sure you're okay?"

Kat laughed. "I'm not dying, Charlotte."

"I know, Mom. Sorry."

Smiling, Kathryn kissed her daughter's cheek. "I'm fine, Lotty. Don't worry about me."

Charlotte nodded, averted her gaze, and took a step back. That little frown was still on her lips. Kathryn's heart just about melted; even though Charlotte was the younger daughter by two years, she'd always been the worrier—even when she was Megan's age.

"Are you okay, Gramma?" Megan asked.

Kathryn looked down at her granddaughter and squatted, holding her arms open for another hug. The little girl moved in without hesitation. Kat held Megan close, closed her eyes, and took in a deep breath. She was amazed every day how much her family had grown. "No need to worry, Megan. I'm perfectly fine. Grandma just needs a nap."

"'Cause you're old, right?"

Kathryn, Charlotte, and Taylor laughed before Kat feigned offense, pressing a hand to her chest. "I'm not *that* old."

Megan delicately touched a finger to the corner of Kat's eye. "But you have wrinkles."

"I prefer to call them laugh lines."

"Because you're happy?"

Kathryn smiled and affectionately smoothed her hand down Megan's hair. "Yes. Because I'm happy."

She said her goodbyes and made her way toward the long, floating dock that jutted out into the water from the base of the cliff. Before she understood what she was doing, she turned her head to look back at the place where she and Ector had conversed, but the green kraken was already gone. She quickly faced forward and sped her pace just a little. Even if no one else knew what that glance over her shoulder had been about, she did, and she'd not shaken her embarrassment over the whole thing.

She climbed the steps that led up onto the dock. A wide path cut up through the rocky cliffs to her left, leading up into town, and to her right was the dock with all its boats moored and bobbing in place. She turned her head to look at the vessels. Even now, all these years later, she knew which of those boats Colin had built. For a long time, seeing them had roused a painful pang in her chest. But now they just instilled a sense of...of what? Yearning? Restlessness?

Setting those unexplored feelings aside, she turned left and started up the path. The waves sighed behind her as though gently asking her to come back, to embrace this strange wanderlust that was blossoming in her heart.

The rock faces towering on either side dwindled as she moved up the ramp. How many people had walked up and down this concrete pathway since The Watch was founded almost four hundred years ago? How many times had Kathryn walked it in her fifty years?

What's going on with me today? I'm not dying, damn it.

She rounded the bend and walked up the second ramp, which turned right into the town proper. Most of the buildings here were a blend of new and old—many had been built during the original colonization, and generations of townsfolk had added onto them to suit growing families and changing needs, turning The Watch into the place Kathryn called home. And this town *was* home, without a doubt. How could she be so certain of that and yet still feel so restless?

Kathryn turned right at the first intersecting road and followed it the short way to her home—a small house nestled in a cluster of small houses, almost all of which were occupied by fishermen and their families. The people that Colin had worked alongside every day. People Kat had known for her entire life.

She entered her home and closed the door behind her. For a moment, Kathryn stood there with her back against the door and studied her cozy surroundings. There were sofas and chairs, blankets and rugs, and the dining and side tables were adorned with flower-filled vases. Paintings hung on the walls, knick-knacks were displayed on the shelves, and her eclectic collection of décor, built slowly over the years, somehow all came together into something cohesive and harmonious. She'd cooked countless meals on the stove in the far-right corner, had always kept her preserves in the left cupboard and her dishes in the right. This place was familiar. It was home. It was...

Empty. So very, very empty.

There were times when Kathryn had relished the quiet, especially as a single mother of two girls who often bickered and screamed—never as much as they had in the couple years immediately following their father's death. That period had been the hardest on all of them. Kathryn had craved the silence that bedtime brought. But now, with her daughters gone, that silence was oftentimes deafening.

Pushing away from the door, she walked to her favorite chair—the one she kept turned toward the sea-facing window— sat down, and picked up the book she'd started reading earlier that week. It was some old novel she'd borrowed from the little library in the basement of the town hall, and it had sucked her in. She ran her eyes over the text now, knew every letter, every word, but somehow, they lacked meaning. She soon found herself reading individual sentences over and over again without any understanding. After struggling through two or three pages in what must've been twenty minutes, she finally admitted defeat.

"Just not in the mood, I guess," she said with a sigh. She replaced her bookmark on the page at which she'd started and set the book aside.

Pushing herself out of the chair, she set to tidying up the house—a task that mostly involved her frowning at things, wiping up a few specks of dust, and occasionally adjusting the position of a trinket by a millimeter or two. It had been terribly easy to keep the house neat since Allison and Charlotte went to live with their husbands; it was in stark contrast to the days of her daughters' youth, when there'd perpetually been a mess to clean up.

When she eventually accepted that there really wasn't anything to tidy up, her restlessness had only intensified. For lack of anything better to do—but needing to occupy herself regardless—she entered the bathroom and took a shower. She lingered for a while, something that she never would have done in the past, but now that she had hot water—thanks to the efforts of Theo, Kane, and Arkon—she couldn't resist.

When she was done, she dressed in loose, cozy pants and a shirt and stepped out into the hallway. The house had darkened considerably since she'd come home. In the kitchen, she lit a candle and plucked a winefruit from the basket on the counter. She peeled it quickly, placing the violet slices on a plate, and tossed the peel into the compost bin.

Picking up her plate, she bit into a wedge of sweet fruit and moved to the window overlooking the ocean. The darkening sky was violet, blue, and pink, with a thinning ribbon of fiery gold-orange where the sun was sinking on the horizon. This window had always been her favorite spot in the house, and during those rare moments of silence, she'd often found herself here, staring out at the endless water.

Had this longing been in Kathryn's heart all along without her realizing it? Was something out there calling to her, or was she just feeling…trapped?

She closed her eyes and leaned her forehead against the window frame. Distant, faint sounds—voices and music—drifted up from the beach, which was out of her vision from here. In her mind's eye, she could see everyone, humans and kraken alike, dancing and playing in the sand, bathed in the warm orange glow of bonfires and torches. They'd celebrate until the rising tide chased them away, which wouldn't be until well after the light of Halora's two moons turned sand and sea silver.

What would Ector look like beneath the moons, with droplets of sea water clinging to his velvety skin?

The thought startled her, and she opened her eyes and lifted her head. Her cheeks flushed in shame. What must he think of her after she'd run away from him?

Does he think that I find his touch repulsive? That I find him repulsive?

Kathryn groaned. "Way to go, Kat. A male compliments you, and you get skittish and run like you couldn't get away fast enough."

She hadn't found him repulsive in the least. He was different, but not off-putting. And if she hadn't come to her senses… Well, she likely would have explored a little farther south. That she'd been intimately touching a stranger—in public, no less—was embarrassing, but she couldn't deny that it was also titillating. He certainly hadn't seemed to mind. And despite Ector's obvious differences, Kathryn's body had reacted to him in a way it hadn't to anyone in years.

She'd harbored this growing desire for some sort of change for weeks, for months—if not longer—but it had always been vague, and she'd never really known what she wanted. Did Ector represent what she was after without her even knowing, or was her reaction to him simply a symptom of a larger problem that she'd yet to find the heart of?

Kat was lonely, yes; she could admit that to herself. But taking a man to bed wasn't necessarily going to fix that—though the appeal of it only grew with each passing moment. No, she needed something more significant, something more meaningful than a single night of sex. She needed to break the rut she'd been in for so long. She needed to change the routine that had come to define her life. Her family, this house, her work...as much as she loved all of it, she was ready for a change.

She was ready to feel young again. To have an adventure. To be...*alive*. Ector's flirtation had given her a taste of it, but she wanted more. Needed it for herself.

If only I hadn't been such a coward...

Her gaze returned to the water; she felt the sea calling again, felt that pull toward...toward whatever was out there. The ocean couldn't wash away her scars like it could footprints on the beach, but perhaps it could renew her. Perhaps it could give her whatever she'd been missing.

Kathryn had spent so much time just being a mother that she'd forgotten she was also a *woman*. A woman who'd hunted the wilds with her father when she was young, a woman who'd sailed those blue waters, a woman who was capable and independent and adventurous. A woman with desires, with needs. A woman with cravings.

And if those cravings happened to turn toward a big, green-skinned kraken...well, that was fine, wasn't it? There were many townsfolk who'd entered relationships with kraken, male and female alike. And there was no sense in trying to deny it—Kathryn found Ector sexy, tentacles and all.

But she knew at heart this wasn't about him. It was about Kat herself. Despite those aches that had cropped up over the years, despite her daughters being grown and her grandkids getting bigger and bigger all the time, she wasn't *old*. She wasn't done. This was just the beginning of a new phase of her life, a new chapter.

She dipped her gaze slightly, letting it fall on the boats bobbing along the dock, which was long enough for her to see despite the harsh drop of the cliffs.

She wasn't going to let the rest of her life pass her by. She'd chosen the path that had brought her here—she'd fallen in love with Colin all those years ago, and when Allison was born, Kat had decided to give up what she'd known since she was a little girl. She'd stopped hunting and trapping and become a seamstress instead because she wanted to spend every moment she could with her daughter, caring for her, nurturing her. Colin had died too young, too suddenly, but Kat would always treasure the fourteen years they'd had together.

After he'd passed away, she'd found herself the sole caregiver for her two daughters. It hadn't always been easy, but they'd made do—and they'd made countless good memories. Her friends and neighbors had always helped, and Alli and Lotty were good kids, even if those first few years after Colin's passing had been rough.

But as much as she'd loved all those years—she didn't regret a moment—Kathryn could look back and clearly see that she'd left little for herself. Sometimes it felt like there was little *of* herself left. She'd given her all to her family and her community. Now she was ready to choose a new path, if only for a little while. She was ready to rediscover herself, to figure out who she was and who she could be again.

She was ready to follow this wanderlust into the unknown and see where it led her.

CHAPTER 3

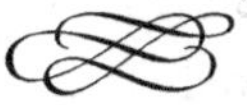

KATHRYN TUGGED HER JACKET CLOSED AND CROSSED HER ARMS over her chest to ward off the early morning chill. The sky was that unique shade of gray it only achieved just before sunrise, when the world was quiet but for the songs of wind and sea. She'd come to cherish times like this, when everything seemed to collectively hold its breath, as though Halora itself didn't dare move before feeling the first warm rays of the sun.

She walked briskly along the path down to the dock. Most mornings—so long as the wind was right—she could hear the fishermen starting their day, and this morning was no exception.

As she neared the landing, she lifted her gaze to look down the length of the dock. Boats of many shapes and sizes were moored all along it, several of which were being prepared by the fishermen. A splash of color, oddly vibrant despite the early morning gloom, was visible closer to the end of the dock—a group of kraken, likely waiting to assist the fishermen in their work.

Kat's eyes fell on a kraken with drab green skin. Her heart fluttered, and her skin prickled in a way that had nothing to do with the morning chill. He was talking to his companions, gesturing with both arms, and she watched the play of the muscles of his back and shoulders as he moved. All at once, she recalled the way his large hand had cupped her breast, the way he'd held her against his solid chest, and the way his flesh had felt beneath her bold touch.

Kathryn sucked in a sharp breath and averted her gaze. Ector was turned away, wasn't looking at her, but she didn't want to draw his attention, didn't want to make eye contact—didn't want him to know how much he affected her. She was here for a specific reason, and it wasn't to see Ector.

Fortunately, the person she *was* here to see was standing beside one of the boats near the midpoint of the dock, and he was plenty big enough to shield her from the kraken's gaze should Ector glance this way.

Kat balled her hands into fists at her sides and strode onto the floating dock, heading straight for her oldest friend—Breckett Sinclair.

Her boots thudded on the dock's surface. Several fishermen greeted her as she passed them, offering waves, friendly smiles, and *good mornings*. Kathryn returned their greetings with a smile of her own.

Breckett didn't look her way until she was within a few paces of him. He glanced at her briefly and looked back to the rope he was neatly coiling, only to snap his head toward her with eyebrows low. He dipped his gaze to her hands—her empty hands—and then back up to hers. "What're you doing down here this morning, Kat? It's not Tuesday yet, is it?"

She brought meals for the fishermen to take with them almost every Tuesday morning; most of these men were her friends or the children of her friends, and many had worked with Colin all those years ago. She couldn't recall having come down to the docks for any other reason over the last eighteen years—and clearly Breckett couldn't either.

He was a tall, burly man with thick, dark hair, a big beard, and a brooding face that was completely at odds with the gentle, kindly soul behind it. He was at once the most intimidating and kindest person she knew.

Kathryn's smile widened as she stopped in front of him. "And a good morning to you, too, Breckett."

He frowned; she knew it by the way his beard moved, though it covered most of his mouth. "Morning, Kat. It's good to see you, but it's probably been close to twenty years since I saw you down here without a basket of food in your hands. Not that I'm ungrateful for all that, or upset that you're here empty-handed, of course."

"I know, Breck. I just wanted to catch you before you left for the day. I'm sure it could have waited until this evening, but... I came to ask a favor."

Breckett turned away only long enough to toss the rope into the nearby boat. "Anything, Kat. What do you need?"

She took in a deep breath. There was no sense in skirting around it, was there? "I need a boat."

His brows fell low again. "What for?"

"Sailing."

He shook his head. "Obviously for sailing, Kat. You wanting to take the grandkids out for an afternoon or something?"

"No, though I'm sure they'd enjoy it." She raised a hand and swept her hair back, but the wind just blew strands of it back into her face as soon as she lowered her arm. "No, this is for me. I want to take it out. Alone."

Breckett turned toward her fully and drew in a deep breath that swelled his barrel chest. "You have too much to drink last night, Kathryn?"

"Did I have..." Kat's brow furrowed before she narrowed her eyes at him and crossed her arms over her chest. "And just what are you implying, Breckett Sinclair?"

He crossed his arms, too. "Just that you must be out of your damned mind. You're not going out there alone. No."

"And how many times have *you* gone out there alone?"

Breckett grunted, shook his head, and spun toward the far end of the dock. As he started walking toward the kraken, he said over his shoulder. "I go out there every day. When was the last time you were even on a boat?"

Kathryn dropped her arms and followed him, needing to move her legs twice as fast as Breckett's to keep up. "That doesn't mean I forgot how to sail."

"No, Kat. I can't allow it."

"Colin helped build half these boats with his own hands, and I rode with him on every one he made. I know what I'm doing."

Breckett slowed to a stop, tension stiffening his shoulders, and tilted his head back with a sigh. "It's too dangerous."

Kat stopped behind him. "It's the dry season, Breck. That's the safest time to sail."

He turned to face her again. "Where are you sailing to? And why now, after all this time?"

Kathryn drew in a lungful of briny air. "I miss it."

He raised his big, rough hands, palms turned up. "So I'll take you in a few days, when we're not fishing. All day if you want."

She shook her head. "I'll be gone for more than a day."

Breckett's expression darkened. "What do you mean you'll be gone for more than a day?"

"I need to go away for a little while. I want to explore what's out there." She searched her oldest friend's face. "I need to find...*me* again."

If Breckett had frowned any deeper in that moment, Kat swore it would've swallowed up the entirety of his bushy beard. "So going out on a boat for the first time in almost twenty years isn't dangerous enough? What're you going to do, Kat? Camp out there on your own? You know what it's like in the wilds."

"I do know, and that's precisely what I plan to do."

"You don't—"

"I grew up out there, Breckett," she said. "I started hunting in that jungle almost as soon as I could walk. I'll bring a rifle, and I'll be careful, but this is something I need to do."

He shook his head again, bringing up a hand to tug at his beard. "And what do I tell your kids?"

"Nothing. I'll tell them I love them and that I'll see them when I get back."

"If you don't come back, that's on me for letting you go."

"I don't need your permission, Breckett. I'm a grown ass woman and can make decisions on my own. I'm only asking because we're friends and I'd rather you not come down here one morning, realize a boat is gone, and wonder where it went."

"I'm not letting you go out there on your own, Kathryn. No." He swiped a big hand through the air, attempting to instill his words with a sense of finality. "You're not doing this."

"I *am* doing this, Breck," she said firmly; she knew he was just worried about her safety, but that didn't curb her frustration.

"I lost one daughter to the sea forever and almost lost the other," Breckett said, voice strained. "I don't intend to give it a shot at anyone else I care about."

Kathryn's irritation fled her in that moment. This was her friend, and he'd been her friend since she was a child. His first child, Sarina—who'd been so sweet, caring, and intelligent—had been swept out to sea by a riptide a year after Colin's death. As though that weren't bad enough, his younger daughter, Macy, had disappeared while at sea during another storm, and had been thought dead for weeks before her kraken mate returned her to The Watch. And he'd been close friends with Colin on top of all that. He was worried because he cared, because he knew firsthand what that worst-case scenario was.

But Kathryn knew, too.

"I can't promise anything, Breckett, but I don't mean to let the sea have me. You all risk yourselves every time you go out there, and I know deep in your heart you love it despite the risk. I have that in me, too. And all your worry didn't stop you from letting Macy back out, because you *know* it's worth that little risk. We can't let fear stop us from living."

Is that what I've been doing this whole time?

He sputtered for a few seconds, face turning red. Then he swept a big hand over his face and said, "Damn it, Kat, at least take someone with you. Maybe Randall or one of the other hunters will be willing to go."

"I would gladly accompany you," said a familiar voice.

Breckett stepped aside and turned to look back, revealing Ector. Kathryn's heart leapt as her eyes met the kraken's. She didn't understand why a simple glance from him could make her feel this way, didn't understand how he could have such an immediate, powerful effect on her, didn't understand what had changed in the last day to allow him that effect to begin with.

Was it because of that accidental intimate touch?

Because despite their differences—and her lack of understanding regarding her feelings—Ector was a man, and she was a woman, and even if age had granted her some wisdom it hadn't made her immune to her basic desires.

"You aren't supposed to encourage her, Ector," Breckett said.

"But you just told her to take someone with her."

"I was trying to dissuade her."

Ector's lips curled into a smile that sparked heat in his eyes. "I have a feeling Kathryn is not so easily dissuaded from anything she decides to do."

Finally shaking herself back to her senses, Kat pointed at Ector and raised her eyebrows at Breckett. "See? He gets it."

Breckett tilted his head back again and let out a frustrated huff. "I don't think either of you gets it."

Kathryn clamped her hands together and held them up. "Breckett, please. I need this."

When Breckett met her gaze, Kat held it. She'd known him almost her entire life; whenever she hadn't been out hunting with her parents, she'd been playing with Breckett and their group of friends. And because Breckett and Colin had worked together so closely, her friendship with Breck had continued strong into adulthood.

She had no desire to get into her reasons for needing to do this—they were too complex to articulate, and she wasn't entirely sure of them herself. But he must've seen enough in her eyes to understand, if only a little.

Breckett's shoulders sagged, and he let out a heavy sigh. "Fine. But only if Ector goes with you."

"Thank y—" Kathryn's eyes widened. "Wait, what?" It was only then that she realized what Ector had said before, and she turned her face toward him. He was watching her, golden eyes bright, still wearing that gentle smile as the ends of his tentacles restlessly shifted. She had a feeling he was holding some of their movement back.

"You require an escort, and I am more than willing to fill the role," Ector said, moving a bit closer. "I do not have much else to do as of late, and I would be lying if I said the company is not appealing."

Oh, damn.

Kathryn's cheeks flushed, and she shifted on her feet. She offered him a smile. "That's very kind of you Ector, but I...I don't *require* an escort."

Breckett once again folded his arms across his chest. "No Ector, no boat."

Kat snapped her gaze to Breckett. "You can't do that!"

Even to her own ears, she sounded like a petulant child.

"Kat, I will have someone stand watch on this dock day and night if I have to." Breckett tipped his head toward Ector. "He's experienced, and I trust him with my life. Ector and his people have made a big difference out there. We haven't lost anyone in the last couple wet seasons thanks to them. I still think this is crazy, but at least knowing Ector is with you will put me a little at ease."

"I do not mean to impose, Kathryn, but Breckett is correct," Ector said. "It will be safer if I am with you. We can look out for one another."

Kathryn looked between the two of them. They were right, no matter how much she wanted to protest—going by herself would be foolish. Her gaze settled on Ector. There was an eagerness in his gaze, in his posture, suggesting he wanted nothing more than for her to say *okay*.

Though this was a very personal trip for her, what was the harm in having the kraken join her? She had no reason to mistrust Ector, especially if Breckett trusted him so wholly. And...it would be nice having some company along the way. Wasn't she already lonely enough?

Kat glanced at Breckett with an expression that said *you win* before focusing on Ector again. "Thank you, Ector. I would love for you to join me."

Ector grinned wide, displaying those sharp teeth of his. "I consider it an honor, Kathryn."

A flicker of heat sparked within her, and she grasped the sides of her skirt. A few years ago, such a smile might have sent chills through her—she wouldn't have known if he was being friendly or if he wanted to eat her. Now... Well, him *eating* her didn't seem so bad, did it?

That heat within her flared just a little hotter.

What the hell am I thinking? It's just a smile. Focus, Kat!

"Give me a couple days to get a boat ready," Breckett said. "How long a trip are you planning, Kat?"

Kathryn swallowed thickly and tore her gaze away from Ector to look at Breckett. "I'm not sure."

Breckett muttered something to himself, beard bobbing as his mouth moved. "It's not too late to change your mind, Kat."

That sobered her. "I don't plan to. I want this, Breck. I just don't know how long I'll be gone."

"I just don't want it to be forever," Breckett said in a low, tight voice.

Kathryn smiled softly. She stepped closer and slipped her arms around Breckett. His burley arms enfolded her in an embrace. Kathryn had grown up with five siblings, all of them sisters—though they'd all moved away with their parents to a town in need of competent hunters shortly after Kat and Colin had joined. Breckett was basically the brother she never had. He and his wife, Madeline, had been there for Kat when Colin had died; they'd been a solid, sturdy presence that kept her grounded. Kat wasn't sure that she would've made it through those first few years as a widow were it not for Maddy's help with the girls.

"And it won't be, my old friend. I need some time away, but I *will* be back." She released him and stepped back, turning her smile toward Ector. "Ector will help make sure of it."

Ector dipped into a shallow bow. "I will protect you with my life, Kathryn."

Her eyes flared briefly at the conviction in his voice. "Oh. Um, let's not let it come to that, shall we?"

As he rose, Ector's lips took on a mischievous slant that complimented the gleam in his eyes. "Of course not. I have confidence in our ability to overcome the many dangers of land and sea with minimal injury."

Breckett grunted; Kat could hear his frown falling impossibly lower in that sound.

Kathryn bent toward the kraken slightly and lowered her voice to a playful whisper she was sure Breckett could hear. "That's not helping, Ector."

Ector chuckled, his grin widening. "Perhaps this is one of the rare cases when I would do best to stop talking?"

She returned his grin. "Yes, I think so." Kat turned her face back toward Breckett. "So, I have a boat, then?"

Breckett narrowed his eyes and muttered, "Against my better judgment, yes."

Excitement spread a wave of warmth through Kathryn's body, and she caught her lips between her teeth to keep from grinning like a damned fool—or *even more* like a damned fool, at least. She had a feeling that if she let too much of her anticipation show, Breckett would think she really had gone mad and change his mind.

"Should be ready in two or three days," Breckett said. "I'll let you know, Kat."

Kat forced herself to remain still, to keep her feet grounded when all she wanted to do was dance up and down dock. "Thank you, Breck."

He let out another heavy sigh. "Thank Ector. He's the only reason I'm giving in to you. You can thank me when you're back here safe."

Kathryn looked at Ector. His eyes were still upon her, and they still contained that glimmer of heat that had been haunting her thoughts since yesterday. "Thank you, Ector."

He nodded, and one of his tentacles slid a little closer to her feet. She could help but remember how it had felt against her skin.

"I should thank you, Kathryn," he said. "You have given me some purpose, if only for a little while."

She sensed deeper meaning in his words, but she dared not delve into it now; this was a small victory, but one she'd needed, and she wasn't going to overshadow it by examining the attraction she and Ector felt toward one another. There'd be plenty of time later to consider the potential consequences of being alone with this kraken for several days.

Something...she found herself looking forward to.

~

THE DAY PASSED INCREDIBLY SLOWLY. It wasn't for a lack of work; Kat had a steady stream of garments to mend, alter, and tailor on most days. The people of The Watch were hard on their clothing, especially those who were mated to kraken. Kathryn had seen an increase in the amount of torn clothes over the last couple years, and she suspected it was due to the kraken people's...passionate nature. At first, she'd been concerned, but that concern had faded after noting that many of those women came into the shop carrying shredded clothing but wearing wide, satisfied smiles—even if their cheeks were often colored pink by embarrassment.

Usually that steady work helped the time pass. She guessed everything felt so sluggish today because of her anticipation; she had something to look forward to.

In a few short days, she'd be leaving The Watch.

It was as thrilling as it was terrifying. Though she'd explored, hunted, and camped in the surrounding jungle in her youth, she'd never been more than a couple days' hike from The Watch. Now, this grand adventure with Ector awaited her. She was nervous about being alone with the kraken, mainly for the same reasons she'd been skittish with him on the beach—Ector looked at her as though she were a woman he desired, and Kathryn didn't have a clue of how to respond to that.

When was the last time she'd felt like a woman? Not just a mother, a grandmother, or a friend, but a *woman?*

It was late in the evening by the time Kathryn decided to put down her work and head home.

The air outside was warm and muggy like it was most days, and the town was bathed in the orange glow of a sun fast sinking toward the horizon. The breeze that flowed through the streets was refreshing, but it never felt quite the same as the wind directly off the open sea—as though the buildings took something invigorating away from the air as they cut the wind. Boisterous voices and music spilled into the central plaza from the town hall, where many people gathered to drink and socialize most nights, and there were still some people in the streets. Kathryn offered everyone she saw a smile and a greeting as she passed them.

As she turned onto her road and her home came into sight, Kathryn arched a brow. The front window was lit from within. That likely meant one of her daughters had stopped by, but they usually let her know when they planned to visit. Suspicion tickled the back of her mind, but she shrugged it off, walked to the front door, and entered her home.

Kat's eldest daughter, Allison, was sitting on one of the living room chairs, reading the book Kat had left out the night before. As Kathryn closed the front door, Allison turned to face her.

"Allison! What a lovely surprise." Kathryn swept her eyes over the room—the incredibly *quiet* room—which was lit by the gentle glow of a lantern and a few candles. "Where are the kids?"

"It's just me," Allison said, setting the book aside and rising from the chair. Her brown hair was gathered in a thick braid that lay over her shoulder.

Kathryn stilled as a spike of worry pierced her chest. It wasn't like Allison to visit without her children, Colin and Emma. "Everything okay, Alli?"

"Of course. Why wouldn't— Oh!" Allison smiled and closed the distance between them, pulling Kathryn into a hug. "They're fine. The hunters came home early today, so the kids are at home spending time with Jackson." She pulled away and lowered her arms, her smile fading. "It's *you* I'm worried about."

Kathryn frowned. "Why are you worried about me? Is it because of yesterday? Did Charlotte make a big fuss about me leaving the festival early?"

"Well, she did mention that you were tired when I asked her

where you were last night, but no, this isn't about that. It's about what I heard today."

Kat shouldn't have been surprised that word had traveled so quickly. Telling Allison had likely been Breckett's last attempt to dissuade Kathryn from taking this trip. She couldn't blame him, though she would rather have been the one to tell her daughters about it.

Kathryn stepped around her daughter and sat on one of the cushioned chairs. She gestured at the seat Allison had risen from. "Sit back down, Alli. What was it you heard?"

Allison moved to the chair, gathered her skirt close, and sat. Her dark brown eyes met Kat's. "That you were taking a boat and leaving The Watch."

"I am," Kat said.

Allison stood so abruptly that she nearly knocked her chair over. "*What? Are you insane?*"

Kathryn scowled, leaned back in her chair, and folded her hands in her lap. "I'm thinking quite clearly, Allison."

"B-But you're—" Allison raised and hand and pinched the bridge of her nose as she closed her eyes, seeming to gather herself. After taking a deep breath, her arms fell to her sides and she opened her eyes again to look at Kathryn. "Mom, you can't be serious. What you're doing is dangerous. It's—"

"It's no different than when Jackson goes out to hunt."

"But mom, you're...*old.*"

Kathryn stared at her daughter, brows low, and mouth agape in utter disbelief. It wasn't that word itself, but it was the way Allison had said it—as though aging were some crippling disease that had left Kat entirely helpless.

Not that fifty is all that damned old anyway!

"So what does that mean, Alli? That I should sit in a rocking chair and spend my days staring wistfully at the sea? That I need to move in with you and Jackson so you can take care of your feeble old mother?"

Allison cringed, and at least had the good sense to look contrite. "You know that's not what I mean, Mom."

"Then what?"

"That you're not young anymore, and that it's not safe for you."

"That's just it, Alli." Kathryn pushed herself to her feet. "I don't want safe. I've been safe for years and years and I'm bored of it. I need adventure. We each have only one life to live, and I want to *live* mine, not passively watch it go by."

Kathryn closed the distance between herself and her daughter and took Allison's hands. "I have loved almost every moment of my life, and the bad times only make the good shine all the brighter. I love that I was blessed with two beautiful daughters and so many grandchildren. And guiding you and Charlotte as you grew into the wonderful young women you are today has made me so proud.

"But you don't need me to hold your hands anymore, and I need something beyond this routine I've fallen into. I need more than working every day and coming home to an empty home. I need to figure out who I am again." Kathryn released one of Allison's hands and reached up to brush her fingertips across Alli's temple, tucking a stray lock of hair behind the younger woman's ear. "And I don't plan to go away forever. It's only for a short while."

Tears shone in Allison's eyes. "But what if I lose you? We already lost dad."

Kathryn's eyes stung with the threat of her own tears. She smiled softly and cupped her daughter's face in both hands. "Oh, sweetie, we can't live our lives around what-ifs. We'd never do anything worth doing if we did that. I have every intention of coming home to my family. Besides…I won't be going alone."

Allison reached up and took hold of Kathryn's wrists, gently drawing Kat's hands away from her face. "Who is going with you?"

Kat chuckled. "Didn't hear that juicy little tidbit, did you?"

"Mom."

"Ector is accompanying me."

Allison glanced away, brow furrowing. "Ector. That name sounds so famil—" Her eyes rounded. "The kraken?"

Kathryn nodded, smiling wide. "He offered to join me, and Breckett made it a condition if I wanted to take one of the boats."

"But isn't he also…old?"

Kat tilted her chin down and eyed her daughter.

"Well he is!"

"And he's also a strong, experienced hunter who'll keep me company while keeping me safe."

He also happened to be pretty easy on the eyes, with muscles Kat could stroke for days—not that Kathryn had any intention of saying that aloud.

Allison released a long, slow breath. "Fine. At least you're not going by yourself. But for the record, I would rather you didn't go at all."

Chuckling, Kathryn leaned forward and pecked a kiss on her daughter's cheek. "Well, it's a good thing I don't need your permission, then."

Allison rolled her eyes, but wrapped her arms around Kat, holding her tight. "Promise me you'll be careful."

Kathryn closed her eyes and embraced her daughter. "I promise."

"I love you, Mom."

"Love you, too, Alli."

CHAPTER 4

BEYOND THE LONG SHADOWS OF THE SHORESIDE CLIFFS, THE SEA shimmered with golden morning light. On a normal day, the fishermen would've already departed by now, but this was a day of rest for them. The dock was rarely so deserted, rarely so peaceful. Everything was blanketed in the soothing sound of the water lapping against the shore.

Ector took a deep breath of sea-scented air and stared out over those gently rolling waters. There was an odd heat and tightness in his chest—eagerness. As the years had passed, he'd often felt there was less and less to look forward to, but that had all changed when Jax and Dracchus brought Macy to the kraken's ancestral home. In the time since, Ector had seen and experienced things he could never have imagined—some of it tragic and painful, much of it awe-inspiring and exhilarating.

This was a new adventure. He'd hunted the waters near the Facility, but he'd rarely ventured beyond those familiar hunting places. He'd always had a vague idea of the vastness of the sea, but viewing it from land, knowing that it stretched farther than his eye could see even from high ground...

In sixty years, he'd only seen a tiny, insignificant portion of the ocean—a tiny, insignificant portion of the *world*. Ector had been uncertain the first time Dracchus had led the kraken people to The Watch, with no real notion of how the first true encounter between his kind and the humans at large would go, but that uncertainty had been underrun by the same sort of eagerness he felt now. There was a thrill in pushing past the artificial boundaries the kraken had created for themselves and exploring the unknown.

His tentacles twitched and curled over the surface of the dock involuntarily, itching to move in response to his anticipation. Forcing them to still required more willpower than he would've guessed.

Though he'd often admonished Jax for his wanderlust, Ector had come to understand it well in the last couple years. He'd come to sympathize with it. And now he was gladly giving in to it. He felt like a youngling about to partake in his first hunt.

Yet he couldn't deny that the company he'd enjoy was even more alluring than the journey ahead.

Despite his increasingly introspective mood over the last several months, he'd not taken much time to contemplate his attraction to Kathryn. He didn't need to. The significance of his wanting her was immense after decades of doing his duty for his people and mating with any female who chose him. As much as he'd enjoyed mating, he'd never wanted any female like he wanted Kathryn—and he could accept that for what it was. There was no need to overanalyze it.

A grunt from behind called Ector's attention away from the endless sea. He turned to see Breckett standing in the small boat he'd prepared for Kathryn, fussing over the ropes securing the supplies. Ector couldn't help but smile; between Breckett, Dracchus, and Kronus, grunting was a language all its own, as expressive and complex as both human speech and kraken sign language. Ector wouldn't have been surprised if the three males could have entire conversations without speaking a word.

"I imagine it is just as secure as it was the last time you checked it half a minute ago, Breckett," Ector said.

Breckett straightened and buried the fingers of one hand in his thick beard, tugging it absently. He grunted again. "Yeah. Just need something to do while I wait. Don't ever feel impatient or anxious when I'm out on the water, but anywhere else…"

"I understand. The patience of a hunter does not necessarily extend to other endeavors."

"Something like that." Breckett stepped out of the boat, his heavy boots thumping atop the swaying dock. He moved closer to Ector and met the kraken's gaze, frowning deeply. "You're going to keep her safe, right?"

Perhaps when he'd been younger and more hotheaded, Ector might've taken that as a questioning of his competence and prowess—reason enough for an immediate challenge. But Ector understood Breckett's concern. Even if Ector hadn't grown up knowing the sorts of friend and family relationships the humans did, he'd experienced enough of it lately to sympathize with this man.

Ector placed a webbed hand on one of Breckett's burly shoulders, gave it a squeeze, and nodded. "I was not lying when I said I would protect her with my life if necessary."

Breckett's frown deepened, and he nodded, placing his own hand on Ector's shoulder. "I know. I'm not sure if *man* is the right term, but you're a good man, Ector. It's just that Kat is like a sister to me. And when Madeline and I lost our daughter"—his eyes shimmered, and he dropped his gaze—"Kat was there for us, even though she was still hurting from Colin's passing. She's…good people, is what I'm trying to say."

Ector pressed his lips into a tight line. Breckett was a big, strong human, in so many ways the ideal specimen—and he regularly wore his feelings on his face. This man had helped Ector learn one of his most important lessons since coming to

The Watch—emotions, especially emotional connections to others, didn't *have* to be private, and they weren't a weakness. And however brief, this little story spoke of an inner strength Kathryn possessed that Ector had guessed at. He couldn't help but admire it deeply.

"She is," Ector said. "And while we are out there, *she* will be my purpose. You understand what I mean by that, as a kraken?"

"I do. Ever since Jax saved my Macy." Breckett lifted his hand briefly and gave Ector's shoulder a pat before stepping back. "Couldn't ask for a better person to look out for Kat."

Ector chuckled. "I am not quite as fast as I used to be, and my bones ache a bit more than I remember, but the sea has not yet reclaimed me. I will have fight in me until the very moment it does."

Breckett smiled, displaying white teeth that were in startling contrast to his dark beard. "I don't doubt that. Hell, I even get why she wants to do this. I still don't think she should, but... here we are."

Grinning, Ector nodded. "Here we are." Movement from the shore caught his eye, and he looked past Breckett to see Kathryn walking down the stone ramp that led to the dock. His grin widened. "And here she is."

Her silver hair was pulled back into what Ector believed was called a *ponytail*, and she was dressed in a simple button-down shirt and durable looking pants not unlike what many of the fishermen usually wore to work—her attire was nothing like the dresses or skirts he'd seen her in previously. Though her clothing hid the pale flesh of her shapely legs, the smile on her face, which was apparent even from this distance, more than made up for it. She had a big backpack slung over her shoulders and a hand grasping each strap.

As she neared, Ector couldn't help but notice that her excitement was shining in her bright blue eyes, making them even more radiant than before. The tightness in his chest flared. Beautiful seemed too mild a word to describe her.

"Good morning, Kathryn," he said.

"Morning, Kat," said Breckett.

"Good morning," she replied, her already flushed cheeks darkening further when she met Ector's gaze. She turned toward Breckett and chuckled. "Oh, quit looking at me like you broke your favorite fishing rod."

Breckett raised a hand and leveled his finger at her. "This isn't a time for joking, Kat. You need to be careful out there."

Kathryn stepped closer to Breckett, rose on her toes, and pressed her lips to his cheek—a kiss. "I will be careful. I promise."

An uncomfortable pang briefly soured the anticipation thrumming in Ector's chest. Despite his knowledge of Breckett and Kathryn's history, despite knowing that their relationship wasn't romantic, despite having witnessed with his own eyes that such kisses between humans could be entirely innocent gestures, he couldn't help that flare of jealousy.

She is mine.

The realization struck Ector hard and knocked the strength out of his jealousy. Somewhere deep inside, he'd already recognized Kathryn as his mate, and it didn't matter if it was instinctual or not. He'd already claimed her. All that remained was for her to claim him...and he'd have time to show her why he was worthy during their journey.

Breckett nodded and took a step back from Kathryn. "I hope you find what you're looking for out there."

Ector couldn't pry his eyes from her. *I think I have found what I am looking for right here.*

"Thank you, Breckett." Kathryn turned her smile toward Ector, and it widened just a little more. "Are we ready to go?"

Ector dipped into a slight bow and offered her his hand, palm up. "At your command, Kathryn."

She stepped closer and placed her hand in his without hesitation. Her skin was warm, and though her fingertips were calloused, her touch was gentle. That warmth spread up Ector's arm to blossom in his chest. She leaned lightly on his hand as she climbed into the waiting boat.

Kathryn withdrew her hand and reached for her backpack's straps again. The boat wobbled beneath her, and Ector nearly darted forward, convinced she was about to tip over the side. But she rode the motion confidently and swung her pack off, placing it beside the stowed supplies.

Breckett made a soft sound—more a hum than a grunt—and Ector turned his head to find the man staring at him.

Breckett's eyes were intent and thoughtful, and one corner of his mouth was upturned in a slight smirk. "You two behave yourselves."

"Breckett!" scolded Kathryn, her cheeks flushing.

Though he chuckled, Breckett still toyed with his beard absently, a sure sign of his remaining concern. "You're adults. What you two do out there isn't any of my business."

"You're right. It isn't." Kathryn glanced at Ector, and the light in her eyes was suddenly brighter; it lit a fire deep inside him.

Ector's anticipation increased to a level he'd previously thought impossible, and he couldn't stop his tentacles from writhing over the surface of the dock.

Kathryn opened her mouth as though to speak only to hesitate and draw in a soft breath before any words emerged. "Would you like to join me in the boat, Ector? Or, um, would you prefer to swim? Whatever is most comfortable for you. I don't want to for—"

"I would very much like to join you in the boat," he said as warmth spread through his chest. "May as well give these old bones as much rest as I can before we get to the difficult parts, right?"

She chuckled and sat on the bench near the aft of the boat.

Her eyes raked over his body, and their light intensified. "For what it's worth, you don't look so old from here."

Ector's hearts quickened, and an instinctual color change threatened to sweep across his skin. He held it back only because of Breckett, who reminded them of his presence by clearing his throat.

Kathryn twisted to face Breckett. "Give Maddy my love. I'll keep an eye out for something to bring back for her."

Breckett nodded. "Just bring yourself back, safe and sound. Both of you."

"We will," Ector promised. He extended his fore tentacles, curling them over the side of the boat, and hauled himself into the vessel. It dipped and swayed under his weight. He'd traveled in boats many times since he'd come to The Watch, but that motion had never quite felt natural to him. He was far more comfortable being *in* the water than being *on* it.

Ector shifted and contorted his tentacles to seat himself on the secondary bench, facing Kathryn, as Breckett untied the mooring rope. Ector met Kathryn's gaze. "Here's to a new adventure."

She smiled. "A grand, new adventure."

For a few moments, Kathryn studied the boat's rigging, and her eyes sparkled with a new light—as though something that had been missing up until that moment had been returned to her. She nodded to herself and set to work, tugging ropes to partially hoist the sail before adjusting the boom to catch the wind. The boat lurched forward.

Kathryn let out a nervous little laugh and dropped a hand to the tiller, swinging it aside to turn the ship away from the dock —avoiding a collision by the length of a finger.

"You sure you know what you're doing?" Breckett asked, brows low.

"I guess we'll see, right?"

She continued the turn as the boat picked up a bit of speed, clearing the other vessels moored along the dock before altering her course to follow the dock toward its end.

Breckett's boots thudded as he walked, keeping pace with the vessel. "Kathryn…"

Kathryn laughed, raised her arm, and waved. "Too late now, Breck! Goodbye!"

At the mercy of the wind, the boom shuddered. Ector's hearts froze for an instant. He shot forward quickly and caught the boom in his hand before it could swing into Kathryn's face.

KATHRYN'S BREATH hitched as the boom stopped mere centimeters from her face. Cringing, she lifted her eyes to Ector's. "Oops."

They stared at each other, and for that brief moment, everything was laid bare; they were just two people who hoped they knew what they were doing. They were two people desperate for some change, for a taste of something they had lost along the way—or perhaps it was for a taste of something they'd never truly had.

And then their lips curled into smiles, and they both laughed. Their laughter only intensified when Breckett yelled Kathryn's name again.

"If we don't get out of this bay quick, I might give him a heart attack," Kathryn said as her laughter eased into chuckling.

"And this whole time I thought *we* were supposed to be the ones in danger," Ector replied.

Kathryn felt a stab of guilt for worrying her old friend. Perhaps she was a *little* rusty, but she was sure it would all come back to her.

Ector kept a hand on the boom, adjusting it to hold the wind as Kathryn steered the boat past the end of the dock, where Breckett stood glaring at Kat with his mouth—undoubtedly turned down in an immense frown—hidden in his thick beard. Grinning, she waved at him again.

He only shook his head.

Kathryn turned the boat, angling it to clear the bay and follow the coastline, and Breckett gradually became a featureless figure in the distance, solid and unmoving.

"I would ask where we are going," Ector said, "but I know nothing of the lands beyond The Watch."

She filled her lungs with sweet sea air. "This is all new to me, as well. I just planned to follow the coastline and see where it takes us."

"That sounds perfect to me."

The boat finally broke past the long shadows cast by the seaside cliffs and entered the golden sunlight, which bathed Kathryn in warmth. She closed her eyes and tilted her head back to let the light fall on her skin. The wind blew from over her left shoulder, toying with her ponytail and the fabric of her shirt. Though The Watch would still be in view if she looked toward land, she already felt as though it were far behind. She already felt...free.

That feeling came with another pang of guilt. She loved her family, and she would miss them during this trip...but how could she explain this sense of freedom to her daughters and grandchildren without making it sound like she saw them as some kind of burden? How could she talk about any of this without sounding selfish?

She lowered her head and opened her eyes, fixing them on Ector. He was twisted to look ahead, likely watching the rocks jutting from the water near the shoreline, and his normally drab green skin was vibrant in the morning sunlight. Her fingers twitched with the memory of how that velvety skin had felt beneath them.

It's okay to be selfish sometimes. Sometimes it's necessary.

And she knew, somehow, that Ector would understand even if no one else could.

She let those thoughts brew until the boat was out of the bay and the only part of town still visible was the towering light-house atop the promontory.

Kathryn's attention soon strayed from the lighthouse to return to Ector. She studied his profile. He had a strong jaw and brow, and though his nose was flatter and less prominent than a human's, she didn't find him wanting. In fact, the more she looked at him, the more handsome he became. Though there was room enough in the boat for two more adult passengers, Ector's presence seemed to fill up the leftover space. His tentacles were spread out across the floor, shifting and moving slowly, constantly; she was sure to touch them if she stretched out her leg.

She trailed her gaze back up his body—his tempting, muscular body—and licked her suddenly dry lips. "Ector? You're...an elder to your people, aren't you? A leader, like the members of our town council?"

He turned to face her fully, and she didn't miss the way his eyes dipped and rose as though he were taking Kathryn in just like she had him. He nodded. "Our lives were always quite dangerous, before. Few lived to my age, so elders were respected. We were always more guides than leaders, I suppose, though we were called upon to resolve disputes when a consensus could not otherwise be reached."

"I can't help but notice you said all that in the past tense."

He smiled softly, perhaps even a bit wistfully, and turned the palm of his free hand skyward. "Much has changed for us recently, as you know. There have always been strong kraken who have assumed leadership of our people as was necessary, but we kraken were not always willing to be led. Dracchus has changed that. Strong as he is, it is his innate wisdom and humbleness that make him perhaps the best leader we could ever have had. His generation has come into their own. My guidance…well, they do not have much use for it, these days."

Kathryn smiled softly. "There's nothing quite as amazing and heartwarming as watching your children grow. And there's nothing quite as bittersweet as realizing that they've reached a point when they can get along just fine without you. But I think they'll still look to you for guidance."

"All true. I suppose what defines that moment is not the realization itself, but how you react to it."

Kathryn chuckled. "Like taking a boat and sailing out into the wilderness?"

Ector laughed, rekindling the fire in his eyes. "Yes, like taking a boat and sailing into the wilderness."

She swept her gaze over her surroundings. The shore was still in view—she didn't intend to let it out of sight at any point during this trip—but there was enough water between the boat and the land for her to feel like she was properly at sea. Perhaps the start of the journey had been a little bumpy, but now that they were sailing, it all felt right. Everything Colin had taught her long ago was already coming back to her.

She dipped her eyes to the preventer line—a rope that ran from the boom to the bow and then back along the port side of the boat to an anchor point near Kathryn's seat. She shook her head and used her free hand to pull the slack on the line before tying it off on the metal cleat beside her. "Should've remembered this sooner."

"I must confess that as many times as I have seen this done by Breckett and the others, I have never partaken in the process," Ector said, eyes intent upon her. "What is that rope for?"

"It's a preventer line. It's meant to stop the boom from swinging across the boat and damaging the mast—or any people who happen to be in the way."

Ector's brows lifted, and his smile took on a mischievous tilt. "That might have been helpful earlier, yes."

Kathryn's cheeks warmed despite his easy, lightly teasing tone. "Thank you, by the way. For catching that."

The corners of Ector's mouth lifted further, displaying those sharp teeth of his. Everything about his appearance should've been unsettling, frightening, off-putting, but she only found herself increasingly captivated.

"That is what I am here for, Kathryn."

Kat glanced down and fiddled with the hem of her shirt. "I… might not have been thrilled about someone babysitting me when Breckett refused to let me go on my own but"—she looked back up at Ector—"I'm glad you're here."

"And I am glad to be here." He tipped his head to the side, and his brow furrowed. "Babysitting means watching a child, does it not?"

"It does," she replied with a snicker.

"I would imagine that you are not in need of babysitting, but someone to look out for you… Everyone needs that."

Kathryn tilted her head, her smile fading as she regarded him. "Do you have someone looking out for you, Ector?"

"If you count my people as a whole, yes. But in a more direct sense"—he swung his gaze skyward and shook his head—"no. It was not the way of my people to form such relationships."

"That sounds…lonely."

He lifted his shoulders in a shrug, and his tentacles moved restlessly at the bottom edge of Kathryn's vision. "It was simply the way my people lived until recently. We crave solitude and social interaction at the same time. These…joinings your people have suit those conflicting drives in several ways, but it simply wasn't practical for us before."

"Why wasn't it practical before?"

"We have always had few females, and birth rates have always been low for our kind. Mating has been a matter of necessity for most of our existence. Mates typically stayed together for short periods, often separating if the female grew bored of the male, or if she failed to conceive after a few months."

Frowning, Kat tucked loose strands of her hair behind her ear—though she might as well not have bothered, as the wind blew them back into her face within a few seconds. She had to remind herself that kraken society was different from her own, that Ector's people lived by a different set of rules, that they weren't human despite their similarities. Mating for the sake of breeding… In some ways, that seemed worse than simply being alone.

"What changed? Was it…us?" she asked.

Ector nodded and finally settled his gaze upon her again. "Macy was the first human any of us had ever seen. Her relationship with Jax was unlike anything my people had known, and none of us truly understood it at first. He called her his mate. That seemed foolish to many of us. The point of mating was to produce younglings and carry on our species, and he could not do so with a human. But Jax had always done things his way. He had always resisted the traditions of our people to follow his own path.

"I suspected there was some value in her that Jax could perceive but I could not. She displayed it to us when she saved a youngling…but there was so much more to it. The two of them showed us what *love* meant. They defined the word. It was something that many of us had felt in our own ways, in different ways, yet had no name for. But it took Macy and Jax to show us just how deep and profound it could be. Those two showed us that we could lead fulfilling, meaningful lives outside of that need to procreate for survival. And once we discovered that she was carrying a youngling…it gave hope to the kraken that we had not known in a long, long while."

Kathryn looked down at the tiller and brushed her thumb

over its smooth, dark wood. She remembered the first time Jax had come to The Watch, carrying Breckett's daughter, Macy, who'd fallen ill after a terrible wound. Everyone had thought the young woman dead, lost to the sea just like her older sister, Sarina. Just like Colin.

Kat also remembered the fear that had swept through the townsfolk after their first glimpse of what they'd perceived as a monster. There had always been stories told by fishermen and hunters about monstrous creatures lurking in the deep jungles and beneath the waves, but the kraken... No one had known of their existence. They'd stayed hidden for centuries, living in fear of humans—fear and hatred for what humans had done to them.

"Do all the kraken agree with such joinings?" she asked, lifting her gaze to Ector.

"Many of my people continue to live by the old ways, but lasting relationships are becoming more and more common. These changes, though..." His lips fell into a contemplative frown. "Getting to this point nearly tore us apart. Many died along the way. Those who remain are at the very least tolerant of humans and kraken joining. I think we all just want peace, by now."

Ector's bright, golden eyes were full of wisdom, passion, and sorrow, so familiar and yet so different because of their oblong, horizontal pupils. They paired with the rawness of his voice to make his pain evident, to make Kat feel the weight of loss he carried on his shoulders. Her heart ached for him.

"There are still some humans who don't agree with all this, who don't see you as people. They believe human and kraken joinings are unnatural and consider you...abominations." She reached across the space separating them and placed a hand on the upper portion of one of his tentacles.

The muscle beneath her palm flexed, and Ector's eyes flared briefly in surprise.

"But I don't," Kathryn said softly. "I see you as the person you are, and I am so, so sorry for your loss, Ector."

He lowered his hand onto hers. With its green skin, long black claws, and webbing between each finger, that hand looked utterly alien—but it was also gentle and warm despite its size and appearance. "You do not need to be sorry for our trials, Kathryn. I wish it had not cost so much, but we are better for all of it."

Kathryn turned her hand beneath his until their palms were touching. She curled her fingers; and due to the webbing between his, only the tops of her fingers could lace with his. "I know all too well that it's never easy to deal with sudden change, but we usually come out stronger in the end."

He smiled again, and that light that was in his eyes so often when he looked upon her returned. It was a welcoming light, an alluring light. He stroked his thumb along the outside of her hand. "And we often find things we may never have discovered otherwise."

Kathryn's lips parted as warmth filled her and her heart stuttered. Spending this time with Ector reminded her of what she had been missing all these years. She had her daughters and their husbands, who had become like sons to her, had her grandchildren, but this... This was *different*. She'd been fortunate to have received unconditional love and support from her friends and family over the years, but no one in all that time had looked at her like Ector was right now. Like she was a woman— a *desirable* woman.

Something slipped beneath the cuff of her pants to stroke the skin of her calf just above her boot; she knew without looking that it was one of Ector's tentacles. It coiled around her leg slowly, like it had on the beach, as if he was giving her a chance to pull away. She didn't. For a second time, she felt the gentle kisses of his suction cups. They were rhythmic, sensual, and stimulating. Kat's breath quickened, and her sex clenched with sudden need.

Kathryn curled her lips inward and ran her tongue along them. "Ector, I—"

The boat dipped, and a wave struck the hull, sending spray of water over the side to splash Kat. The cold water was a shock. She straightened with a gasp, pulling her hand out from under Ector's. Her hair was wet, her shirt soaked and plastered to her back, and there was a pool of water beneath her.

Her wide eyes remained locked with Ector's through several seconds of stunned silence before laughter bubbled up from her belly. Ector laughed along with her, seemingly unbothered by the droplets of water glistening on his skin.

"I suppose I should get used to getting wet again," she said, brushing the water off the bench onto the floor. She paused for a moment as she considered her choice of words given her body's reaction to Ector just before the sea had intervened. Her eyes flared, and a flush stained her cheeks. "I mean, the *ocean* getting me wet."

Ector's brow furrowed, and he tilted his head. "What else would get you wet out here when it is not raining?"

Kathryn blinked at him, her own brows falling. Did he not...? The fishermen would have been in an uproar after hearing her words, turning them into a crude but good-humored jest. "Well, it could be taken to mean...um... You know what? Never mind."

He shook his head and laughed again. "This is a case of one of those double meanings you humans have for so many words, is it not? I have learned of so many dual meanings during my time here, and I am always interested in learning more."

Kathryn pressed her lips together to hold in her laughter— and to stop herself from telling him. She knew she could get the words out if she really wanted to, but she wasn't sure if she could face the potential embarrassment...or the rekindling of the heat that might have followed the explanation.

"Well... We'll see how things go over the next few days," she said with a grin. "Maybe you'll have a chance to learn firsthand."

Wait a second. What *did I just say to him?*

She'd held back saying one thing only to blurt out another. She'd basically told him that there was pretty damn good chance they'd be having sex—not that he would know it due to his lack of understanding regarding the initial innuendo.

He narrowed his eyes, and his smile took on a sly tilt. "Something tells me this mystery will be more exciting to solve than most."

Kat's cheeks burned as she forced her eyes away from him. "Perhaps."

She wasn't used to flirtation—whether directed at her or coming *from* her. But, despite her embarrassment, she found herself eager to follow this new path, to see what would develop between her and Ector.

She also couldn't deny that she hoped he solved this little mystery. Soon.

CHAPTER 5

THE DAY PASSED QUICKLY, SPED BY KATHRYN'S ELATION AND THE easy conversations she and Ector fell into—none of which grew quite as heated as the exchange that had been interrupted by the sea itself. She'd donned a wide-brimmed hat to protect her from the sun, which she'd had to tie beneath her chin to prevent the occasional gust of wind from stealing it off her head. Ector left the boat a few times to swim ahead, vanishing beneath the surface to scout for rocks and other hazards hidden in their path, and she couldn't help worrying whenever he departed. But he always returned before long and pulled himself back into the boat with a grin.

And she couldn't stop her eyes from straying over his glistening body every time.

As the afternoon passed, Kat increasingly turned her attention toward the shore, seeking a good place to camp for the night. She found it just as the first evening colors crept into the sky. Though flanked by sheer cliffs on both sides, the section of beach she'd spotted was backed by a gradual slope that rose in uneven tiers on its way inland. The next tier up from the sand, which looked easily accessible in several spots, was covered in long, swaying grass and large rocks, the latter of which would provide some shelter from the wind. As an added perk, it was at least a hundred meters away from the jungle.

When the boat neared the land, Ector dropped into the water. "Stay there."

He clamped his hands over the side rail and guided the vessel onto the beach. Kat turned her head to watch as his powerful tentacles flared and snapped shut, propelling the boat forward. The receding tide soon halted their progress, dropping the boat fully onto the sand.

Ector moved around to the front of the boat and slowly went farther inland, sweeping his tentacles from side to side and creating a wide track. Kathryn watched him, unsure of what he was doing but grateful for another chance to see him move—to see that play of muscle beneath the skin of his corded arms and strong back. When he reached the bare rock that separated the beach from the first swathe of grass, he turned and came back along the same path, repeating the process.

This time, she noticed his tentacles occasionally digging deeper into the sand to pluck out a stone and toss it aside with a dull *thump*.

When he reached the boat, Kathryn frowned and pried her gaze away from him to study their surroundings. "The tide line is too far inland to—"

The boat lurched forward. She clamped both hands on the side rails to steady herself as she rocked back. Twisting around, she looked back to find Ector behind the boat, both hands pressed to the stern.

"Sorry," he said, offering her a smile. "I just needed to find the right spot." Ector slid his hands a little lower. The muscles in his arms and torso flexed, his tentacles sank into the wet sand beneath him, and the ship slid forward again—much farther this time.

He was *pushing* the boat.

She'd seen it done plenty of times, but a boat this size would've been a struggle even for two men in their prime. Ector barely made a sound as he continued forward at a slow but unwavering pace, tentacles constantly in motion. Kathryn could only maintain her hold on the sides and stare in awe.

When he finally stopped, dropped his hands, and straightened, the bow was within a couple meters of the end of the sand. His shoulders rose and fell a little quicker than before, but he seemed otherwise unaffected by the exertion.

Ector brushed his palms together. "That should keep the boat out of the tide. The water level will be higher in the morning, at least, so we'll have less distance to push backward."

Kathryn rose, glancing around before returning her gaze to Ector. "Ector...wow." She laughed. "I would've had to anchor offshore and swim if I were alone right now."

He chuckled and leaned toward her. "I am just happy to be of use."

"Oh, you've been *very* useful."

"If you find me blathering endlessly to be of use, I will not complain."

Smiling, Kathryn lowered the sails and secured the lines before she bent and unfastened the ties on some of the supplies. She grabbed one of the larger packs, lifted it over the side, and held it out to Ector. "You don't blather, Ector. I've enjoyed your company."

He accepted the pack and slung it over one shoulder. "I suppose we had best get everything set up to your satisfaction while you are still enjoying my company, then."

She turned back and was reaching for another pack when something caught her eye. Tilting her head and kneeling, she dragged the pack aside, revealing the airtight crates that had been behind it. There was small black bundle tucked between the two crates. Kat grasped the bundle and tugged it out. It immediately unfurled, and something clattered to the floor. She picked up the fallen object with an arched brow; it was a curved piece of glass with a thin, metal black frame and two slitted attachments at the bottom corners. Recognition struck Kat.

She turned the black fabric and raised it higher. It bore a faint hexagonal pattern, a round device on the chest, and another device on one of the sleeves.

It was a diving suit.

There was one of these in the museum in The Watch; such suits had been used by Halora's early colonists. As far as Kathryn knew, there hadn't been another like it until the kraken brought more suits to The Watch from the Facility. The functioning suits that were now available were usually reserved for specific occasions—like when humans mated to kraken needed to travel between the Facility and The Watch, or when humans accompanied the kraken on deep water hunts. They'd even been used to perform repairs on a few of the larger boats over the last year or so.

"Everything all right, Kathryn?" Ector asked.

Kat turned toward him and lifted the suit. "I didn't think Breckett would have packed a diving suit. He thinks me being on the surface is dangerous enough, but below it?"

"Which is exactly why I did not allow Breckett to see it when I slipped it in with the other supplies," Ector said with that mischievous light in his eyes.

Her mouth dropped open briefly before she laughed. "You sly, sly man. I won't tell him about it if you don't."

He chuckled and dipped his head in a deep nod. "I never planned to."

"You'd never hear the end of it." She turned back toward the crates, folded the suit around the glass mask, and tucked it away. Grabbing her personal backpack, she slung it over her shoulder and stood. As she walked toward Ector, she said, "Breckett means well, though."

Ector raised a hand to her, palm up. She placed hers atop it and used it to steady herself as she swung her legs over the side of the boat, moving herself into a sitting position.

Before she could hop down, Ector placed his hands on her hips and lifted her effortlessly. Kat sucked in a sharp breath and braced her hands on his shoulders—not that there was any need to. His hold on her was stable and sure as he gently set her on her feet in the sand.

"He does mean well," Ector said, "but that does not mean he knows best, does it? None of us do, not really. But I would like to think that we at least know what is right most of the time."

She smiled. "I try to tell myself that all the time when it comes to my daughters. It's...hard letting go."

"Yes, it certainly is." His hands flexed around her hips, giving Kat the sense that he meant it was hard to let go of *her*.

A delightful shiver rippled through her at the feel of his claws through her clothing, and that now familiar warmth blossomed on her cheeks. She had to delay this at least long enough to prepare a camp before dark...didn't she?

"So...what made you decide to sneak the diving suit aboard?" she forced herself to ask.

His gaze dipped, trailing over her body, before he replied. "I knew you were after an adventure, and I remembered how wondrous The Watch was when I first came to it. Many of the humans who have come below with us have viewed the ocean with the same wonder. So, if you are up to it...perhaps I will show you my world during one of the coming days."

Kathryn beamed; the thought of exploring the mysterious world beneath the waves had her brimming with excitement. Such exploration had been an impossible thing for most of her life, something she hadn't considered even in her wildest imaginings. "Oh, Ector, I'd love that! Thank you so much!"

Ector's smile stretched into a grin to mirror hers. "Then I am glad to have mustered enough wisdom to bring it along."

She patted his shoulder. "A very wise decision, indeed."

"We shall have to endeavor not to prove Breckett correct in his concerns."

"Well...we did establish that whatever we do out here is none of his business, so I wouldn't worry too much about it." She smirked and stepped back, out of Ector's hold. "Shall we set up camp before it gets dark?"

He tipped his head toward the grassy area nearby. "Lead the way, Kathryn."

ECTOR LOWERED his tentacles to the sandy bottom and dragged himself toward the beach. His head broke the surface first as he reached shallower water, followed soon by his shoulders and chest. He lifted his gaze to the patch of grass just above the pale sand. Though the sky was rapidly shifting toward the oranges and reds that would dominate it as the sun fell into the sea, the orange glow of the fire stood out against the green grass and dark rocks.

He shook excess water from his skin and continued forward, raising his catch to ensure it didn't end up coated in sand by the time he reached the camp. The boat that had brought them here was still resting in the spot to which Ector had pushed it. Its sail was furled, its lines secured, and it showed only the slightest hints of movement in the persistent sea breeze. For a moment— a ridiculous moment—Ector was a little jealous of the vessel for its complete, undisturbed rest.

His greatest exertion today had been pushing the boat onto the beach, but even that had resulted only in minor aches in some of his joints—nothing he wasn't used to. He'd seen more physical activity than this during most every other day of his life. But he was tired, nonetheless.

No, not really tired, he corrected. *Just ready to relax.*

Relaxation was one of those words the kraken had always

known but had never had use for. Everyday life had been about individual survival, about the survival of their entire race. They had to monitor food, go on hunts, defend the waters around their home, teach younglings the skills they would need to live in their harsh underwater world. What time had there been to relax?

But things were different now. There was little question as to whether there'd be food to eat; the kraken partnership with humans had resulted in excessive bounty. Ector's people had been afforded time to learn new skills, to build new relationships, to enter a new age.

And here he was with a fat fish in hand, having fulfilled that old kraken tradition of providing for a female for the first time in at least fifteen or twenty years.

He chuckled to himself as he moved past the boat and climbed the rocky slope toward the grass. What was it some of his new human friends were fond of saying?

The more things change, the more they stay the same.

Though he more and more frequently felt every year of his age, Ector still felt like a young, virile male in many ways. Perhaps he'd gained wisdom and perspective over time...but he still felt like the same kraken he'd been thirty or forty years ago. And being around Kathryn only strengthened that feeling. There was a certain youthfulness to her that was impossible to resist—as impossible to resist as her beauty.

He was glad she'd found the diving suit, was glad she'd been eager to swim with him. He'd been excited about the idea from the moment he'd conceived it. He'd have to wait until he found the right place to introduce her to his world—which meant he would have to look at the sea through *her* eyes as he scouted over the coming days. Even that prospect had him brimming with eagerness, in part because they were already in waters he'd never traversed. This was all as new to him as it was to her.

And, when he finally took her below...he would dance for

her. He'd not had reason to in a long, long while, and he found himself thrilled to have the chance. He couldn't be sure how she'd take it, but it would happen.

As he crested the small rise, Kathryn came into view. She was sitting, rifle laid across her lap, on a low rock in front of the fire she'd built, which itself was near the canvas tent they'd erected together. She'd removed her boots and head covering. The supplies she'd deemed essential enough to bring to camp were arranged beside the tent.

"I have returned"—Ector raised his hand, displaying the fish he'd caught, which was as long as his arm—"with the bounty of the sea."

She turned her head toward him and grinned, setting the rifle carefully on the ground. "It's been a long time since someone brought me dinner."

"If I knew how to cook it, it would be the perfect gift." He stopped near the fire. The heat it gave off was both pleasant and disconcerting; spending his life in the water had made such sensations foreign to him, and he was still growing accustomed to them even after two years in The Watch.

Kathryn chuckled. "It's still a gift all the same—and it saves our food stores." She rolled up her sleeves, baring her arms. "Come, I'll show you how to cook it."

She tugged a knife from her belt and took the lead. The process humans went through to *clean* a fish was still baffling to Ector. He watched with fascination, and couldn't resist eating many of the parts she cut away as though they were refuse. Her little cringes as he ate those morsels made him chuckle more than once.

"I'm sorry," she said, shaking her head. "I don't mean to make faces or insult you, but…"

"It is all right," he said, offering her a smile. "I know humans do not find all parts of these creatures palatable."

She laughed. "We don't find them *edible*."

From that point forward, she handed the bits she removed to him directly. That warmed his hearts in a way he'd never imagined possible—it was a small but powerful show of acceptance.

But more interesting than what she was doing—or the morsels she was feeding him—was her skill. Her hands moved with practiced ease, making the blade seem as natural an extension of her body as Ector's claws were to his.

Within short order, she had several thick fillets cooking at the fire. Ector found the aroma of cooking meat an enticing one. Though he'd never imagined that taste could be altered so drastically by such simple processes and methods, he'd come to enjoy such flavors during his time amongst humans. And, despite the nibbles he'd already had, the smell of roasting fish made him realize just how hungry he still was.

He and Kathryn washed their hands and sat beside one another to wait until the food was ready.

"I've seen so many sunrises and sunsets through the years, but they never lose their beauty," Kathryn said softly.

Ector glanced at her. Her eyes were focused toward the sea, and he turned his head to follow her gaze. The sun was a red-orange disk on the horizon, its bottom curve barely touching the sea, and the sky was stained with lovely colors that only seemed to exist during this time of day. The reds and oranges gave way to pinks and purples amidst the clouds, and everything darkened toward the land—deep blues, grays, and violets spreading as night followed in the day's wake. All those colors were reflected—albeit darker—on the water.

"You are right. They never do," he said, but his attention returned to her. There was a hint of wonder in her eyes and serenity in her expression; she exuded a sense of peace and fulfillment that only enhanced her allure.

Ector shifted a tentacle toward her and loosely curled it around her ankle. Its tip brushed beneath the cuff of her pants, and his suction cups tasted the salty sweetness of her skin; he craved more. "And I can think of no one better to enjoy it with."

The pink on her cheeks deepened as she looked at him, and the corners of her lips curled upward. She didn't pull away from him. "Neither can I."

Whenever she graced him with one of those smiles, he couldn't help but mirror it. Together, they returned their attention to the sunset, and sat in comfortable silence as the fiery orb continued its descent and the sky darkened. Finally, the sun sank beneath the horizon, and the only light touching Ector and Kathryn was the warm orange glow of the fire. It wasn't long before the first little stars became visible through the gaps in the clouds.

They ate when Kathryn declared the meat ready. She ate relatively slowly, seeming to take her time to enjoy each bite, and Ector forced himself to match her pace. Eating as though any given meal could be his last had been a habit for his entire life, and it had proven difficult to break even after experiencing the abundance of food in The Watch. Still, despite his efforts, he devoured the flakey meat well before she finished hers, licking the remaining juices from his fingers when he was done.

Kathryn raised a hand to cover her mouth as she laughed. Her eyes, shining in the firelight, crinkled at the corners endearingly. "I'll take that as a compliment."

Ector chuckled and angled himself toward her. "It was *good*."

She lowered her hand, finished chewing what was in her mouth, and swallowed. "I can't claim to be a great cook. Honestly, my cooking leaves a lot to be desired. I'm glad my daughters didn't take after me. But there's just something about roasting meat on an open fire that awakens my hidden culinary skills." She tore a small piece off the fillet in her hand, ate it, and held out the remaining meat to Ector. "Here. Have some more."

He shook his head. "No, that is your share. You finish it."

"I insist." Her eyes dipped down his body, lingering on his

chest. "You, uh, have a much...*larger* body that requires...more. More, um, sustenance."

The heat in her gaze surpassed that of the fire, and it suffused Ector's blood. One corner of his quirked. "Shall I take that as a compliment?"

Kathryn's eyes met his again briefly before shifting away. Her cheeks, already flushed from the fire's warmth, reddened further. "I, uh, don't see why not. You're certainly appealing, and you've likely had no problem attracting the attention of female kraken. I'm sure you have plenty vying for you, considering your, well, um, your..." Kathryn cleared her throat. "I'm rambling, aren't I?" She lifted the food in her hand again, offering it to him. "Take it."

For the first time in a long while, Ector found himself having to actively resist an instinctual color change—the shift to maroon that would display his desire for her. Normally, he kept firm enough control on his emotions to prevent such changes, which he believed had granted him more credibility as a guiding force to his people. But he could not deny that his forwardness on the beach a few days before had likely frightened Kathryn away and cut their encounter short. She was signaling that she was interested, that she was attracted to him, but she needed more time—and though much had changed, he still believed in many aspects of the old ways.

It was the female's choice. All he could do was present himself to her and show her why he was worthy of her time and attention. His impatience for something new, for something *more*, had pushed him toward her initially, but if left unchecked it would not serve him well.

There were other matters to address now—like the fact that his female was attempting to reduce her portion of food for his benefit. As much as he appreciated the gesture, he didn't want her to deny herself for his sake.

He lifted his hands, displaying his palms to her. "I have had my share, Kathryn. You eat yours."

"I've had plenty, if that is what you're worried about."

He lowered his brows. "You have hardly eaten anything. Eat."

"Ector," she tilted her head, narrowing her eyes, "are you calling me a liar?"

"No," he said with a chuckle, "just overly generous."

Kathryn rose from her seat and eased closer to him, moving the fillet closer to his face. She grinned. "Come on, Ector. You know you want it."

There was a hint of playfulness in her tone that made Ector's hearts beat a little faster. Perhaps looking at it from the outside, his excitement—which bordered on giddiness—would've seemed foolish, but he could not deny that seeing this side of Kathryn only enhanced his attraction to her.

He leaned precariously away from her, tentacles bunches to one side, and shook his head. "I do not want it as much as you need it, Kathryn. You will have to maintain your strength if you are to keep up with me over the coming days."

Kathryn gaped at him, eyes flaring wide in shock. "Now you're calling me weak!"

Ector grimaced. "For someone who has no feet, I certainly seem prone to putting them in my mouth."

She chuckled. "You could put this food in your mouth, instead." She moved as though to step closer, but his tentacle—still wrapped loosely around one of her ankles—was in the path of her leading foot. Her toes caught on the underside of the tentacle, and before either of them could react, she pitched forward with a gasp.

Kathryn fell on top of Ector. Her slight weight was enough to upset his balance. He dropped backward, wrapping his arms around her, and accepted the impact of the fall on his back. They both grunted—and the fish fillet flew from her hand and landed on his face, covering his eyes and nose.

A few moments of silence passed, during which Ector was struck by the absurdity of the situation. This little human had tripped and knocked him to the ground, there was a rock digging into his back, and a piece of meat was draped over his face…but he couldn't help enjoying the feel of her soft, warm body sprawled atop his. How could something be so comical and arousing at once?

"You missed my mouth," he said.

An abrupt, snort-like sound escaped Kathryn, and then she was laughing. She buried her face against Ector's chest, and her warm breath fanned his skin as her entire body shook with her laughter.

Ector added his laughter to hers. It felt *good*—not just laughing together, but having her body against his, feeling her heat, experiencing a closeness that, at least at that moment, transcended the physical.

The warmth of her breath faded as she propped herself up. She lifted one side of the fillet to uncover one of his eyes. She was still chuckling as she met his gaze.

"I'm afraid you're going to start seeing me as nothing more than a clumsy human," she said.

He raised a hand and gently closed it around hers, guiding her arm up until the fish was lifted off his face, leaving the fillet to dangle above him. "You are so much more than that, Kathryn."

Her expression softened.

The strain placed on the flaky meat proved too much just as he finished speaking, and the bottom half of it tore away.

Kathryn started, her arm tensing. "Oh!"

Ector quickly shifted his head, opened his mouth, and caught the meat between his teeth. He chewed and swallowed before offering her a smile. "I suppose you win, after all."

Her body shook as she laughed again, creating delightful friction against his closed slit. "I suppose I do."

He kept his eyes locked with hers as he opened his mouth again, lifted his head off the ground, and ate the remaining fish, lips and tongue briefly brushing her flesh. After a moment's consideration, he slowly licked the juices from her fingers.

Kathryn's laughter was cut short by a sharp inhalation. Her eyes dipped to his mouth, and something lit within them, something heated and wanting.

Ector very well understood his potential double meaning when he said, "Delicious."

Her other hand, which was still resting on his chest, moved up, lightly brushing over his skin. When it reached his face, she traced his jawline, lips, and nose with the tips of her fingers. That touch—so simple but so powerful—nearly stole his breath.

Of their own accord, a few of his tentacles curled up to wrap around her legs, and his cock pressed uncomfortably against the inside of his slit. He clenched his jaw to maintain control; extruding now was very unlikely to endear him to her. His time amongst humans had taught him that they usually didn't appreciate genitalia being openly displayed.

Finally, Kathryn flattened her palm against his cheek, smiled, and met his eyes with hers. "We should get some sleep so we can get an early start tomorrow."

He knew she was right, and part of him wanted nothing more than to sleep right there with her nestled securely atop him. It would have been worth the discomfort of having a rock digging into his back for the entirety of the night. "Indeed, we should."

Kathryn lingered upon him, stroking his cheekbone with her thumb, and Ector breathed in her sweet, floral, sea-kissed scent.

Lowering her face, she kissed his cheek. "Goodnight, Ector."

He released his hold on her hand and legs with a surprising amount of reluctance as she pushed herself up and climbed off him. Cold had never bothered him, but the air felt unreasonably cool in her absence—contrasted by the warmth lingering on his cheek in the wake of her kiss.

"Goodnight, Kathryn," he said softly.

She walked to the tent, paused at the entrance, and looked back at him over her shoulder. The corners of her mouth rose in a small smile. Then she ducked through the canvas flaps, exiting his view.

With a groan, Ector dropped his head onto the ground and pressed a hand over his aching slit. He'd not felt quite so strong a need for release since he was on the cusp of adulthood many, many years before. He forced his gaze skyward.

Little points of light twinkled amidst the field of dark blue, purple, and gray, and the first hints of moonlight were reflected on the landside edges of the clouds. Those stars were not unlike little flecks of halorium sometimes found floating in the deep, dark parts of the sea. Beautiful as the sky was, it could not fully distract him from the female only a few meters away from him.

He couldn't be sure of the best way to move forward with Kathryn, couldn't be certain of how to win her favor or whether her favor could be won to begin with, but he knew one thing without a doubt—he wanted her. More than that, he was already thinking of her as *his*. His female, his mate. And he knew that building a bond between them would be the most fulfilling part of this new adventure.

CHAPTER 6

THE NEXT COUPLE OF DAYS PASSED PLEASANTLY AND WITHOUT
incident. Kathryn and Ector fell into an easy routine—though
she wasn't sure *routine* was the right term for it. She'd been
stuck in a routine back at home, doing the same things at the
same times every day even though the faces and the conversations were often different.

But out here, with Ector, routine was a malleable thing.
They had certain things they needed to do—watch for hazards
in the water as they sailed, prepare meals, set camp—but they
were free to accomplish those tasks whenever and however they
pleased.

Plus, the sights were ever-changing; each hour brought new
sections of the coastline into view, and Kat would hold all of it
in her memory for the rest of her life. The Watch was home, and
it would always hold a particular beauty for her, but the rest of
Halora was beautiful, too. Kathryn was glad she was finally
seeing more of it.

The one part of their routine that had remained solid,
however, was proving to be her favorite. Each evening, she and
Ector lounged beside the fire, shared a meal, watched the

sunset, and traded stories about their lives and their people as the moons and stars came out. Each night, Ector moved a little closer to her, and his touch grew a little bolder and more familiar.

And each night, she welcomed it, *craved* it, just a little more.

But like every night for years before this trip, Kat went to bed alone. And no matter how exhausted she was, she'd lie awake in her tent, her body throbbing with need. For the first time in forever, she'd found herself tempted—tempted to touch herself, to bring herself to completion knowing that Ector was right outside, possibly listening. Part of her thrilled in the thought of him hearing her and entering her tent...thrilled in the thought of *him* being the one to bring her to completion.

And those thoughts, those *fantasies*, shocked her.

She hadn't experienced this kind of sexual drive in a long time—and had never imagined someone like Ector pleasuring her. Before their brief conversation during the Dryfall Festival, Kathryn would never have considered the feel of tentacles on her bare skin, could never have imagined herself attracted to a kraken. But now those tentacles were simply another *very* intriguing part of a male she was coming to care for very deeply. Though she harbored lingering uncertainties, she wasn't repulsed by Ector or his body. Her hesitance was about her own insecurity. Her own cowardice. She'd gone so long without any desire for a relationship, for sex, that they were daunting concepts now.

Her body had changed in the eighteen years since her husband's death; it had changed *a lot*. No one had seen her naked in all that time. Would Ector like what he saw when the time came, especially considering that she must've looked as alien to him as he did to her? And yet an undeniable anticipation thrummed within her at the notion of Ector's golden eyes taking in her naked body.

The fourth day of their journey dawned bright and clear,

bearing only a hint of the chill that often gripped Halorian nights throughout the wet season. Both sky and sea stretched out to the horizon, endless and impossibly blue. Kathryn and Ector took their time eating breakfast. There was no need to rush when their only destination was *farther along* and they didn't have to be there until whenever they arrived.

After they were done eating, Kathryn plucked a purple leaf from the stalk of star mint she'd picked near camp and slipped it into her mouth. Its cool, refreshing flavor swept through her mouth once she chewed, erasing the lingering taste of her meal.

"What is that?" Ector asked, cocking his head to the side.

"It's star mint. It cleans your teeth and makes your breath smell nice." She plucked another dark purple leaf from the stem and held it out to him. "Want to try one?"

A crease formed between Ector's brows as he accepted the leaf. He held it up between forefinger and thumb and turned it slowly, examining it as though with deep suspicion. After a final glance at Kat, he slipped the leaf between his lips, and the muscles of his jaw bulged as he bit down. His eyes immediately widened. He turned his head and spit the partially chewed leaf into the grass.

"Don't like it?" she asked, chuckling.

"How can something be hot and cold at the same time?" he demanded before sticking out his tongue to scrape a few violet flecks off it.

Kathryn continued chewing her star mint, unable to suppress her grin through her giggles. "Guess it's just an acquired taste. Come one, let's pack up camp. It should get your mind off the taste."

The sun was already shining just above the vast inland jungle by the time everything was loaded and the boat was back on the water. Ector swam ahead, keeping close to the surface to guide Kathryn past any potentially dangerous obstacles—submerged rocks were the most commonplace of the dangers thus far, but there'd been at least two reefs that had been large and vibrant enough for Kat to spot from above through the relatively clear coastal waters. She relied on Ector more than her own eyes, however, as his perspective from beneath the surface allowed him to gauge the depth and positioning with much greater accuracy than she could achieve from the boat.

Once the vessel was in deeper water, Ector hauled himself over the side and sat down across from Kathryn. Sailing proved a somewhat difficult task while the beads of water clinging to Ector's skin sparkled in the bright morning sun. Kat's eyes roved over his body repeatedly—sometimes by conscious choice but more often of their own accord. She imagined not only her fingers running over those sculpted muscles, but her lips and tongue.

Her only comfort—and perhaps the only thing that saved her from death by embarrassment—was that his hungry gaze was just as often on her. She might've been made uncomfortable by the lustful light in his eyes were it not a direct reflection of what must've been in her own. Fortunately, she was able to eventually force her attention to the task at hand.

The sea was calm and the breeze gentle; progress was slower than it had been on the prior days, but the serenity was more than worth the reduced pace, especially when paired with the pleasant warmth of the sunshine.

Kathryn and Ector passed the time like they had over the first few days, with easy conversation that was broken only by occasional, companionable lulls during which Ector sometimes left the boat to scout the surrounding waters. With Ector, Kat had found none of the awkwardness that usually accompanied silence; so many people seemed to think that every moment had to be filled with conversation or sound to have meaning. She and Ector didn't *need* to talk. The bond forming between them already transcended the need for words. Even when he was silent, Ector was still *present*. He was still there with her. He was still there for her.

It was early afternoon when Kathryn spotted the perfect campsite situated on a stretch of beach where the rocky slope leading inland was far gentler than most places. As ideal as that was, the stream flowing directly onto the beach and into the ocean was the feature that really caught her eye. Its path took it through a small, rocky ravine, and despite the outcroppings of bare stone around it, the stream's banks were lined with lush grass and vegetation.

Though this was the fourth day of their trip, Kat and Ector had yet to venture very far inland. In addition to acting as a source of fresh water, the stream could serve as a natural path leading into and back out of the jungle, and Kathryn was excited to explore the wilderness like she'd done in her adolescence.

When she told Ector she wanted to make camp near that stream, he scanned the area she'd indicated and nodded. They conducted their landing procedure with practiced ease. Once they were closer to shore, he dove into the water and guided the boat onto the beach, where he went through his usual check for rocks and other obstructions under the sand that might've damaged the boat's hull. He pushed the boat ashore and past the tide line along the path he'd established.

An onlooker might've thought she and Ector had been sailing together for decades rather than days. And Kathryn almost felt like that was the truth—all of this felt so natural and effortless that she could've believed she'd been doing it forever.

Ector accompanied Kathryn as she searched for the right spot to set up the camp. He didn't need to ask which supplies needed to be brought to the site after she selected it; he knew by now and moved everything quickly and efficiently. Within short order, they were established on a low, grassy rise overlooking the beach, only about twenty meters from the stream. Ector had even arranged a ring of stones at the center of their little campsite, and Kathryn filled it with driftwood and spare firewood from their last camp.

With the preparations complete, Kathryn turned toward Ector and grinned. "Feel like exploring?"

He smiled and held up a hand, palm turned skyward. "Lead the way, and I shall follow."

Kathryn picked up her rifle, slung it over her shoulder, and gestured to the water filtration jugs standing beside the tent. "Would you mind grabbing those?"

Ector moved to the tent—giving Kat another opportunity to watch his strange but almost hypnotic movement on land—and looped the end of a tentacle around each jug. He lifted them to his hands, offered her another smile, and followed Kathryn to the stream.

Kathryn remained mindful of her footing as she started up the gentle incline leading inland, where the stream widened and ran through a patch of loose rocks on its way to the beach. Bare stone and dirt rose to either side of the water, creating the small ravine she'd spied from the boat. The ground was interspersed with patches of vegetation, and the stream's banks were bristling with greenery closest to the water, but there was a narrow strip of relatively clear ground on each bank that offered only the occasional cluster of rocks as an obstacle.

The lazily twisting stream led up the slope and eventually into the jungle about a hundred meters onward. The grass along the banks was sprinkled with pretty little indigo flowers that usually grew near the sea—capeweed, which was often used to make dye for cloth Kathryn used in her work.

"Right here is good," she said as they reached a spot where the stream ran a little deeper. She carefully knelt on the smooth rocks, swung the rifle off her shoulder to prop it beside her, and held out her hand. Ector passed her one of the jugs. She twisted off the cap and dunked the jug into the stream.

Ector sank down to fill the other jug. "Even after two years, I cannot quite understand the need to drink water. It is strange."

Kathryn glanced at him with a smile. "And I don't understand not needing to drink. It only takes a few days without water for a human to die of dehydration."

"I find it curious that you are land creatures but are so dependent upon water for your survival."

She chuckled and lifted the filled jug out of the water, screwing the cap back on. "It is strange, isn't it?"

He removed his jug from the water, too, and resealed it. "Stranger still is that despite kraken being part human, the very water you depend upon is dangerous for us."

Kat frowned, and her brows knitted in worry as she skimmed her gaze over the stream. "Just by being inside it?"

"For long enough, yes. But my understanding—based on information Arkon found—is that it would take quite some time." He flicked the end of a tentacle over the surface of the stream. "Mere contact will not do me any harm. No need to worry, Kathryn."

She released a huff of laughter. "You really had me worried for a second there, Ector." After setting the jug down about half a meter from the water's edge, she planted the butt of her rifle on the ground and used it to help herself stand up. "We can leave the containers here while we go farther inland. No sense in hauling them through the jungle when we have to come back this way later."

Ector twisted at his waist and placed his jug beside Kat's. His tentacles drew together and pushed his torso upward in a smooth, effortless motion. As velvety-smooth as their skin was, as gentle as their touch could be, Kathryn couldn't imagine the amount of strength held within those tentacles, couldn't imagine the strength Ector exerted constantly just to remain upright on land. Kraken were made for the water but being out of it didn't seem to slow them down much.

Kathryn's eyes traveled down Ector's body.

It's no wonder their bodies are so muscular, so strong, so...

When she lifted her gaze again, he was staring right back at her with a knowing smile on his lips.

Heat flooded her cheeks. "I was staring again, wasn't I?"

"Yes, but I do not mind." He eased closer, raised a hand, and brushed the backs of his fingers across her cheek to tuck a few stray strands of hair behind her ear. A moment later, one of his tentacles rose, and he plucked something from it—a vibrant capeweed flower, which he slipped into her hair. He curled a clawed finger beneath her chin and tilted her face up toward his. "I very much enjoy looking at you, too, Kathryn."

He towered over her, but she wasn't afraid; he made her feel small but *safe.*

Kat's lips parted as she searched his eyes. They were warm and glowing, and he looked at her as though she were the most beautiful thing in the world. As though she *was* his world. She lifted a hand and loosely curled her fingers around his wrist—it was too big for her fingertips to meet—and, without thinking, closed her eyes, rose up on her toes, and pressed her mouth to his. Heat flared along Kat's lips and spread through her, leaving pleasurable tingles in its wake.

He started and released a surprised breath, but he didn't pull away as she molded their mouths together. His lips were warm and firm, and she tasted salt and sea upon them, but Ector was still—so still that Kathryn feared she'd done something wrong. That *this* was wrong.

Dread washed over her, cold and sobering, and she broke the kiss, pulling away and releasing her hold on his wrist.

But Ector looped an arm around her back, halting her retreat. She looked up to find his brow furrowed and his lips turned down in a shallow frown. He plucked the rifle from her grasp with his free hand and passed it to a tentacle, setting it aside.

"I did not do that correctly, did I?" he asked.

Kathryn's mouth fell into a frown of her own as she settled her hands on his shoulders. "You didn't... What do you mean?"

"I have never *kissed*," he replied softly.

Kat's eyes widened. "Oh." She tilted her face a little closer, keeping her eyes locked with his. "But don't kraken kiss? I've seen so many with their mates..."

"Something they learned from their human mates." He smiled, and his tongue slipped out to run over his lips. "And I... would like to learn, also."

Her gaze dipped to watch his tongue move, catching a glimpse of his sharp teeth, and a spark of arousal flickered in her core. She tightened her grip on his shoulders. Those wicked teeth didn't dampen her desire to feel his mouth against hers again—they intensified it. And, though playing the role of tutor in such intimate matters was strange, she couldn't deny that it was also thrilling.

"You want me to teach you?" she asked, her voice surprisingly husky.

Ector lifted his free hand to her face, cupping her cheek with his warm palm while one of his tentacles coiled around her calf. He drew her body flush against his. "Yes. You are the only one I want to kiss."

Kathryn's breath hitched, and her heart fluttered. The spark at her core flared, sending a wave of anticipation and desire through her body. She leaned her face closer, leaving their lips a whisper apart, and stared up at him.

"Think of it...as a dance." She grazed her lips back and forth across his. "A kiss can be slow and sensual." She kissed him more firmly, caressing his lips with her own, exploring his mouth, before nipping at his lower lip and sucking it into her mouth to stroke with her tongue.

Ector's breath caught, and both his arm and his tentacle tightened around her. The tips of his claws lightly scraped the skin of her lower back through her shirt; the sensation only heightened her arousal.

She released his lip and skimmed the tip of her nose over his. "One leads and takes control. Kiss me, Ector, like I showed you."

Kathryn returned her mouth to his. The difference was immediate.

Ector leaned into the kiss, responding to the movement of her lips and complementing them with his own. He seemed tentative at first, but as the kiss continued, his confidence improved—and her need grew along with it.

A heady sensation spread from Kathryn's mouth to suffuse her body, making her feel heavy and warm. Her sex throbbed, her nipples were tight and achy, and shivers stole through her as the subtle movements of his chest created sweet, teasing friction against those sensitive buds.

"Or," she whispered against his mouth as she slid her hands to the back of his neck, "a kiss can be raw and passionate."

Kat pulled him down and claimed his mouth in a hungry, desperate kiss, feeding into the fierce need for intimacy that he'd awoken within her. Her tongue slipped past his lips to flick and stroke his tongue and dance across the sharp points of his teeth. She tasted the sea, and she tasted *him*. And she wanted more.

Ector's calm shattered. He crushed her to him, seemingly unable to get close enough, and his mouth took hers with startling intensity. She was no longer in control. He kissed Kat with reckless abandon, moving his mouth over hers, devouring her, and what he lacked in finesse, he made up for with passion and eagerness.

She hugged him closer, needing to feel his solidness, his strength, his heat. His hands fell to her hips, and before she could guess what he was doing, her feet were off the ground. She instinctively wrapped her legs around his waist. Something long, thick, and solid pressed against the apex of her thighs, directly over her clit.

Urgency drove her to grind her pelvis against him. There was no conscious thought—only pleasure, only feeling, and she rocked her hips again and again, following that sensation, chasing it, *needing* it.

Ector growled, sliding his hands to her backside. His grip on her tightened as he shuddered. He slanted his mouth over Kathryn's, kissing her deeper, harder. His tongue danced with hers, exploring the recesses of her mouth. His tentacles coiled around her legs to tug her against him even more firmly.

Her breaths were short and shallow, turning into small moans as the sensation between her legs built into something intense, something blistering, something consuming. Sheer pleasure pierced her core. Kathryn gasped and tore her mouth away from Ector's. She barely registering the little flash of pain it caused as pleasure wracked her body, making her cry out. Her sex spasmed, and liquid heat flooded her.

Ector tensed and sucked in a sharp breath. For a moment, he was utterly still. Then his hips bucked, his powerful body shook, and a growl tore from his throat. Kathryn was hit by a fresh wave of heat, but this one was not from within herself. The new warmth soaked through her shirt to wet her belly. Ector clutched her ass tightly enough for his claws to prick her skin through her pants, pressing her pelvis firmly against his. His chest heaved with ragged breaths as he curled around her, his body trembling and jerking in his release.

Panting, Kathryn pressed her face into his neck and clung to him, feeling sated and weak, but still...not wholly fulfilled. There was an emptiness within her, and she knew exactly what her body craved—*him*. Ector. Inside her.

His tentacles slid along the backs of her thighs, supporting her weight as he lifted a hand from her ass. He hooked a finger beneath her chin, leaned back, and tilted her face toward his.

Kathryn looked up with half-lidded eyes. His gleaming gaze held hers for a few seconds before dipping to her mouth.

Ector's brow furrowed, creating a worried crease above the bridge of his nose, and his skin changed from deep maroon to its normal drab green. She hadn't noticed the initial color change, but the concern in his expression was all she could focus on—as well as the smear of crimson on his lips.

"You are bleeding, Kathryn."

All at once, she was aware of the slight sting on the inside of her lip.

Ector unwound his tentacles from her legs and gently lowered her. She set her feet on the ground; her legs were weak and unsteady, and she was immediately thankful that his hold on her remained firm. Lifting a hand to her mouth, she pressed the tip of a finger to the tiny cut on the inside of her lower lip. Her finger came away wet with blood.

"I cut you," Ector said, voice thicker than usual. The oblong pupils of his eyes dilated. "I am sorry, Kathryn. I did not mean—"

Kat pressed the fingers of her free hand to his mouth, quieting him. The cut was insignificant compared to the bliss she'd experienced. She chuckled. "I guess we just need to be more careful the next time we kiss."

He covered her hand with his own and guided it down. Confusion joined the concern in his expression. "You wish to kiss me again, even after this?"

"Ector," Kat turned her hand and laced her fingers with his as much as his webbing allowed, "*this* was perfect. We were both, well, in the moment, and it was an accident. One I don't regret."

Her eyes dipped down his body. Wetness glistened on his abdomen, but it wasn't sweat. Her gaze dropped a little farther to his pelvis, where his cock had emerged from its slit. It was long and thick, hard even after he'd reached completion, and glistened with its own secretions. It was a darker green than the rest of his skin, though it lightened at the tip. He had no scrotum, at least none that she could see, but there were thin, five-centimeter long tendrils at the base of his shaft that were slowly writhing, their tips repeatedly reaching toward her as though they had appetites of their own.

The breath fled Kathryn. She knew *exactly* where those would have touched had he been inside her. A thrilling shiver raced through her, and she squeezed her thighs together, but it did nothing to alleviate the needy ache between them. Her sex still pulsed in the aftermath of her orgasm.

The sight of his cock might have shocked her a year ago, maybe even a few months ago, but now, she yearned for it. She'd already grown used to Ector's alienness, and this part of him only intrigued her further.

His green skin took on a violet tint, decidedly different from the maroon he'd displayed before, and he withdrew from her, breaking their physical contact. "I am sorry, Kathryn. This is... I..."

Kathryn looked up at him and frowned. "Ector, what's wrong?"

Ector's eyes were locked on her—or rather more specifically, her abdomen. He wore a frown of his own, the expression decidedly strained. "I have demonstrated all the control of a youngling."

Brows lowering, she glanced down and lifted a hand to her stomach, where her shirt was plastered to her skin. Yep. She was soaked all right. Nearly the entire front of her shirt was wet—from his seed.

Her lips slowly spread into a wide smile, and she laughed. Startled by her own reaction, she snapped her wide eyes to his —she knew how he might take her reaction—but she couldn't stop. The laughter kept coming.

"I'm sorry," she said between laughs, covering her mouth. "I'm not…not laughing at you. I promise. Well, kind of not."

His brow furrowed again, and he tilted his head. His cock—with a bead of his seed gathered at its tip—twitched in the open air, its tendrils still moving restlessly. His tentacles writhed over the ground in similar fashion. "I do not understand, Kathryn. I… You deserve better than what I have done. You deserve better of me."

His words sobered her, and she shook her head. "No. Don't talk like that, Ector."

She moved closer to him. In her peripheral vision, she saw his tentacles reaching for her, but he seemed to hold them back.

Kat lifted a hand and cupped Ector's jaw, brushing her thumb over the smear of blood on his chin. "I'm sorry. I didn't mean for you to get that impression. I was laughing because… we were *both* acting like teenagers. Which isn't a bad thing." She moved her thumb up to caress his bottom lip. "It's…been a long time since I felt anything like that."

Ector's expression softened, and he leaned slightly into her touch as his color returned to normal. He tentatively dropped a hand to her hip and brushed the pad of his thumb across the fabric of her shirt. "I have *never* felt anything like that."

Kat's heart skipped a beat. In some ways, she hadn't felt anything like it either. She'd loved Colin with all her heart, had been passionate with him, had mourned him for many, many years after he was gone, and she would always have love for him. But what she had with Ector was new, and it was fiery and intense. She knew already that it could easily become love even though it seemed absurdly early for that. It was neither better than nor lesser to her feelings for Colin, it was just different.

And who's to say it's too early, anyway? I'd say I'm grown up enough to decide that without anyone else's input. I've waited long enough.

Kathryn smiled and slid her hand around the back of his

neck, tugging him down. He lowered himself without hesitation. When she brushed her lips over his, a shiver stole through him. Knowing that the simplest of her touches, the lightest caress, could rouse such a reaction in him made her feel confident and sensual.

"Why don't we get cleaned up?" she asked. "We can find a deeper part of the stream and rinse off."

He kissed her gently, letting the contact between their lips linger for several seconds. His nostrils flared with a deep inhalation. He closed his eyes and groaned. "But that would mean washing away your alluring scent."

A flush heated her cheeks, and she laughed, giving his chest a playful smack as she drew away. He opened his eyes and grinned, flashing his teeth. Despite what those teeth had done, his words and that wicked grin excited her.

Her shirt wasn't the only thing that was wet.

Before those thoughts could push her to leap into his arms and grind against him again—*God, I really am acting like a horny teenager*—Kathryn bent down to pick up her rifle, slung it over her shoulder, and forced her feet to move, continuing their trek upstream.

The vegetation to either side of the water thickened as Kat and Ector moved uphill, but there remained enough space along the bank to allow them easy passage. They stopped when they reached a spot where the stream flowed over a bare outcropping of rock in a little waterfall that couldn't be more than a meter high. The stream was bloated beneath the waterfall, which had likely carved a deeper pool over hundreds or thousands of years. There were many trees nearby now, creating interesting patterns of shadows and light both on the water and the surrounding foliage, but it was another ten or fifteen meters before the jungle properly began.

It was a beautiful spot.

Kathryn swept her eyes over the area. Capeweed and long,

green stalks of naba grew amidst the grass around the edges of the pool. She'd have to remember to gather some naba on the way back to camp. She took a few moments to scan the wider area, looking for any signs of danger. Many of the more dangerous Halorian predators kept to the deeper jungle, but there were always exceptions. Fortunately, the plants here weren't thick enough to conceal any large animals, and the landscape, while sloped, was open enough to allow clear lines of sight in almost all directions.

"This is perfect," Kat said, flashing a grin over her shoulder at Ector. She sat on a low boulder, stood the rifle against it, and bent forward to unlace her boots.

CHAPTER 7

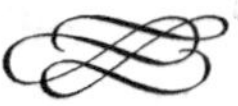

She is perfect.

Ector watched as Kathryn removed her footwear, unable but to marvel at her form and figure even as she performed so mundane a task. He discovered some new point of beauty each time he looked upon her. Whether it was the multiple hues of blue in her irises, the various shades of silver in her hair, the little, joyous lines that formed at the corners of her eyes when she smiled and laughed—or a hundred other things—she was beautiful in her entirety.

The kisses they'd shared, however brief, had only heightened his desire for her. Something had passed between them while their lips were pressed together, something powerful and profound. It had been unlike anything he'd ever experienced; the intimacy and affection of that simple contact had transcended everything he'd known, had woken something inside him that must always have been dormant, awaiting Kathryn.

Though minutes had passed since they'd kissed, his lips still tingled in the aftermath of it. He fixed his gaze on her mouth. Kathryn's lips were swollen and red, sparking his hunger anew, rekindling his need to taste and touch her.

But as much as he longed to watch her, as much as he longed to take her in his arms and kiss her again, he needed to remain alert. He needed to keep her safe. The ocean and the coast had their own dangers, some of which Ector and Kathryn had already navigated during this trip, but the jungle introduced a new set of threats—many of which were unfamiliar to him. Kathryn herself had expressed a cautious and respectful stance regarding the jungle, as did many of the humans in The Watch.

And this was the closest Ector and Kathryn had come to the jungle thus far.

So, he pried his gaze away from her and forced himself to study his surroundings with the same attentiveness he'd have maintained in the ocean. He didn't know the names of all the plants, didn't know what animals they were likely to encounter, and wasn't even sure if this spot was actually considered part of the jungle, but none of that mattered. He had instincts—instincts that had been honed over decades. Instincts he trusted.

Some of which had pushed him—or was *pulled* the better word?—to Kathryn.

Once her boots were set aside, Kathryn stood up. She unbuckled her belt and placed it, along with the sheathed knife and small pouch attached to it, atop the boulder. Offering Ector a smile, she walked to the edge of the pool. She stopped there, with smooth rocks and flattened grass beneath her feet, and lifted a leg. Ector tilted his head, attention once again solely upon her.

Kathryn dipped her toes into the pool and held them there for a second. Then she nodded and stepped forward, plunging her foot into the water. The leg of her pants darkened as it absorbed moisture. Her other foot followed, and she walked to the center of the pool, where the water came nearly to her hips. She crouched, submerging herself up to her shoulders, and let out a slow sigh.

When she rose, fire flowed through Ector's veins. The material of her shirt, now thoroughly soaked, clung to her body, perfectly sculpting over her sides, her belly, her full breasts and hardened nipples. He caught his bottom lip with his teeth, but even the string of sharp teeth against soft flesh wasn't enough to break his stare.

It was Kathryn herself who broke his trance when she asked with a laugh, "Are you going to come in or just gawk at me all afternoon?"

He curled the ends of his tentacles tight and pressed the tips of his claws into his palms. "My apologies, Kathryn."

Though he'd learned much about humans and their ways over the last few years, that knowledge remained relatively new to Ector, and many aspects of it did not occur to him naturally. This was an instance in which he'd required a reminder—humans clung to what they called *modesty* and often felt shame, embarrassment, and uncertainty when it came to displaying their bared bodies. For kraken, lack of clothing was the natural state. The only state. But humans were private with their nudity.

Ector couldn't guess how such matters would be viewed as humans and kraken became more integrated—both in culture and blood—over the coming generations.

He forced his gaze away from her again and entered the water, moving slowly; the fresh water smelled different, tasted different, *felt* different on his skin, and he could not bring himself to plunge into it like he would have the ocean. Still, it wasn't unpleasant—especially given the company.

Once he was far enough in, he spread his tentacles and submerged himself fully. He brushed his hands over his abdomen and was immediately reminded of his shameful performance. Strength and control—those had been the traits necessary for the kraken people to survive. Strength not just of body, but of willpower, of resolve, and control of one's actions and emotions. He'd failed on both fronts, and he couldn't help but be embarrassed even if Kathryn had ultimately been appreciative and amused.

A small part of him still saw spilling his seed outside of a womb to be wasteful. His people had always struggled to reproduce, and so self-pleasure—or pleasure not the result of intended reproduction—had always been seen as selfish.

But everything is different now, isn't it?

Everything certainly had changed, and Ector's views hadn't been spared alteration. So what if his control had faltered for a little while? He'd been lost in a passionate moment with the female he intended to take as his mate. There was no shame to be had in that situation.

He rose, lifting his head and torso above the surface, and glanced toward Kathryn. She was standing at the waterfall now, holding her shirt from its lower hem and stretching it out in front of her. The tumbling water landed directly atop the taut fabric.

An unexpected pang pierced Ector's chest. For a little while, Kathryn had been marked by the combined scents of their arousal, of their shared pleasure, and it had been far sweeter and more satisfying than he could've imagined. Knowing that those scents were being washed away from her and himself alike roused both a hint of sadness and a growing, possessive urge in Ector— the first whispers of an instinct demanding he mark her again.

Kathryn turned her head toward Ector, caught his eyes, and smiled. She dropped the hem of her shirt and waded toward him. "You look as though you have something on your mind."

He nearly flashed violet again with a flare of embarrassment —not due to the nature of his thoughts, but for his failure to mask them. He clenched his fists at his sides.

She stopped in front of him, and her smile slowly fell as she searched his face. "Do...you regret it? What we did?"

Ector's eyes widened, and he shook his head. He closed the

remaining distance between them and placed his hands on her shoulders. "No. Not at all, Kathryn. It is just new, and I do not want to…*misstep*. That can mean to make a mistake, correct?"

She reached up and settled her hands on his forearms. "It does, but you didn't misstep or make any mistakes, Ector."

"My people have always moved quickly when it comes to mating. I do not want to make what I feel for you, or my intentions, seem shallow."

"And what do you intend?"

He shifted a hand to her face, brushing the pad of his thumb over her cheek, relishing in the softness of her skin. "I want you as my mate. In the…new sense. The human sense."

Her smile, her beautiful smile, returned, spreading wide. It brightened her face and made her blue eyes sparkle. She tilted her head, pressing her cheek into his palm—into his touch. "You want that? With me?"

The light in her expression made Ector's hearts quicken. He nodded without hesitation. "I do. But the choice remains yours, and I do not expect you to decide so soon."

Her eyes dipped, and her smile waned. "I…want this. I do. I just… It's been so long since I've been with anyone, I just don't know how to do this anymore."

He gently combed his claws through the strands of her hair that had come loose from their tie. "If it makes any difference, Kathryn, I have *never* done this. But I do not consider myself too old to learn something new."

Kathryn returned her gaze to his. "Then we'll take it at whatever pace feels right at any given moment." She moved a hand to his chest, placing it over one of his hearts. "Being with you… feels natural."

Ector leaned down and pressed his lips to hers tenderly, just as she'd shown him, sampling her taste and savoring her softness. His eyes drifted shut during that contact. When he broke the kiss and pulled his head away, he found her looking up at him with half-lidded eyes.

Her smile stretched a little wider, and she said a bit breathlessly, "You're nothing if not a fast learner."

"Well, it *is* my duty to please my female."

Kathryn's cheeks reddened, and she trailed a finger down his chest. "And is my male pleased, as well?"

Heat unfurled in Ector's chest and rushed outward to suffuse his entire body, followed by a swelling of pride that poured fresh strength into his muscles. Simply hearing Kathryn refer to him as her male was nearly enough to urge him to action. His cock, which had finally receded during their journey to this pool, strained against the inside of his slit. "For now."

The light in Kathryn's eyes intensified, and the warmth of her body grew along with it. Before he could act upon that, movement in Ector's peripheral vision caught his attention, making his hearts skip a beat.

A clump of grass at the edge of the pool shook, and something made a shrill call from within it. Instinctively, Ector placed himself between Kathryn and the creature to shield her with his body, his skin shifting turning crimson. His tentacles flared out to the sides, the rearmost rising to curl around Kathryn's waist protectively, and he bared his teeth.

With a high-pitched squeal, a tiny, furry creature leapt from the grass and darted away, its stubby legs pumping desperately. It quickly disappeared in the thicker vegetation, its frightened calls fading with distance.

For a few seconds, Ector's body thrummed with unspent energy, strength, and heat; he was ready to fight, to destroy. Then the ridiculousness of the situation—getting so worked up over a tiny, likely harmless creature—crashed down on him. The source of the warmth within him shifted to embarrassment, and he couldn't keep a violet tint from his skin.

Kathryn shook against his back; he felt her vibrations

through the tentacles around her waist. Finally, giggles escaped her.

She flattened her palms against his back and leaned forward, peering around Ector's body to look up at him. "We can relax. I don't think that ravenous beast will be coming back anytime soon."

Ector released a heavy breath and chuckled, shaking his head. "For our sake, I hope it does not."

He reluctantly loosened his tentacles and withdrew them from her waist. Kathryn waded around to his side, and he turned his head, meeting her gaze briefly before she looked in the direction in which the creature had fled. She paused, eyes narrowing.

"What's that?" she asked, walking toward the edge of the pool. Water sloshed around her legs, growing noisier as more of her body rose above the surface.

Ector furrowed his brow and followed her. "What is what?"

She raised an arm and pointed to a place well beyond the pool, where the trees and foliage were thicker. "That right there. Do you see it?"

He leaned toward her and followed her gesture with his gaze, scanning the jungle. Everything was a mess of green, purple, and brown, thick with life but even more chaotic than the sea. He narrowed his eyes. What was he missing?

"The dark shape within the trees," Kathryn said. "I...I think it's a building."

Ector frowned and forced himself to adjust his focus. It was only when he stopped looking at the jungle as a collection of leaves, vines, and tree trunks and saw it as a whole that the shape she'd indicated became apparent. It was tucked beneath the shadows of the jungle canopy, made indistinct in the darkness, but he couldn't deny its presence. It was at least as tall as a full-grown human and as wide as two adult kraken stretched end-to-end.

"It could be a large rock," he said, but the suggestion, however reasonable, didn't sound right.

Kathryn looked back at him and smiled. "I guess there's only one way to find out."

She waded past Ector, crossing to the opposite side of the pool, and stepped onto land. After wringing excess water from her shirt, she bent down beside her belongings. The material of her pants pulled taut, granting Ector a delectable view of her backside; he bit back a groan. She pulled on her boots one by one, swiftly tying them before she straightened, fastened her belt around her waist, and grabbed her rifle.

Kathryn walked to the narrow spot where the pool emptied into the stream and crossed the shallow water. "Ready?"

Ector extended his front tentacles and dragged himself out of the pool. He shook excess moisture from his skin, reminded himself to ignore the tastes of the ground and plants beneath his suction cups—a mental feat at which he'd become quite adept—and nodded. He had no idea what they would find in the jungle, even just twenty or thirty meters ahead, but he couldn't deny his curiosity.

Kathryn took the lead, picking a path through the vegetation. As much as Ector wanted to focus on their destination—or even better on Kathryn's shapely backside—he forced himself to monitor their surroundings. There were animal calls in the air, mingling with the sounds of rustling leaves and creaking branches. Though he'd heard some of those calls before, they all belonged to creatures for which he had no name and had never seen with his own eyes.

It was the unfamiliar tastes and scents that concerned him more. His understanding was that most all land creatures required fresh water to survive, and this stream likely served as a primary source for many of the animals in the area. Traces of their passages lingered on the ground and grass, communicated to him in fleeting, tiny hints through his suction cups, some much fresher than others.

Their path grew meandering as Kathryn navigated various obstacles—trees both standing and fallen; thick tangles of vegetation; gnarled tree roots rising from the dirt. Some of the latter resembled unmoving tentacles and seemed to grab at Kathryn's feet, making her stumble and mutter, on the few occasions when she didn't notice them soon enough to avoid them.

Ector's hearts leapt when her foot finally snagged fully enough to make her trip. She pitched forward, but he lunged quickly enough to catch her by the arm before she could hit the ground. She gasped as his hold brought her to an abrupt halt. The rifle slipped off her opposite arm and fell. Ector wrapped a tentacle around her waist and righted Kathryn, only releasing her when she was steady on her feet.

"There I go being clumsy again." Kathryn smiled shyly up at Ector, tucking dangling hair behind her ear. "Thank you. I guess I'm feeling a little waterlogged."

"Waterlogged?" He stretched a tentacle, curled it around her rifle, and lifted the weapon, holding it out to her.

She accepted the rifle, taking it in both hands. "Feeling heavy with water."

"Ah. I often feel that way when I leave the water, too, though I suspect the reason is different."

"And what do you think the difference is?"

He pressed his lips together for a second or two, seeking the right words to convey his meaning. "Movement in the water is...unrestricted. I can go in any direction—up or down, left or right, backward and forward. I can swim toward the sun high above or to the darkest depths. I can twist and flip and spin. I do not mean to say there are no limits, but..."

"The water makes you feel free?"

Ector nodded, smiling widely. "Exactly."

Kathryn returned the smile. "And you don't have these

clumsy moments we humans experience, stuck on the ground as we are." She faced forward and continued walking, tilting her head down every few steps as though studying the ground in front of her. "The way you describe it makes me think of flying. People used to be able to do that."

"Humans could fly?"

"Well, not like kraken can swim. We had machines that could soar through the air back when we first came to this world hundreds of years ago. Machines that could fly between the stars. That's what the history we're taught in The Watch says, anyway. It's what brought us here. Sometimes when I was a girl, I'd look up at the clouds and wonder what it would feel like to soar through them. To reach out and touch them." She chuckled. "I wondered if you could squeeze them and force out the rain. It seems silly now…"

Ector's hearts ached for her. Perhaps those dreams could never be made true, but if swimming and flying were anything alike, he would bring her as close to soaring in the clouds as he could.

"It does not seem silly to me," Ector said gently. "I admire that sense of wonder. I wish I had been exposed to it much sooner in my life—or maybe it is more accurate to say that I wish I had been more open to it much sooner."

Kathryn stopped and turned to face him, still wearing a soft smile on her lips. "Things are different now."

He made no effort to prevent his gaze from dipping to take her in again. "They certainly are."

She turned away, and they continued onward. The jungle filled in around them; within a minute or two, they were standing in front of the object Kathryn had spied through the vegetation. While it had stone components, it certainly was not a rock. Kathryn had been correct—it was a building.

Its cracked and crumbling foundation was constructed of countless stones that must have once fit together neatly, and much of it was obstructed by a thick overgrowth of vines and low vegetation. The logs forming the walls atop that foundation were rotting with age; many of them had sagged or broken, leaving large gaps in several places. More vegetation clung to those logs, though it was not as thick as around the foundation.

Ector and Kathryn slowly walked around the structure. A portion of the side facing away from the stream had collapsed, leaving a pile of loose rocks across which lay several broken logs, their cores dark and decaying. Something about the shape of the opening suggested that this had once been an entryway.

In his mind, Ector could *almost* picture this place as having looked like one of the buildings in The Watch, but there was something about it that spoke of a cruder construction.

Kathryn stepped closer, placed a hand on the wall beside the gaping hole, and leaned inside the building. "I've never heard of anyone living alone this far outside town. I wonder if this place was used by traveling hunters or something."

Ector studied the ruined wall she was currently using for support and frowned. The Facility his people had called home for hundreds of years was old, but it was not in anywhere near as deteriorated a state as this building. "Do your hunters usually rove this far?"

"From The Watch? No, never this far. There's plenty of game closer to town. My family and I never hiked more than a day or two away when I was younger." She turned her head to look at Ector. "But...there could be another town near here. Regular communication broke down between the settlements on Halora a long time ago, but there are still several towns we trade with, probably even more we don't know about. I'm just not sure where we are in relation to any of those places."

She leaned back slightly, swung her rifle over her shoulder, sweeping it behind her back, and braced her now free hand on the other side of the wall gap.

Something tightened in Ector's chest. "What are you doing, Kathryn? This building does not look safe."

Kathryn paused and shoved against the log wall. It didn't budge. "It's sturdy enough. Anyway, I'm just going to look around for a minute." She stepped over the rubble at the base of the entry and entered the dark interior.

Though he may well have hesitated to enter this building if he were alone, he did not delay in following Kathryn through the gap. Of course, the passage that she made look so effortless was somewhat more difficult given his larger body, and he was forced to carefully twist and contort himself in an effort to avoid the jagged pieces of broken wood to either side as he entered the building.

A flare of pain on his right shoulder signaled that he'd failed in those efforts. Once he was clear of the entryway, he paused and turned his head to look down at the cut. It was a minor wound, about half the length of his forefinger, but it was already oozing crimson.

Kathryn stepped up beside him, placing a gentle hand on his bicep. "Oh, Ector. We'll get this patched up once we get back."

"It is nothing," Ector said, Laying his hand atop hers. "We kraken heal quite rapidly. There will be no trace left of it within a few days."

Her frown said that she was skeptical—and the set of her brows said she'd be patching up the cut regardless—but she didn't press the matter. Together, they turned their attention to their new surroundings.

The hints of light visible through the cracks and gaps in the walls were just bright enough to cast the contents of the single large room in a gloomy glow; Ector's eyes adjusted quickly. He assumed the heaps of broken wood scattered around had been furniture of some sort many, many years ago, though they were well beyond his ability to identify in their current states. A thick layer of dirt and dead leaves covered the floor, and the slight give beneath it suggested wood planks of some sort that had gone soft with moisture and time.

Kathryn's eyes were wide, her pupils so dilated that they swallowed up her irises. She stepped deeper into the room carefully, almost reverently, as though she were afraid to disturb anything within. As strange as this place was to Ector, it was Kathryn who caught his attention. Her reaction—her wonder—was fascinating.

She approached a formation of stone that ran from the floor to the ceiling on the far wall with a large, cavern like opening at its base, and gently set her hand atop it. After a few seconds, she turned her head and swept her gaze over the rest of the space. "This place has been abandoned for a long, long time."

Ector looked the room over again, struggling to see it through her eyes. Time passed at the same speed both above and below the waves, but its ravages were different here.

"How long?" he asked as he moved toward a large piece of collapsed furniture in the far-left corner. He folded his tentacles and lowered himself to study the remains. All that was left of the item were a great many branches and sticks, all thick and crudely whittled down—and none quite straight.

"Longer than either of us has been alive, at the very least," Kathryn replied. "Colin always used to talk about how most Halorian wood is very resistant to rot. That it could go untreated for decades and still hold its strength. That's one of the reasons our boats last so long. So, given the state of this place…it has to be *old*."

Ector chuckled. "Well, that's the second thing to make me feel young in the last week."

"What's the other?"

"You."

Kathryn smiled and tilted her face down, but she wasn't quick enough to hide the blush staining her cheeks.

A fresh swell of pride filled Ector's chest. He knew that

human skin often turned that pinkish-red shade when they were angry or embarrassed, but he also knew that wasn't the case now. Her flushed skin was a good sign—she was flattered by his words.

But his unease about this building lingered; this was neither the place to reflect nor to act upon his feelings for her.

Turning back to the collapsed piece of furniture, Ector tilted his head. Though many of the sticks were broken and likely out of place, they were arranged in a large, vaguely rectangular shape with a deep pile of debris filling the middle—mostly leaves, but a few bits of what might've been fur were mixed in. Thicker branches—logs, really—lay near the corners of the formation. His brow furrowed. Somehow, this ruined thing seemed familiar to him, as though he should have known what it had once been.

Kathryn's footfalls were quiet save for the occasional creak of hidden wood as she approached Ector. She crouched beside him. "I think this was a bed."

Now he could see it, now he could rearrange the pieces well enough in his imagination to visualize the shape it might once have held—a frame with thick posts standing at each corner.

A strange, gloomy mood overcame him in that moment. Generations of kraken had lived and died on this world, but were they to vanish, what proof of their existence would remain? How would anyone know who they had been or that they'd *been* at all? What had been crafted by kraken hands and tentacles in all that time?

The gloom fled quickly, chased away by a resurgence of pride. Perhaps such thoughts were suitable a generation or two ago, but no longer. There would be a kraken legacy left behind thanks to individuals like Arkon.

A thoughtful look settled on Kathryn's face. "If someone did live here, I wonder why they isolated themselves."

Carefully, Ector extended a tentacle into the debris gathered at the center of the fallen bedframe, sifting through it. "I can understand a want for solitude. It is my people's nature. But I wonder now whether it is actually a desire for...privacy, not isolation." He turned his head to look upon her again. "I find no value in isolation."

A soft smile curled on her lips. "It's okay to be alone sometimes...but no one wants to be lonely."

The light in her eyes gave those words immense meaning, rekindling that warm, tight feeling in Ector's chest. Perhaps two or three years ago, he'd have mistaken the sensation for something negative—alarm or fear, perhaps. Anxiety. But he knew this was different. It was far deeper, far more complicated...and there was nothing negative about it.

"Come on," she said, placing a hand on his forearm and rising to her feet. As she stepped away, she trailed her fingers along his arm, up to his shoulder. "Let's head back to camp."

He nodded and was withdrawing his tentacle from the debris when it bumped into something hard and cold beneath the relatively soft pile. Brow furrowing, he looked down at the pile and curled his tentacle around the object; it had four flat sides, smooth beneath the grime clinging to them. Ector lifted the object free. The rotting debris rained from atop it to reveal a small metal box.

From front to back, it was as wide as his hand was long, and twice as big from side to side. He shifted it into his hands and rose, turning to face Kathryn. Holding the box atop one palm, he brushed away some of the dirt from its lid with the other. He'd seen boxes just like this more times than he could count— they were all over the Facility.

"Look at this," he said.

Kathryn paused, her body silhouetted against the light coming in through the gap in the wall, and turned her face back toward Ector. Her brows lowered. She cast another look at the room around them before her eyes fell on the box. "Well, that certainly doesn't belong here."

Ector tilted his head. "What do you mean?"

She gestured vaguely around the room. "Look at this place. It's all crudely built, made by hand. Everything here was made from materials available just outside, and it's all rotting away and being reclaimed by nature." She pointed at the box. "Everything but that."

He trailed his gaze around the space before returning it to the box. "And…anyone who had access to this should have had access to more advanced tools. Should have been able to build things like your people have in The Watch."

"Or someone might have found this place like we did and hid that here. Though that would still leave the question of who built this to begin with. All the colonists should've had access to the same tools, right?" She stepped closer to him and brushed the tips of her fingers across the box's lid. "It's going to start getting dark soon. Let's get back to camp, and we can try to open it there. Maybe there are some answers inside. And anyway, we still need to take care of that cut."

"That seems as good a plan as any," Ector said, smiling at her again. The cut had already lost most of its sting; had she not mentioned it, he probably wouldn't have remembered it at all.

She returned the smile and gestured toward the opening in the wall. Ector tucked the metal box beneath his left arm and preceded her through the gap. Thankfully, he avoided cutting himself again. Once he was clear of the opening, he moved aside to allow Kathryn space.

The fallen rocks laying across the entryway clattered softly as she emerged. She stopped beside him and brushed her fingertips over his wrist. "Hopefully those hinges aren't rusted closed or anything."

Ector turned his head to look at her. "We will figure it out one way or another, Kathryn, even if—"

A harsh hiss cut off Ector's words. Kathryn started, jerking back from the sound, and both she and Ector snapped their wide eyes toward the source.

Two yellow eyes gleamed amidst the foliage not five meters away. The leaves and branches shook as a creature emerged. Its body was sleek and powerful, with a long neck and tail, and each of its four legs ended in wicked talons. The beast was covered in dark scales in shades of green and violet that matched the surrounding vegetation. It opened wide its jaws, which were lined with sharp, curved teeth, and hissed again.

"A vriga," Kathryn whispered.

Ector extended an arm and swept Kathryn behind him, skin going crimson. He released his hold on the box. Its fall was muted by the blanket of leaves on the jungle floor.

The creature hesitated in its advance and lowered its head, yellow eyes locked on Ector. A long, thin tongue darted out from its mouth and whipped through the air. It slowly moved one of its legs forward.

"A predator?" Ector asked, keeping his voice low.

"Yes," Kathryn replied. "It probably scented your blood."

Keeping his movements slow to match the vriga's, Ector spread his tentacles, bracing himself. His hearts thumped in anticipation of the battle that was likely to commence, filling his limbs with thrumming energy.

"I need you to crouch. Get lower to the ground," Kathryn said.

The vriga took another step in its cautious advance, long tail swinging behind it slowly, fangs still bared.

Ector shook his head once. "I will not expose you."

"Trust me, Ector."

He clenched his jaw, and his nostrils flared with a deep, frustrated inhalation. It went against his every instinct to do as she asked, but he *did* trust her. Though this creature was utterly alien to him, Kathryn knew what it was. It only made sense to follow her lead in this—while remaining prepared to protect her.

He spread his tentacles farther and eased his torso down. The vriga dipped its head lower to follow his progress. A clear, glistening liquid gathered on its foremost fangs.

The barrel of Kathryn's rifle entered Ector's peripheral vision. A moment later, she lowered it onto his shoulder, aiming directly at the creature.

"This is going to be loud," she said softly. "Don't move."

The vriga opened its jaws wider and released another hiss. The scales around its head flared open and swept forward; Ector's instincts took it as an overt display of aggression, as a challenge, but he forced himself to remain still.

Suddenly, the beast leapt toward Ector.

The vriga's feet had barely left the ground when the rifle boomed. The weapon jolted back slightly, and the vriga crashed to the ground in a heap. A ringing filled Ector's ears for several seconds, drowning out all other sounds. The creature's legs and tail twitched, rustling fallen leaves and living vegetation alike, and then the beast went still.

Ector released a slow breath, muscles tense as he stared down at the fallen vriga. It remained unmoving; even the slight rise and fall of its chest that most animals exhibited while breathing air was absent. Behind him, Kathryn released a heavy breath of her own, which fanned across the side of Ector's neck, warm and oddly soothing.

"That was a bit intense," she said. Though her voice sounded distant—Ector's hearing was still recovering—it was perfectly clear.

"Just a bit." He couldn't help but chuckle; that chuckle turned into outright laughter that shook his shoulders as the energy that had tensed his muscles dissipated. His body felt unsteady and weak in the wake of that energy—from a high to a low, just that quickly—but he knew that feeling would pass soon enough. Sometimes it took longer than others, but it always passed.

Kathryn withdrew the rifle and stepped around Ector to face him with head cocked and brows furrowed. "Why are you laughing?"

He rose on his tentacles to a more comfortable height and rolled his shoulders, trying to shake the lingering discomfort out of his arms. "I was just appreciating your understatement."

She snickered. "Okay, so maybe it was *a lot* intense. But hey" —she pointed at the creature—"I caught us dinner."

Ector fixed his gaze on the scaled creature. "Have you ever eaten one of these vrigas before?"

"I have, but not often. We don't go out looking for them, but they're dangerous, so the hunters usually take care of these things when they get too close to The Watch."

"And no meat is left to waste."

Kathryn nodded. "Not as long as we can help it."

Ector smiled; his time in The Watch had taught him that there were many differences between humans and kraken beyond the physical—but there were a great many similarities, as well, and a good number of those had been unexpected. This was another small example, one that he chose to take as proof that ultimately, their people wanted the same thing—peaceful lives of plenty.

He turned toward her and opened his mouth to speak, but stilled, his brows dropping low.

Kathryn was pale, much paler than she'd been before. Her hands were white knuckled around the rifle, which trembled in her grasp.

Frowning, he moved to her and placed his hands on either side of her neck, brushing the pads of his thumbs soothingly along her jaw. "Is it nerves or fear?"

She huffed a laugh. "Both, I think. It's just... It's been a *long* time since I used a gun, and..." She took in a deep, shaky inhalation and slowly released it; somehow, her gaze remained solidly locked with his throughout. "I was scared I was going to miss, and that it'd hurt you. They're poisonous. A single bite from one of them can be lethal."

Ector slid one of his hands higher, sweeping back the loose strands of her silver hair, and stared into her bright eyes. "But it did not, and you were brave. You are a huntress at heart."

She covered his hand with her own and rubbed her cheek against his palm, smiling. "Give me a moment for my hands to stop shaking and I'll get the vriga dressed and ready to take back to camp."

"Dressed? I do not understand, Kathryn."

"Field dressed," she said, smile widening. "It doesn't mean what it probably sounds like…it's a good deal messier than that. But it's a necessary part of the process to keep the meat from spoiling. It should only take about ten minutes."

He dropped his other hand to wrap his arm around her waist, curled a tentacle around her calf, and drew her close. "Take all the time you need, my huntress."

CHAPTER 8

KATHRYN RECLINED AGAINST HER BACKPACK, WHICH SHE'D wedged between herself and the boulder behind her keep the hard rock from digging into her back. While it hadn't taken her long to field dress the vriga, skinning and butchering it once Ector carried it back to camp had been a lot of work. She'd had to reteach herself as she went, making it a messy, clumsy process, and now every one of Kathryn's muscles was sore. She was exhausted, but she still felt good. She was proud of what she'd accomplished.

After seeing to Ector's cut—which had surprisingly already started closing—Kathryn and Ector had briefly split up. He'd gone to the sea to wash while she'd taken a real bath in the stream, using the soap she'd packed. Now, her hair was clean and damp, hanging around her shoulders, and she was wearing fresh, dry clothes—a loose button-down shirt and a pair of shorts.

The soothing heat and welcoming glow of the fire chased away the chill of the deepening twilight, and the meat roasting on spits over the open flame added a delectable aroma to the briny air. Not for the first time, she appreciated her aches, her weariness; she'd earned it all today.

She hadn't hunted since she was a teenager, and she'd nearly forgotten the simple satisfaction of enjoying a meal she'd had to catch herself—especially when she and Ector had come closer than she cared to admit to becoming the vriga's meal instead of the other way around. Not that she doubted Ector's skill and prowess. The kraken were immensely strong and capable, but even the smallest nick from the vriga's venom coated fangs could've been enough to kill him; even a victory on his part might have ended in tragedy. The chance that he wasn't as susceptible to the venom due to his species wasn't one she was willing to take.

She opened her canteen and took a drink of cool water, glancing skyward. Only a hint of light remained on the horizon, the last embers of a sun that had already sunken into slumber, and the night's first stars twinkled directly overhead. There were no clouds to be seen, and the sea was calmly singing its ceaseless lullaby. There was undeniable beauty all around her.

Kat looked at Ector, who sat beside her—not that the position kraken got into when they settled down could quite be called *sitting*, but that word was close enough. His tentacles were curled up and swept to the side opposite her save for one; that lone tentacle was draped over her knee, gently brushing over her skin. She loved that simple touch—especially those whisper-like kisses from his suction cups.

The rational part of her mind still whispered that things were moving too fast between them, but she knew that such matters rarely had much to do with rationality. She and Ector were irresistibly drawn to one another. They'd been growing closer and closer each day, and today's events had accelerated that process. Their kisses and their shared pleasure beside the stream had only been the start. And after the run-in with the vriga…

She released a slow, quiet sigh. Kat felt like she'd known Ector for her entire life, like she was closer to him than should've been possible. They'd shared something profound today. They'd looked into the eyes of death and come out alive —together. But...that brush with death was not something she wished to experience again.

Breckett will have a fit when he finds out.

Kathryn snickered.

Ector turned his face toward her and smiled. "Amusing thought?"

"I was just thinking about how Breckett would react if he knew what happened today."

Ector chuckled, and his tentacle coiled briefly around her leg, giving it a gentle squeeze. "I imagine we will find out when we return."

She grinned. "He'd never let me touch a boat again. He'd rant and go on and on about how he told me so, and how dangerous and stupid this was."

"He was not wrong. Life itself is dangerous, but this trip...we are taking many unnecessary risks."

Kathryn's smile faded as she looked away from Ector to stare down at the tentacle around her leg. Tentatively, she brushed her fingers over it. His skin there was as soft and velvety as everywhere else.

"I know," she said with a sigh.

He eased closer to Kathryn until his arm was touching hers and tipped his head to the side, resting it atop her hair. "We both knew, and yet we both came. I know why I did. Why are you here, Kathryn?"

Kat closed her eyes and allowed her body to relax into his. Without hesitation, he slipped his arm around her shoulders and tugged her against him. He put off as much heat as the fire, and tingles of pleasure pulsed from every place their bodies touched. She cuddled just a little closer to him.

Why was she here? Why had she come on this journey? What exactly was she looking for?

She opened her eyes and looked past the flickering fire, toward the sea. "Honestly? I don't know. Validation, I guess, that I...that I am still who I used to be." She shook her head. "No, that's not quite right. I already knew I'm not who I used to be. I'm someone different. I just wanted to find out who that person is, find out how much she resembles the me I remember. Who I am *now*."

The pads of Ector's fingers glided up and down her sleeve. "You are Kathryn. Who else could you be but yourself?"

Kathryn couldn't help but smile. "I know, but..." Why was it so hard to explain? "For thirty-two years I've been a mother, and for most of that time, I spent my every moment caring for, teaching, worrying over, and raising my daughters. They were my life. *Are* my life. As are my grandchildren. But for several years now, every morning I wake up and there's this...emptiness. This void. There's no laughter, no voices, just...silence. Every day, I go to work, whether mending clothes or tending crops, and then I go home to that same silence. It's deafening at times. My girls aren't there anymore. They're living lives of their own with their husbands, with their children, while I..."

The fire in front of her was a wavering blur, breaking into wild shards of distorted light. Her vision cleared only when she blinked, forcing out the tears she hadn't realized had welled in her eyes. She pressed her lips together, lifted a hand, and wiped the tears away. Ector turned his head and gently kissed her hair. That silent comfort—small, yet so powerful—was enough to urge her on.

"I just didn't know what to do with myself anymore. Before I became a wife, a mother, a grandmother, even a seamstress, I was a hunter. That's what I did when I was young—I went out of town with my parents and spent my days in the jungle, hunting and trapping. I chose to leave that behind when I got pregnant. I'm proud of my life, and I'm proud of my kids, and I don't regret a single moment of it.

"But I needed to know if that's still me. If I'm still the same woman who hunted without fear, who sailed open water. I needed to know if it was still inside me. Because living alone in that empty house, I just felt...lost. Purposeless. I could move in with either of my daughters if I wanted to, but they need to have their lives. And I...I needed to figure out if I could still have one of my own, too."

She sniffled, curled her fingers around his tentacle, and stroked her thumb over it. "Does all that make sense? Or am I being...selfish, making my family and friends worry over something foolish?"

A deep, thoughtful hum rumbled from Ector's chest. He picked Kathryn up and shifted his body; when he lowered her a moment later, his tentacles were beneath her, and her back was leaning against his chest. He wrapped his arms around her and coiled a couple of his tentacles around her legs, blanketing her in his warmth.

"It may be selfish," he said after a long silence, "but it is also right. One of our traditions has never changed, even after contact with humans. Hunters always eat first."

Kathryn chuckled and turned her head to look at him. "I think I know where this is going."

His lips curled up, and he chuckled as well. "Then I can save some of my breath. You need to take for yourself sometimes, or you will have nothing to give." He raised and hand and ran his claws through her hair, gently working out the small tangles. "You have given much, Kathryn, to everyone you care for. If this is what you need in return, who is to argue?"

Kat searched his golden eyes. They were so gentle, so caring, so expressive...and she had a sense they were only for her. Her heart fluttered, and she was all the more aware of how he held her.

"And what about you?" she asked. "Why did you volunteer to go on this crazy adventure with me?"

Ector shifted his gaze toward the fire. The flames reflected in his eyes, making them molten gold—but they remained as welcoming as ever. "I have felt much the same as you as of late. Lost. Without purpose. I look upon my people with pride for all they have accomplished, for how far they have come, and I know they no longer need me to move forward. I have guided them as best I can for a long while, but all the younglings I taught are grown. They are intelligent and creative, and they are shaping our future. They have outgrown me.

"I have been their teacher, their elder, for so many years... They have already innovated on the things I taught them, have already improved. They have surpassed me. I cannot hunt with them, for I know I would only slow them down. Their wisdom is greater than my own. What role do I serve in this world? What is my place?"

Kat's chest clenched. Ector understood everything she felt; he'd experienced it himself. Learning that he was going through the same thing, that he had the same feelings, the same doubts at a similar point in his life eased the burden of worry she'd been carrying. She wasn't the only one.

He nodded and returned his gaze to her. A new light was in his eyes. "But it would be dishonest to say that those are my reasons for coming. I have only one reason, and it is the only one that matters to me now." He curled a clawed finger beneath her chin. "I came for you."

A new flood of tears flowed from her eyes. "For me?"

With a gentleness belying the immense strength she knew he possessed, Ector wiped the tears from her cheeks with the pad of his thumb. "For you."

"But why? You didn't know me. We barely ever spoke, and I swear I must've insulted you during the Dryfall festival."

Ector chuckled, shaking his head. "I have always thought

you were beautiful, Kathryn. Your hair especially has always drawn my eye." He caught a strand with his claw and lifted it, rubbing it between his fingers. "For a long while, I thought my mating days were well behind me. Even living amongst humans, I did not realize there could be more for me than duty to my people. But what pushed me to speak to you...it was that wistful look in your eyes while you were staring out at the sea. That yearning for something more. I felt it within myself, too."

She smiled wide and turned until her body to face his, straddling his lap. He dropped his hands to her waist and curled his fingers around her. There was a possessiveness in the way the tips of his claws pressed against her through her shirt and shorts, a whisper of danger that created delightful tingles on her skin.

Taking his face between her hands, she pressed a kiss to his lips. "I am so very glad you did. When you touched me..." Heat blossomed on her cheeks as she traced the tip of a finger over one of his siphons, which widened and contracted. "It was the first time I felt desire in a long, long time."

Ector's nostril's flared, and his pupils dilated. His grip on her tightened, and he dragged her closer, grinding her covered sex over the solid bump beneath his slit. Kathryn's breath hitched from the friction against her clit.

A low growl rumbled in his chest. The sound vibrated into her, making her nipples harden and ache.

It was at that exact moment that her stomach decided to grumble loud enough to overcome the sounds of wind, fire, and sea.

Kathryn stilled, eyes wide, before laughter burst from her.

"Seems my female has other needs I must tend to first," Ector said, trailing his tentacles over her bare legs.

Damn you, stomach.

Kat sighed morosely, brushing her thumbs just beneath his

bottom lip. "I suppose we should eat before the meat burns and it all goes to waste."

With a muffled groan, Ector lifted Kat off him and set her on the ground in her original spot. His tentacles lingered on her legs as though he were reluctant to break contact with her. She felt the same reluctance. Her eyes dipped to his slit; it was partially open, and the dark, glistening head of his cock was visible. Her sex clenched with the need to feel him inside her. She caught her lower lip between her teeth.

"If you keep staring like that, our food *will* burn," Ector said huskily. "And I will not let my female go hungry."

Kathryn snapped her eyes up to his, seeing her desire reflected in those golden depths. She really was tempted to say food be damned, but he was right. It'd been a long day and they needed to eat.

She grinned. "Okay, okay."

Kathryn leaned closer to the fire and plucked out the skewers one at a time, using her knife to ensure the meat was fully cooked. The thicker fillets were still raw on the inside, but she passed those that were done to Ector, who propped them up against the rock. When she was done, she settled back down against her backpack, and she and Ector ate in companionable silence, listening to the crackling fire and crashing waves. The meat was flavorful, but tough—though Ector didn't seem to have any trouble tearing into it.

They ate until they were full—with Ector eating at least three times as much as Kat—but there was still a lot of meat left over. She could've smoked the leftovers, allowing them to be taken on the next leg of the journey, but that would've required digging a pit, filling it with coals, and tending it for hours to prevent flare ups and ensure the meat cooked properly. With it already being so late—and Kat already being so worn—it simply wasn't feasible. Throwing it all away didn't sit well with her, but she didn't feel like she had much choice. She had Ector take the remains farther inland, unwilling to keep a pile of raw meat near camp. And at least *something* would eat it this way.

Kathryn was tidying up their little camp when Ector returned. The twin moons, both bright crescents hanging over the jungle, cast a silvery glow on him that highlighted the edges of his form, allowing her to appreciate it anew. His eyes reflected the light, and Kathryn knew they were focused on her. Warmth pooled low in her belly, and something more spread through her chest, making her heart flutter and her pulse quicken.

She took a step toward him; her foot bumped against something cold and hard. When she looked down, her eyes fell on the dingy metal box from the abandoned cabin, which they'd set aside and forgotten while they tended to the vriga and bathed. Kat crouched and turned the box onto its side. She ran her fingers along the seam to each of the two latches. They were locked.

"Hmm," she said.

A soft rustling of grass nearby caught her attention, and she looked up to see Ector enter the camp, his skin given an orange tint by the firelight. Kathryn smiled and picked up the box as she stood.

"I'd forgotten all about this," she said, turning the metal box in her hands. Its contents, which clearly had a bit of weight to them, slid around, but it felt like something was padding the impact when they bumped into the side of the container. "Shall we try to open it to see what's inside?"

Ector tilted his head. "Yes. I have been quite curious about it."

Kat sat down next to her backpack, placing the box on the ground upside down. She picked up her knife and wedged the blade beneath one of the latches. "See if you can find a fist sized rock."

After a brief search, Ector sank close to the ground, scooped up a stone, and passed it to her. She thanked him as she took the rock and hammered it against the knife's handle. After a few minor alterations to the blade's angle and the force she was using, the latch finally popped open. Anticipation rushed through her as she repeated the process with the remaining latch.

Kat set the knife and rock aside, flipped the box over, and lifted the lid. It offered a bit of resistance before it opened, releasing a quiet groan.

A faded cloth filled the inside of the box, its folds tattered and worn. Kathryn reached inside and carefully took hold of the cloth—it was thin, almost threadbare in places. She peeled the sides away to reveal a small collection of objects around which the cloth had been bundled. Kathryn's brow furrowed as she removed the first item.

It was a small, heart-shaped shell with a little chip near its narrowest point. Kat held it delicately between her forefinger and thumb and lifted it into the firelight. Though the orange glow of the flames made the shell's colors difficult to discern, its underside shimmered with the promise of opalescent beauty that she couldn't wait to examine in the morning.

"A curious thing to lock away," Ector said.

Kathryn turned the shell again, making its underside glint. "People value many things based on emotional significance, even if it's as simple as finding something pleasing to look at."

She glanced up to find, unsurprisingly, Ector looking at her. The heat in his eyes was not merely the result of the fire being reflected in them.

I find you *pleasing to look at*, those eyes said.

Cheeks warming, she dropped her gaze and carefully placed the shell on the soft, flattened grass beside the box. She would've thought the intensity of his gaze would've lost at least some of its effect on her over the last few days, especially after what they'd done by the stream, but it only seemed to produce progressively stronger reactions in her. Fortunately, the puzzle offered by this box was compelling enough of a distraction to hold Kat's attention—for now, anyway.

She reached into the box and withdrew the next object; a knife. An *old* knife.

There were still blades like this one being used in The Watch. It was crafted of a material for which Kathryn had no name, present on Halora only because it had been brought by the original colonists. Such knives had held their edges through centuries of use, and the people of The Watch had passed them down through many generations.

She plucked a blade of grass from the ground and dragged it across the knife's edge; the grass sliced in half effortlessly.

Kathryn laid the knife flat on her palm and examined it. While the blade was immaculate, the grip was as primitive as the building in which it had been hidden. A bit of dingy cloth was wrapped around a piece of wood that served as the handle, which had been carved into something only crudely ergonomic. Smooth spots worn into the wood perfectly matched where fingers would naturally rest while the knife was in use.

Ector leaned closer to her. "The blade is the same as those in the Facility."

Though she couldn't be sure why, something in his words prompted her to pick up her own knife again, which was made of that same ancient, nameless material. She held the tools side by side. The blades were the same color, but their shapes were noticeably different—and the blade from the chest was at least three or four centimeters longer.

"I've seen a few different blade styles in The Watch, but this *does* look different than the rest." Kathryn slipped her knife into its sheath and ran her fingertips over the other tool's makeshift wooden grip. "Most of the knives we have left have had their handles replaced over the years, but I've never seen any so crudely made."

Setting the knife down beside the shell, Kat removed another item from the box. The object was attached to a loop of frayed, brittle twine, fibers of which flaked and crumbed away despite the delicacy of her touch. She pressed her lips together and slowed her already careful movements further. Her breath caught in her throat and remained lodged there until she had laid the object on her waiting palm.

The wooden pendant was hand carved in as clumsy and amateur a fashion as the knife grip, but its intended form was apparent to Kathryn—it was an ember blossom, a species of orange-petaled flower she'd seen scattered throughout the nearby jungle. The flowers were known for that fiery color and their many lush, thin petals. Though the carving certainly wasn't an example of skill or talent, it spoke of great time and care in its creation.

Kathryn brushed a fingertip over one of the carved petals. The wood was faded to a grayish shade, but it was well-preserved.

"I think a couple lived in that place," she said, returning her gaze to Ector.

He tilted his head and glanced at the carving. "That item makes you think so?"

Smiling softly, she turned the pendant over. The flat back-side showed more wear than the front; a patch of the relatively dark wood had been worn down to reveal the lighter wood beneath. "Just…a hunch. A feeling. This matches the way things were crafted back at the cabin, and it looks like it was worn a lot. I think it was a gift."

Ector extended an arm and ran the pad of a finger across the back of the pendant. "If all this is to remain a mystery, I will choose to accept your speculation."

Kathryn chuckled and arched a brow. "Even if the evidence supporting it is so thin?"

His answering smile was wide and warm despite his sharp

teeth. "Even then. A few years ago, I would not have given it any thought, but... It feels good to think that two people lived in that place together happily."

The warm sensation Ector so often sparked in Kathryn's chest bloomed again, deeper and more powerful than before. There was something subtle in his voice—a hint of longing, perhaps—that made his words resonate with her. His sentiment regarding the matter only endeared her to him further. She hoped he was right, too, and that the mysterious couple she'd speculated had shared happiness here...

She placed the pendant beside the other items on the ground with great care. Each object was a piece of the puzzle, but Kat couldn't see how they could possibly tell enough of the story to answer her questions.

Of course, she also could never have anticipated the final item that had been tucked away in that old cloth.

Kathryn's brows fell low as she removed the last object from the box and held it to the light. It was a small device—not quite as large as her hand—with rounded ends and a shallow depression on top that was roughly thumb width. She felt like she'd seen something similar before and knew it was an old piece of technology, but the work she'd done during her life had never brought her into contact with such objects.

"That almost looks like the wrist controls on the diving suits," Ector said.

"I've never really seen those suits up close apart from the one you snuck onto the boat for me." Even then, she hadn't taken the time to study the controls she'd seen on the suit during her quick perusal of it. Kathryn turned the device over; its underside was smooth and lacked any discernable markings or buttons.

Ector chuckled. "I cannot claim any understanding of their operation, but I believe you brush a finger along the groove to activate it."

She nodded and placed her thumb in that shallow depression. This thing dated at least as far back as the colonization, three hundred and sixty-five years ago. Some of those old devices still functioned. Many more did not. Expecting nothing, she swiped her thumb along the groove.

A holographic screen flashed into existence in the air above the device.

Kathryn started, heart skipping a beat, and raised her free hand to her chest. Her startlement passed within a couple seconds, and she couldn't help laughing at herself. When she looked up at Ector, he was smiling softly, an amused light dancing in his eyes—but it wasn't amusement at her expense. Somehow, she knew he wouldn't be responding this way were it not for her laughter.

"I guess I really didn't expect it to work," she said, returning her attention to the hologram. The screen's bluish glow clashed with the firelight immediately around it, lending Ector's skin a surreal cast. It took a moment for Kathryn to realize what she was looking at—a menu with various icons, most of which were meaningless to her.

"I haven't used anything like this since I was a girl," she said. "We use a few of the working holos and computers in The Watch to teach children—mostly history."

"My people have used the computer in the Facility similarly, though we were long limited by the need for voice commands and the fact that much of the information was locked away. Our younglings have enjoyed listening to old human stories for many generations."

Kathryn tilted her head, studying him anew. "So, you grew up hearing human stories but being distrustful of humans?"

The amused light rekindled in his eyes. "It does sound contradictory, does it not? But so many of those tales went beyond species. They were about strength, courage, defiance of fate and oppression. Many of our names are derived from those stories."

"Was yours?"

"Yes. I am named for a warrior who fought a superior foe in defense of his home."

Kathryn smiled at him. "It suits you. You'll have to tell me the story some time."

"It would be my pleasure."

Her mind flashed back to the day of the festival, the day he'd first approached her. Before their conversation, Kathryn had seen Ector surrounded by children—including her younger grandchildren—as he regaled them with a story. That was another quality humans and kraken shared—the need to share stories.

She shifted her gaze back to the holographic screen. There was a story here, she was certain of it, and this was a rare opportunity for Kat and Ector to discover it together. A chance to, in some small way, make it a part of their own stories, which were currently intertwined.

"Let's see what there is to find in this thing," she said.

CHAPTER 9

MANY OF THE ITEMS DISPLAYED ON THE SCREEN WERE LABELED with strings of numbers that were all similar in sequence but had no meaning to Kathryn. A flick of her finger made that list scroll, revealing dozens of similar icons.

Here goes nothing, I guess.

She selected one of the icons at random.

The hologram changed instantly, becoming a small, three-dimensional image of a room. The place was clean and sleek, bearing some resemblance to a few of the oldest buildings in The Watch, but the hologram didn't seem to encompass the entire room. A uniformed man was seated in a chair close to Kat, his face depicted in stunning detail despite its reduced size. He had short brown hair, a long, sharp nose, and dark brown eyes. He couldn't have been older than twenty-five or thirty.

Kathryn recognized the insignia on his uniform—it belonged to the Interstellar Defense Coalition, the military organization that had been involved in Halora's colonization. Those markings could be found all over The Watch to this day.

Ector's eyes widened, and he moved closer to Kathryn. "That looks just like the rooms in the Facility where the humans stay."

Kathryn's brows rose. "Do you think this is from there?"

"I do not know."

The man in the hologram was leaned to one side with an elbow on the armrest and his chin propped on his hand. His eyebrows were drawn low over unfocused, troubled eyes. It took Kathryn several moments to realize that she wasn't staring at a still image; the man's shoulders were gently rising and falling as he breathed.

At least ten seconds passed before the man tipped his head forward and combed his fingers through his short hair. "I've gone back and forth in my head over the last few months, and it only gets harder every day," he said in a tired voice. "What course of action can I take? What can I do?"

He lifted his hand from his head, fingers splayed in a hopeless gesture. "File a report? This is a top-secret facility. It doesn't officially exist in IDC records. A formal complaint will see me in a cell solely based on the information I'd have to leak to explain the situation. And all the way out here... I'm not likely to get out of that cell while I'm still breathing. Hell, these logs alone violate enough rules to get me stripped of my clearance and tossed in the brig. I'm not supposed to be recording sensitive information of any sort, even on approved IDC devices... which obviously this isn't.

"But..." He threw up both hands, shrugged, and leaned back heavily. "Here I am. I can't just stay quiet, and I don't know if anyone else agrees with me. Talking about it like this again... Well, it doesn't change the situation, but at least I'm getting some of it off my chest. Can't get court-martialed if I don't get caught, anyway.

"What they're doing here is wrong. I'm just a grunt, and I don't understand the science behind all this or how this halorium stuff works, but those things they made... They're not *things* at all. They're people."

A strange, uncomfortable sensation—somewhere between

anxiety and outright dread—pooled in Kat's stomach, making it feel heavy and hollow at once. She glanced at Ector. His expression was solemn, his eyes fixed on the little hologram.

"It's just…" The man in the recording tilted his head back, angling his face toward the ceiling. "Yeah, they don't look like us, but they do at the same time. The staff treats them like animals." He leaned forward, presumable closer to the recording device, and lowered his voice as he said, "What kind of animals can understand what you're saying and talk back? And I don't mean just mimicking words, but having *conversations.*"

The man sighed and fell silent, eyes dropping to the floor. His expression wasn't merely troubled, Kathryn realized, it was conflicted, almost tortured. Whoever this man had been, his inner conflict had been clear at the time of this recording.

After another sigh, the man opened his mouth as though to speak. No words came. He took a breath, hesitated, and shook his head. He reached for something just outside the hologram's view.

The projection reverted to the enigmatic list that had first come up when Kat activated the device.

She looked to Ector again, whose solemn countenance hadn't changed.

He met her gaze with his own. "There is more?"

"I think so. Most of these other items are marked in the same manner." She worried her lower as she compared the numbers between several consecutive icons. "I think…I think those numbers are all times and dates, just recorded in the old pre-colonization calendar."

Ector pressed his lips together for a few moments. His face conveyed a grave thoughtfulness but gave away nothing else. "Shall we continue to unravel this story?"

Kat let her eyes linger on him. Even she—knowing so little of Ector's people and their history—understood that this unnamed man was likely referring to the kraken. The kraken had been mistreated by humans in the past. Kathryn couldn't imagine what it was like for Ector to have this potential window into the world in which his ancestors had lived.

Silently, she touched the next selection on the list.

The hologram once again depicted that same room—the bed against the wall was easier to see now—and the same man. This time, he was standing. He moved away from the front of the unseen recording device and paced back and forth across the center of the room.

"Maybe I'm stupid for doing what I'm doing. I know I'm stupid for logging any of this, so…I guess I have a precedent set, at least. If they find me out, it won't matter either way." The man—a soldier, Kathryn realized suddenly—shook his head and uttered a short, bitter laugh. "Wish I could say this is all to document what's happening here, that it's for some greater cause… but I think it's really just about trying to make myself feel better."

The man paused and threw his hands out to the sides. "I've been talking to them. We all do while we're guarding them— they get ordered around a lot, get told what to do. But I mean I was actually *talking*. Having conversations. And they are so much smarter than anyone seems to think. Hell, I'd guess they're smarter than half the grunts in this place. They know a lot more than they let on, and they know when they're not being treated right."

He lifted a hand and raked it through his hair. "And *she*… She's just beautiful. Doesn't matter how alien she looks. Those eyes, that skin, her voice… They're so much like us it's a little frightening. And I don't think any of them have ever been treated with even a little kindness. The first few times I interacted with them, they were extremely wary and distrustful. But they're capable of hope. If that's not a human quality, what is? Keeping them here like this, *using* them like this, is wrong. They're looked at as slaves. As living tools."

The man paced in silence for several more seconds, locking the fingers of both hands together atop his head. Little tufts of his short hair jutted up from between his fingers at wild angles, giving him a disheveled look. He didn't speak again until he was at the front end of the holographic room.

"I understood when I pushed for my clearance that I'd see some sensitive, questionable stuff, especially if I got a combat assignment. But this...this is so far outside what the IDC is supposed to stand for. This is exactly what we're supposed to be fighting against, isn't it?"

The man frowned and leaned closer to the front of the hologram, eyes even more troubled than before. He extended an arm, and the recording ended.

Kathryn's eyes locked with Ector's again. He nodded once, and she proceeded through the logs. They watched many of the recordings, transfixed by this glimpse into the past, barely noticing as the moons climbed higher into the night sky. They paused between recordings, sometimes to swap meaningful but silent glances, other times to absently feed another piece of wood into the fire. The song of the sea remained a steady ambience throughout.

The pieces of information scattered across the recordings slowly came together to form a clear idea of the soldier and his circumstances. He never directly introduced himself—why would he, if his logs were his personal records?—but a few frustrated mutterings to himself suggested his name had been Luke. He was an IDC soldier who'd lived and worked in the place the kraken called home, often referring to himself as a grunt or a guard. The topics of his recordings varied. He didn't always mention the mistreated creatures—and he never named them or described them directly—but they became an increasingly common subject.

His passion seemed to intensify each time he spoke of the creatures, especially a particular female. Kathryn recognized the gleam in the young soldier's eyes whenever he brought up that female; it was similar to the light in Ector's eyes when he looked upon Kat—full of longing, adoration...perhaps even the first signs of love. Just the memory of seeing those things in Ector's gaze was enough to spark heat in Kathryn's chest.

Luke grew increasingly certain that something had to be done, that some change needed to occur, as the logs progressed. He described his increasingly bold interactions with the kraken —and what else could those mysterious creatures have been? According to Luke, he'd even explained how they could access limited functions through the facility's computer and its voice commands—mostly what he dubbed harmless information like ancient myths and history.

The information brought a soft smile to Ector's face. Could it be that this human, Luke, had been the one to enable the old kraken tradition Ector had described earlier?

As Kathryn continued through the recordings, Luke spoke more and more of the kraken and less and less about anything else—and the female he'd mentioned came up with increasing frequency. His adoration for the unnamed female grew each time he mentioned her, evident in his body language, expression, and tone even though he seemed to be very careful regarding his choice of words whenever he talked about her. Those blossoming emotions sparked a gradually strengthening tightness in Kat's chest and built the tension in her limbs.

Even if she wasn't familiar with kraken history, Kathryn knew what the fate of the humans who'd lived and worked at the Facility had been. Her heart broke a little, but she held back the flood of emotion threatening to overcome her; she didn't know how Luke's story had ended yet. There was a distinct possibility that she would never truly know, though finding this device out here, days away from any town Kat was aware of, gave her at least a little hope.

"She has a name now," Luke said in one of the recordings—

one of the few in which his face was not dominated by obvious worry. He chuckled and smiled wide. The happiness in his expression transformed him into a new person. "Hera. Queen of the gods. If she were human, I'd laugh at the audacity of taking a name like that, but there's no ego involved here. And I guess if I were a little sappier, I would've suggested Helen or Aphrodite... because her beauty is unrivaled."

His smile shifted to something softer, something made impossibly affectionate by the light in his eyes. "But Hera...it suits her. It's perfect. I think the goddess Hera was all about family and childbirth. I don't know, it's been a long time since I was in school, and I don't remember much about all that. All I do know is that Hera's people—*my* Hera's people—were made to have trouble reproducing to keep their numbers controlled. So taking that name speaks of such...*hopefulness* to me."

Luke leaned back in his chair and stared up at the ceiling. Wistfully, he said, "Hera..."

Kathryn's heart ached, and it steadily climbed into her throat as she progressed through the logs. Luke described something akin to an awakening of Hera and her people as they took names for themselves and seemed to organize, and their displeasure with their situation grew with each passing day. For the first time, Luke also referred to them as kraken—a name which they had selected for themselves.

According to the young soldier, the typical response from most of the staff was increased cruelty. He seemed much less conflicted now; he was angry and upset, and before long, was unable to hold still for more than a few seconds at a time during the recordings.

As one such log began, Luke stalked away from the recording device, hands clenched in trembling fists at his sides. His shoulders rose and fell with deep, harsh breaths, and his lips were peeled back to reveal gritted teeth. He moved around the room like an agitated predator; if he'd had fur, it would've been bristling.

"There was an *incident* today," he finally said after what must've been a full minute of pacing. "I knocked another soldier on his ass, and he's damn lucky that's all I did. The kraken weren't moving quick enough for him on their way to their holding quarters. He decided to use his fucking prod, and he hit Hera with it. *My* Hera. And I just…"

Luke finally paused. He lifted a hand to squeeze his temples between forefinger and thumb, blocking his eyes from view.

"I told him to stop. He didn't. So, I just snapped. I punched him. Hard. I fucking *made* him stop. My official report reflects the necessity of my action—the way the kraken were looking at him, I swear they were about to attack. And in close quarters… They're built bigger, stronger, and faster than us. Against a couple of them, a rifle would help, but against a dozen? The idiot was going to start a riot and get himself torn to shreds.

"I'm sure I'll be disciplined, but the officers know what's going on here. You could be deaf and blind and still feel the tension in this place. The pressure's building, and if they keep going like this… One of my comrades is going to start something that won't end until a whole lot of blood has been spilled."

When the recording ended, Kathryn remained still, staring unseeing at the list of icons that again appeared on the projection. The sounds of wind and sea rushed in to fill the heavy silence. She was suddenly aware of the chill that had built on the air. Kat fed another chunk of wood into the fire and shifted a little closer to Ector's body heat.

He responded by slipping an arm around Kathryn and drawing her against him. Several of his tentacles slid over her legs as he tucked her into the shelter of his body, shielding her from the wind and chasing away the cold that the fire could not combat. She gratefully snuggled into his warmth.

"I long expected that not all the humans were our enemies,"

Ector said softly. "My first encounter with Macy was more than enough to instill that doubt."

"Most things are far less simple than they seem on the surface," Kathryn said.

"There is great truth in that. It is unfortunate that it took hundreds of years to learn that lesson."

Kathryn rested a hand on one of his tentacles and gave it a gentle squeeze. She still couldn't understand how the muscle beneath his skin could be simultaneously spongy and firm—as flexible as rubber but as strong as steel. "Your people did the best they could, and my people had no idea you even existed. Really…it's for the best things worked out the way they did. It's not perfect, but humans and kraken are living together peacefully now. Who can say we would've ever reached this point if things had gone differently?"

Ector brushed the back of a finger down her cheek. "You are right. There is much to be thankful for here and now."

Her stomach fluttered with heady anticipation, but this wasn't the time to give in. There was more to explore first, more to learn.

"Shall we continue?" she asked.

"Yes. We have been able to access many records in the Facility thanks to Theodora and Kane, but none have been so…"

"Personal?"

Ector nodded, smiling softly. "Most of the others are what Theodora referred to as *official*. More concerned with documenting occurrences, with protocol and form, than the emotions this Luke has displayed in his recordings."

Luke's tone over the next several recordings was just as dire. He was angry and frustrated—especially when he reported that one of the consequences he'd faced had been temporary removal from the posting that put him in direct contact with the kraken. His only consolations—which Kat agreed were scant comfort—were that Hera was unharmed and the other soldier had also been suspended from duties that brought him face to face with the kraken.

But the separation from Hera seemed to make Luke more distraught as time progressed.

"I think knocking that bastard on his ass definitely cooled things down a bit," he said in one log, "but it's still in the air. All I did—inadvertently—was delay the inevitable. This is going to reach a head soon. The kraken aren't broken, they aren't...*animals* to be tamed. Eventually, they are going to retaliate, and they know a hell of a lot more about this facility and the way we operate than anyone wants to admit."

His words—and the certainty with which he'd spoken them—rattled Kathryn and roused a sourness in her stomach that only intensified as she continued through the logs. The tightness in her chest grew along with her nausea; even from many kilometers and several centuries away, she felt the doom closing in on Luke and the facility in which he'd lived and worked. Thanks to the arrival of the kraken in The Watch a couple years ago, she knew of the kraken revolt, but only as a vague story about a time and place she'd never seen.

But these recordings made it real. It was a real place, they'd been real people, and these events had happened. The ocean of time that had separated Kathryn from those people and their lives had dwindled into a puddle; she was, at least for this little while, right there with Luke.

One recording opened with Luke sitting in his chair, leaned forward with shoulders hunched and elbows on his knees. He hung his head, drew in a deep breath, and released it in a heavy sigh. "I saw her today. Face to face. It was only for a second, but our eyes met, and..." He laughed; the sound was somehow joyous and bitter at once. "I don't understand how a moment of eye contact can feel so good and hurt so much. I'm still a little shaky."

Without looking directly at the recording device, he lifted

his hands briefly, palms to the ceiling. "I realized that for all the times I've talked about Hera, I've never really described her. Sure, I've talked about her beauty. I've mentioned her eyes— they're violet, so vibrant and deep. But all that is the surface. It's not all she is. She's so, *so* much more.

"Hera's strong. I mean, not just physically. She's strong willed and confident, and she hasn't let any of these assholes break that spirit—she never will. She's also...gentle. She doesn't use her strength to attack, only to protect, to uplift. And she's so intelligent, so inquisitive, so eager to learn and discover new things. She's not afraid to look upon the world with almost childlike wonder because it's all new to her, it's all amazing. And sometimes, the way she looks at me...it makes me feel like I'm the most amazing thing of them all. But that's not right. *She* is the most amazing, most wondrous thing in the world. In any world."

Ector held Kat just a little closer, drawing her more fully into his warmth. She melted against him.

Luke laughed again; much of the bitterness was absent from the sound now, but a dissonant note remained. "It's on record now, anyway, so if I end up doing something stupid, this will be here for them to find and use against me. Guess I should say if I do something *stupider*, since this is already so dumb of me. But that's really the ultimate outcome, isn't it? This whole situation leaves me no choice but to do something stupid and drastic to change it, and who am I kidding with that? This is a secret military research facility. They *will* kill me.

"And even knowing that, I can't do nothing. I want to help the kraken, want to help all of them, but I *need* to help her. It's important enough that I'm willing to risk getting shot...which maybe doesn't say much seeing as I voluntarily enlisted with the IDC knowing there's a war brewing in the fringe worlds."

Luke sighed again and leaned back in his chair. "Anyway, my

temporary suspension is finally over in a few days. I can start figuring all this out once I can talk to her again."

When the recording ended, Kathryn remained still, nearly overwhelmed by all she was feeling. Ector's presence—his solidness and heat—was all that kept her anchored to the present, but even that tether seemed tenuous at best.

"Are you all right?" Ector asked, his deep voice rumbling from his body into hers.

"I am," she replied after a few hesitant moments. "This is just...a lot. I'm almost scared to continue, as silly as that sounds."

Ector gave her upper arm a gentle squeeze, and his tentacles settled more firmly over her legs. "It does not sound silly, Kathryn. What we know of history says this story does not end well, but it is impossible not to hope for a happy resolution regardless."

"That's exactly it. I mean...this was left out here, so far away from your home. Someone must've brought it here, right?"

He nodded. "And there's only one way we might find out."

Kathryn took in a steadying breath, turned her gaze to the icon screen, and selected the next recording.

Luke appeared, hands braced on a table very close to the unseen recording device. The look on his face made Kat's heart freeze for a few moments—his skin was terribly pale but for frantic red splotches on his cheeks, his eyes were wide, his brow knitted, and his mouth hung open. Even with his holographic image displaying at perhaps a sixth of his actual size, beads of perspiration clearly shone on his forehead.

He snapped his mouth closed, and his lips peeled back to reveal clenched teeth. There was undeniable anger and aggression in his expression, but there was a certain quality to the light in his eyes that pronounced his obvious worry and suggested fear at his core.

"Don't have long. We're entering emergency lockdown," he

said, voice wavering. "Situation unclear, but… Sounds like one of the other guards got too rough and might've beaten a kraken to death. Don't know who was involved on either side. But the kraken are angry, and no one in command knows how they're going to react. Right now, it's all hands on deck."

Luke swallowed thickly and shook his head. "Fuck. This is so… *Fuck.*"

He reached forward, and the recording ended.

Kathryn didn't say anything; what could she have said? The moment felt too heavy, the air too thick, her chest too constricted. She played the next recordings—each of which was brief—in quick succession.

"Still in lockdown," he said in the first. "Kraken are quiet. Going back on duty after sleep."

In the next, his words were clipped, his breathing heavy. "It was Theseus. He's dead. It's still quiet, but…too quiet."

By the third, Luke looked haggard. His eyes were bloodshot and cradled by purplish bags, and his chin, jaw, and cheeks were lined with stubble. "Five days. No retaliation. I think they're going to give the *all clear* tomorrow to start getting the kraken back to work. Command is stupid, and what's worse is their stupidity is born of ignorance. The kraken haven't just forgotten."

In the next log, he looked a bit better rested, though no less distraught. Easing down into his chair, he drew in a deep breath, raked his fingers through his hair, and shook his head. "Saw her today, but we only had a few seconds. She seemed off, like she wanted to say something but couldn't, not while there were other humans around. Something's going to happen, and—"

A strange chiming sound cut him off. He shifted, leaning to one side, and raised his arm to touch a small device on his wrist. A holographic screen appeared in front of him. His eyebrows drew together, slanting down toward the bridge of his nose, as he muttered, "Communications compromised?"

Luke pressed his lips together, and his jaw muscles ticked. Without another word, he reached forward and ended the recording.

"That was the start of it," Ector said, tentacles flexing.

Kathryn licked her dry lips. "The start of what?"

"The revolt. Other records indicate that our ancestors prevented the Facility from sending or receiving communications when they rose against the humans. They isolated the inhabitants."

That sour feeling in Kat's stomach resurged; it felt like a lead weight was sinking through her belly. "And Luke knew it would eventually happen."

"I would guess that many of them would have known had they seen my people as more than animals or tools. But if that had been the case…perhaps it wouldn't have happened at all."

"I'm sorry, Ector."

He turned his head and leaned down, pressing a lingering kiss atop Kat's hair. "You do not need to apologize, Kathryn. You have not wronged me or my people, and I have not been the victim of any of what my ancestors experienced."

She leaned her head against his shoulder, once again melting into his warmth. "I'm still sorry about all of it. Sorry it happened. Your people didn't deserve any of it."

Ector ran his hand slowly up and down her arm, holding her close. "I am sorry for it, too. Thank you."

Kathryn would've been content to simply sit there, secure in Ector's embrace, but her eyes fell on the holographic screen, and she could not suppress her curiosity. "There are more logs left."

Ector made a thoughtful hum that vibrated into Kat. "So, the story is not yet over?"

"I guess we're about to find out." She selected the next log.

The holographic projection changed, but this time it

depicted a different—and entirely unexpected—scene. It was the same young man, Luke, but he was on some sort of small boat or raft unlike any Kat had seen. The vessel was made of a flexible material instead of wood, colored an oddly reflective white and bright orange. He was only dressed in his uniform pants—no shirt or shoes. A familiar-looking metal box lay beside him in the boat.

Based on the angle and viewpoint of the hologram, he must've been holding the recording device in his hand. Outside the boat was only churning water, dark but for the flickering reflections of light from overhead.

Once again, he looked tired and distraught, like he was stretched too thin, but there was a gleam in his eyes now that suggested he was also rattled.

"She found me. In all that… She found me and got me out. They, uh…" He stared off blankly for a few seconds before uttering a humorless laugh. "They fought back. I said they would, and now they have, and could anyone blame them?"

Luke dragged his free hand down over his face. "Took a PDS to get out. Ditched it as soon as I reached the surface so they can't use it to track me. Tore the distress beacon from this raft, too. I don't think… There's no going back now. And I'm just… glad. Glad to be out of that place, to be away from what it means.

"She's scouting right now to make sure we weren't followed. I think we slipped out unnoticed, just because…it was chaos down there. Going to follow the sunrise. We're only a few kilometers from shore, I think, so it shouldn't take long to reach land. Then, uh… Well, I guess we'll figure it out, won't we?"

The recording ended. Kat wet her lips again as she moved to select the next log. That tightness in her chest was still there, more intense than ever, and she knew it wouldn't ease until this was done. Until she knew.

The next recording began on a beach, but the hologram—as

usual—only spread about five meters from its central point, leaving a featureless patch of sand and a sliver of surf visible. Luke stood at the center of it, still barefoot but now wearing his uniform shirt with its buttons undone. Sand clung to his feet and pants.

"Came ashore about ten minutes ago. I turned off all network features on this device so it can't be pinged, but that also means I can't link with the navigation satellites." He turned to look to his left and slowly swung around to look to his right. "I think Watchpoint Echo is down the coast from here, maybe a day or two of walking away. That's not enough distance. They'll probably be mobilizing troops from there, so we're going to move in the opposite direction. Hopefully."

Luke turned again, this time toward the sea. "Hera should be back any minute. She was pushing the life raft out to open water to sink it. It might've been useful, but…it's too visible. We'll manage without."

When the holographic screen reverted to the icon list, Kathryn didn't waste any time in selecting the next.

THE HOLOGRAPHIC SCENE depicted the sort of vegetation that seemed common along the edges of Halora's jungles—green and violet leaves of various sizes and shapes, blades of grass that moved in the wind like the surface of the ocean, and scattered trees. But none of that fully registered for Ector; his attention was caught instead by the *two* figures within the scene.

One of them was familiar by now—the human named Luke, who wore his dark uniform shirt tied around his waist. The short-sleeved white shirt, which he must've usually worn beneath the other, was stained and damp looking. The man's face bore the short hairs humans called stubble and was smudged with dirt, but he was smiling.

The female kraken beside him looked a touch more bewildered, and Ector understood why. Her big, bright, violet eyes were wide and in continual motion, scanning her surroundings with awe and a hint of unease. Ector had reacted much the same way the first several times he'd been on land.

The female's skin was green, much more vibrant than Ector's drab natural color, and she had dark stripes along her arms, shoulders, tentacles, and head. She was beautiful; Ector couldn't deny it. But she couldn't compare to his female.

He shifted his gaze to Kathryn, who sat with her soft little body tucked against him. From this angle, he couldn't see her face, but its every detail was locked in his memory to be summoned at will. He could stare at her for hours at a time without getting his fill.

But his attention was called back to the hologram when Luke spoke.

"We've been moving along the coast for a few days now."

Hera turned toward Luke, and her brow furrowed. "I know this."

Luke chuckled and glanced at her. "I know you do. I'm just… documenting this."

"I do not understand what you mean."

He lifted his extended hand—the hand that must've been holding the recording device—and smiled. "I'm recording it on here. It'll help us remember these moments."

"Do you require that device's assistance to remember?" Hera asked.

"Well, no, but… This is our story. And maybe, one day, someone will watch this and learn about us."

Hera moved closer to Luke. She tilted her head to the side, arched a brow, and leaned toward his extended hand. "This makes the…holograms?"

"It does."

She reached forward. For a few moments, it seemed like her hand was truly emerging from that hologram, and Ector was almost certain that if he and Kathryn took it, they'd end up in that distant past, right beside Luke and Hera.

Hera withdrew her hand and turned her face toward Luke. She lowered her torso, placing her eyes on level with his, and smiled. "You humans are strange creatures."

Luke laughed, though there was a note of sorrow in the sound. "We sure are. Anyway, I wanted to record this, because… this is the spot. We haven't had an easy time so far, but we have what we need here. There's a stream nearby for fresh water, I've seen some trees with that winefruit stuff growing on it, the same stuff they shipped us from Watchpoint Echo sometimes, and there's some of those naba stalks growing along the stream banks. Lots of animals, too. Hunting will take some time to figure out, but"—he took one of Hera's hands with his, and their gazes locked—"we will figure it all out."

"We will," Hera agreed. "Escaping that place was our greatest challenge. The rest will be simple, for we have one another. Now turn off your device and see to your female's needs, my mate."

Luke grinned, tipped his head forward, and kissed her. He slipped his free arm around her—still holding the device in the other hand—and she wrapped her arms around his neck. When he finally broke the kiss, he smirked. "And just what is it my female needs? Is she *hungry*?"

"No, mate. I want you to—"

Just as Hera was sliding a hand down his chest, toward his pelvis, the recording ended. Kathryn's body heat increased; Ector knew it was not due to the fire. She had needs of her own, and Ector couldn't wait to satiate them for her. But he understood this wasn't the time. They'd come a long way, but she'd not quite accepted the claim he longed to place upon her. She'd not yet made a claim of her own. And it was late, regardless, after a very long day of travel and exploration. They both needed rest.

He tightened his hold on Kathryn just a little more; she physically couldn't get much closer, but he needed her to regardless, needed to feel as much of her as possible.

The symbols reappeared on the screen, nearly as meaningless now as they'd been before. He knew what each number was and could even identify many human letters by their names, but he'd not learned how to put them all together to read. Ector had learned many skills during his lifetime, but reading had only recently become a possibility, and he often wondered if it was simply beyond his capabilities by this point in his life. Despite all that he did not doubt Kat when she'd said those numbers were dates.

Kathryn touched the next symbol on the list.

Once again, Luke seemed to be holding the device on his upturned palm. He looked different—the hair on his face and head was longer, shaggier, and a shade lighter than before, and he was noticeably thinner. His skin had taken on a darker shade, leaving it closer to brown. His clothing was dirtier and a bit tattered. But he was smiling, and his eyes were bright. The little shell Kat had found in the metal box—minus the chip near its narrow end—dangled from around his neck, held in place by a bit of twine.

Thicker jungle foliage crowded around the edges of the hologram, and there was a wood and stone building behind the man. Many of the logs had that pale, fresh color Ector had seen in recently hewn wood back in The Watch. There was an open doorway on the wall with what appeared to be a curtain of grass hanging down from it. Large, fresh leaves covered the roof in overlapping layers.

Ector's eyes widened when he realized what he was looking at. The structure was sagging and rotting now, and creeping plants clung to much of it, but this was an image of the building where he and Kathryn had discovered the box.

"It's just about done," Luke said. "Been a long year, but we finally figured out enough to keep this thing standing. Not bad for only having one knife and a bunch of rocks for tools. Probably have to fill in more of the gaps with mud, but hey"—he shrugged—"it's been keeping us warm and dry."

The dangling blades of grass parted, and Hera emerged from the structure. She looked much the same as she had in the previous recording save for her posture—she seemed much more at ease now. There was something hanging on a string around her neck—the wooden flower that had been in the box along with the recording device, knife, and shell.

"You are using your little device again, Luke?" she asked, moving closer to him. She placed her hands on his shoulders from behind and wrapped a tentacle around his waist.

As she leaned forward, Luke twisted slightly and pecked a kiss on her cheek. "Saving the moment. This is a big deal. We're making it, finally doing more than just surviving. Anyway, I haven't even recorded anything since we found this spot. It's been almost a year already."

"My mate has crafted me a fine den," Hera said. She nipped at Luke's ear.

He chuckled and tilted his head away. "You had a big hand—and tentacles, I guess—in it too, Hera."

"As you say, it is better together." Hera shifted her attention to Luke's outstretched hand. "You will have to teach me to operate your device."

"You'll have to learn to read to get the most out of it."

Hera's brow furrowed. "Read... That means to make sense of those symbols your people use on everything, does it not?"

"It does. Now that we have this place, we'll have more time for that."

"We have been using this shelter for weeks, my mate."

"Well, yeah, but... It was still under construction. That doesn't count." Luke turned to face the building, swinging the angle of the hologram around. Hera moved with him, keeping her hands on his shoulders and her tentacle around his waist.

His smile softened. "We came here with one box of supplies and a knife. I'd say we've done pretty well, all things considered."

"It *is* a fine den." Hera craned her neck over his shoulder and cupped a hand over his cheek, guiding his face toward hers to capture his lips in a slow, passionate kiss.

Just as Luke began turning his entire body toward Hera, the recording ended.

Warmth blossomed in Ector's chest, radiating outward from each of his three hearts. When Kathryn had speculated that a couple had once lived in that old, abandoned structure, he'd easily accepted her assessment, but he would never have guessed it had been a human and a kraken together. He doubted Kathryn could ever have guessed it herself.

The next hologram displayed what must have been the interior of the little house. The stone structure opposite the entrance looked much the same as it did today—though considerably cleaner—but it was amazing to see all the furnishings intact and in their original shapes.

Luke was holding the recording device in his hand again, but the focus of it seemed to be set on the big, wide bed he was standing in front of. The only parts of the bed frame visible were the thick corner posts. It was draped in lush furs, and Hera lounged on her side atop it, her tentacles bundled and curled behind her.

"No more sleeping on the ground for us," Luke said. He beamed at the recording device for a moment before turning his head toward Hera.

Her lips were curled in a smile, too, but her expression was far more heated. "Come, mate, and help warm this bed."

Turning back to the device, Luke raised his arm, giving a

higher angle view of Hera. "I can't yet. I need to capture how beautiful you look right now."

She lifted a hand and bent her fingers, beckoning him. "I was not *asking*, Luke."

Luke faced her fully; the hologram swung around with him, capturing the way his tongue slipped out to slide across his lips. He growled playfully.

The light in Hera's eyes flared. Skin turning maroon, she crawled toward him, teeth bared, and grabbed a hold of him with hands and tentacles. When she suddenly dragged him onto the bed, Luke laughed. The recording device tumbled out of his hand and clattered onto the floor; the underside of the bed suddenly dominated the hologram's field of view, leaving nothing of Luke and Hera visible but for a single dangling tentacle.

Luke's laughter soon gave way to appreciative hums and groans, accompanied by sounds Ector now knew well—kissing.

Ector grew impossibly more aware of Kathryn's feel, scent, and heat, all of which seemed to intensify in those moments, and the ache behind his slit reintroduced itself. The sounds from the hologram continued—also seeming to intensify—and the one visible tentacle curled.

Kathryn cleared her throat, reached forward, and flicked her fingers through the hologram, returning it to the selection screen. For a few seconds, she and Ector simply sat like that, their bodies so close and yet not connected in the way he yearned for.

"Guess they were…caught up in their passion," she said breathlessly.

"Indeed," Ector replied, willing his hearts to slow.

After several more seconds of silence, Kathryn touched the next symbol. Ector didn't know whether to be disappointed or grateful.

The following three recordings offered a heartwarming

glimpse into the life that Luke and Hera had shared, providing little glimpses into what for them had been normal. It was the recording taken during a sunset that resonated the strongest with Ector. Luke somehow changed the way the hologram was captured, creating a two-dimensional image instead of the usual three-dimensional, and had recorded the sun setting over the ocean as he and Hera sat on the beach. Their quiet conversation faded away as the colors in the sky grew more vibrant and varied.

Ector felt a strong connection to the pair in that moment. He and Kathryn had enjoyed several such sunsets thus far, and he looked forward to many, many more.

"Only two more left," Kathryn said when the recording of the sunset ended. Her voice was undercut by emotion, but that emotion was too subtle for Ector to decipher; that barely noticeable quivering, that hint of hoarseness, could've been the result of anger, sadness, disappointment, joy, or a hundred other things.

Ector once more ran his hand slowly up and down her arm from shoulder to elbow; his palm rasped over the fabric of her shirt, adding another tiny layer to the night sounds. "Go ahead, Kathryn. We are almost there."

The next hologram displayed the interior of the little house again. Luke lay in the wide bed, sitting up with his back propped against the wall. Ector was stricken by the man's appearance; the human had aged years over the course of a few seconds.

Luke's hair, once short and dark, was now long and gray, paired with a beard that was a shade or two lighter and which was large enough to rival Breckett's. His skin, as darkly tanned as before, was now lined and weathered. His eyes—still lively and alert—had deep wrinkles at their corners.

Ector frowned and leaned a bit closer to the hologram. There was something off in the man's skin—a sickly, grayish undertone, accented by frantic splashes of color on his face. But that little shell was still secure on its string around his neck—and there was a tiny chip near its narrowest end.

The man chuckled. It was a tired, hoarse sound that nearly broke in a mild fit of coughing. Kathryn sat up straighter and clutched at Ector a little tighter.

Luke's breathing was labored when he finally recovered. He tipped his head back and closed his eyes. "Nearly forgot about this thing. Hasn't seen a whole lot of use through all these years, but…I'm glad it still works. Going through all my old complaining…it reminded me of how fortunate we've been."

He drew in a deep, raspy breath that swelled his bare chest and made his rib bones only more visible through his skin. "Nothing's been easy. We've…we've had to work for everything we have. Had to figure it all out as we went. And there were a lot of times when…when it seemed…" He pressed his lips together and exhaled slowly through flared nostrils.

"There were a lot of times when it seemed like we weren't going to make it. You know, like…well, like now. But we made it this far, and that's more than I could've hoped. I wasn't even sure how long it's been until I turned this thing on." Luke laughed, making his shoulders shake, but he didn't fall into a coughing fit this time. "Thirty-three years since we left that place. Not bad for only having a knife and a couple weeks of IDC survival training, huh?"

Luke shifted his head from side to side as though searching the ceiling for something. "Had things been different, I'd be in some nice apartment right now, maybe on Tau Ceti III or someplace like that, collecting a good IDC pension. Nothing to worry about, no reason to bust my ass for anything… No Hera. And that's the whole problem right there. All that must sound like complaining, because it's easy to focus on the bad stuff, right? But that's not what life has been. Life has been *good*. Yeah, it's been hard, but we've had so much joy throughout those hardships. We made so many great memories.

"And that's why...that's why I'm doing this now. Busted up my leg about a week ago, and it got infected, and I don't know what's going to happen. I just know that I don't want to leave her."

Tears welled in Luke's eyes and spilled down his cheeks. "I want all this on record because I love her, and I don't know if I've told her all this yet. I'm afraid now that I might not have the time to.

"I've never once, not for a single second, regretted Hera. I've never once thought longingly about what...what might've been, because without her...none of it has any meaning. She is my purpose. My everything. I would gladly choose to face all the hardships we endured over the years again and again so long as it meant having her.

"And...whatever I lost in walking this path, she's lost too—and more. She gave up everything she's ever known for me. *Everything*. I don't... I don't deserve that. I've done my best to be worthy of her, but even if I get through this...there's just not enough time left to earn her. But I *love* her, and I'll take whatever she's willing to give."

With faint tremors running through his limbs, Luke lifted his head and sat forward, looking directly at the recording device. "I love my Hera. If anyone finds this someday... I want the whole universe to know it. I can't claim to be a great man, and...and I've always wondered if I..."

Luke hung his head. His long hair fell in front of his face, but it wasn't enough to fully hide the fresh tear drops spilling from his eyes. He took several slow, shaky breaths before he could speak again, his voice now softer, thinner. "Always wondered if I could've done more in Pontus Alpha to stop what happened. To...to save the kraken and make sure they never had reason to do what they did. I spent my time complaining to myself instead of *really* helping. Instead of pushing for change, instead of fighting against a system, a situation I knew was wrong. That makes me just as guilty, doesn't it?"

He fell silent, tears still flowing, shoulders sagging. A deep ache clutched Ector's chest. His memory traveled back over the last several years, returning to the bloody fight that had taken place in the Facility when a group of disgruntled kraken had attacked both the humans who'd taken residence there and the kraken who'd accepted those humans.

The ache in Ector's chest was soon accompanied by a constricting feeling around all three of his hearts. He'd lost himself in contemplation over the events that had led to that terrible night more times than he could count, even knowing the futility of that contemplation. Nothing could change what had already happened. But the same questions that had haunted Luke centuries ago had plagued Ector for a long while now.

Could he have done more to prevent that conflict? Could he have handled everything better, could he have handled it differently? Could he have kept the peace and prevented the loss of life that had ultimately occurred?

He tipped his head aside and rested his cheek on Kathryn's soft hair. When he drew in a deep breath, her scent—now colored by the flowery aroma of the soap she'd used to wash herself in the stream—filled his nostrils, calling him back to the present.

"But no matter what," Luke continued, "no one can say I didn't love her with all my heart and soul. No one can say I haven't put my all into loving my Hera. Don't forget that no matter how else you must judge me—as a coward, a traitor, a deserter—I was also a man who loved his woman as much as anyone can love. And even if I die in the next minute, my love for her will persist. It's undying, it's…forever. I love you, Hera, and that love is bigger than both of us. It's bigger than the land

and the sea, than the moon and the stars. Bigger than...than anything."

The recording ended, allowing the sighing of wind and sea to return to Ector's awareness—but they seemed distant and diminished now, more like hazy memories of a time long past than part of the here and now. The feel of Kathryn's little fingers, so warm and gentle, dancing over the skin of his side was far more immediate, far more demanding of his attention. Luke had known lifelong love with Hera; Ector wanted the same with the female tucked against him. It didn't matter if that meant another year or thirty more. He wanted Kathryn and nothing else.

He couldn't be sure how long had passed when Kathryn finally spoke; it might have been seconds or hours. He knew only that he would've been content to sit with her in silent companionship until the sun rose.

"There's one more," she said, voice barely above a whisper.

Ector stared at that last symbol. Even if those letters and numbers held no real meaning for him, the icon they were attached to did—for better or worse, it meant the end. It was the end of Luke and Hera's story, but it was also a reminder that Ector's story would also come to an end someday. Everyone's did eventually. He wasn't fond of that understanding, not so soon after having Kathryn enter his life.

He lifted his gaze to the dark water ahead, which glistened with reflected light from the twin moons hanging over it.

You do not have me yet. You cannot.

Ector looked back at the screen, extended an arm, and touched the last symbol with the tip of a claw.

Once again, the hologram depicted the inside of the little home Luke and Hera had shared. The place was a bit darker, a bit dirtier; it was on its earliest step toward what it looked like today. Hera was alone now, squatted beside the table upon which the recording device must've been positioned.

Eyes downcast, she remained still but for her breathing, which was slow and steady but raspy. One of her hands was raised to her bare chest, and her fingers were absently tracing the petals of the wooden flower she wore around her neck. There were lines on her face—deep, clear lines earned over a long life. And even in the dim light, it was apparent that her once vibrant skin color had faded considerably.

"I do not know if this is working," she finally said, flicking an uncertain glance at the recording device, "and...I do not know what to say. But this device...it holds my mate, and I wish to speak with him one final time. The sea may have claimed his body, but part of him remains here. I...I must believe that." Her voice was weak, but retained a confidence, a decisiveness, that surmounted its frailty.

Hera raised her gaze and held it up, solid and unwavering despite how thin and frail she now looked compared to the earlier holograms. "My Luke, you are gone, and I have been alone for two years...but I see you everywhere, in everything. I know it is not real, that it is just in my mind. You are in my mind always. You are here"—she pressed a hand over her chest —"always."

She lowered her hand and her gaze simultaneously, leaning her elbows on the edge of the table. "I still do not know who you were talking to when you used this device, if you even knew...but if they are listening, I want them to know about you. About my mate. My Luke."

Ector noticed only then that she was toying with something between her fingers—the small shell that Luke had worn.

"You were brave, and you could be stubborn," Hera said. "You were a warrior but not a hunter, a protector but not a provider—not at first. But whatever I needed from you, whatever role you had to fill, you dedicated yourself to it. You adapted and overcame your shortcomings. You always found a way. Yet none of that is why I love you. Your kindness is what drew me to you, my Luke. That kindness you showed to me and my people in a place otherwise flooded by cruelty.

"From the first time our eyes met to the very last, you looked at me as though there were no greater wonder in the world. I… do not think I have the words to explain how that made me feel. We were looked at by other humans as beasts, as tools to be exploited. You looked at me as a person. As a female. And even the faintest memory of the way you used to look at me is enough to fill me with heat and joy."

Hera lifted her gaze again and smiled. The expression made her eyes sparkle with youthfulness at odds with how tired she appeared. "I am glad you captured yourself on this device, my mate, because it has allowed me to be near you again, to hear your voice, to know what your thoughts once were. These glimpses of you have given me strength to carry on.

"You survived your leg wound, my mate, though the battle you fought to do so was very, very hard, and it cost you much. Your leg was never the same…and neither was your health. You were ill through much of the next rainy season, but it was not until the next year that you finally lost your fight. I know you did not want to leave. But you, more than anyone, deserved rest." Her nostrils flared with a heavy exhalation. She pressed her lips together and closed her hand around the shell. "If you can hear me, you need to know that I have never regretted any of it either. All I left behind was *nothing* compared to you.

"Even if I had to endure ten times the suffering, I would choose to endure it again and again to have you as my mate. I hope the burden of your guilt has been lifted, for you were never at fault. You only brought joy. You made me so, so happy."

She twisted to the side and bent down slowly, wincing as she moved, to pluck up a familiar metal chest from the floor. "But… I am tired. I feel it in my bones. My time is near…and I will soon join you in the sea." Hera placed the chest atop the table and opened the lid. She raised a piece of folded cloth first—no, not just a piece of cloth, but Luke's uniform shirt, tattered and faded from years of use. She tucked the shirt into the chest. Its fabric billowed over the sides. Gently, she placed the shell in the chest.

"I do not know who may one day find this," Hera said as she reached up and removed the carved flower from around her neck. "We have not seen anyone in all our time here. But I want it to be known in this world and any other hiding amongst the stars..."

She took in a shuddering breath and placed the wooden pendant and its twine string in the chest. "My mate was not a coward or a traitor. He was a man who resisted doing wrong even when it was demanded as his duty. He loved me with all his heart, and I still feel that love to this day, long after he had to leave me."

Reaching down, she tugged at something strapped to her upper tentacle—the knife with its crude wooden handle. She placed it in the chest with the other items. "And let it be known to all that my mate was *loved* as much as anyone could be loved. Luke...my love for you will persist even should the ocean dry up and the sun fail to rise."

Features tight, Hera closed her eyes and bowed her head. Her entire body shuddered, and Ector knew that if kraken could shed tears, she would have been doing so now.

She took a deep, shaky breath and reached toward the device. The recording ended.

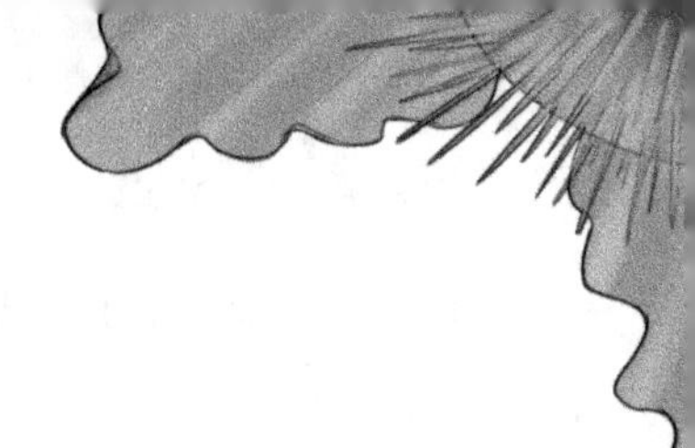

CHAPTER 10

ECTOR STARED AT THE SCREEN, WHICH ONCE AGAIN DISPLAYED human symbols, unable to do anything but feel his hearts thumping in his still-tight chest. The emotion that had been in Hera's voice was so raw, so powerful, so undeniable, that her sadness, pain, and love had seeped into Ector.

Kathryn sniffled and shifted in his hold. Ector leaned forward and angled his face down to look at her. Her eyes and cheeks glistened with tears, which sparkled gold and orange in the firelight, and she was wiping at them with the back of her hand.

Frowning, Ector slid his hand up from her shoulder to the side of her head, smoothing down her long, soft hair with his palm. She set the hologram device on the grass, turned her face against Ector's shoulder, and wrapped both arms around him, clutching him tight.

"Ah, Kathryn." Ector slid a pair of tentacles beneath her legs and coiled them around her thighs, at the same time lowering the arm he had around her. He gently lifted her off the ground and lowered her onto his lap. Her weight was slight, but the weight of her emotion was almost tangible; he felt it doubly so because he was flooded with powerful emotions of his own. He banded his arms around her as she huddled against his chest. Her tears wet his skin, trailing hot down his abdomen.

"I'm sorry," she said, her voice thick and quiet. She sniffled again. "I just… They loved each other so much." She lifted her head, tilted it back, and met his gaze. Her beautiful blue eyes swam with tears. "I…I know what it feels like to lose someone you love. I understand her pain, her suffering. I felt it for years. I never wanted to feel that kind of heartbreak again."

He frowned and lifted a hand, lightly brushing strands of hair back from her face. "I cannot imagine what it would feel like."

"It's like…something was torn out of you, and the hole that's left behind just wants to swallow everything up."

Her words produced a hollow ache in Ector's chest. "You survived that pain, Kathryn. Just as Hera did. Because you are strong."

She laughed, and the sorrow on her face was briefly overcome by amusement. "Stubborn is more likely." Her expression quickly sobered. She reached up and cupped Ector's cheek, biting her trembling lip as she searched his eyes. "I closed myself off. Told myself it wasn't worth it to risk feeling that way ever again. My girls filled that hole for me, and it was enough for a long time. But…I know now that it's never going to heal all the way until I open myself up again. The risk, the pain, is worth it."

Now Ector searched her face, hearts thudding louder than the crackling fire, louder than the sea and the wind. He ran a hand up her spine to cradle the back of her neck. "I… I have lived a long life, Kathryn. There has been good and bad. Whatever I have left, whatever else is to come, I want to face it with you."

Kathryn smiled, and fresh tears fell from her eyes—but there was joy glimmering in her gaze now. "The sea once took someone I loved, but now it's given me you. You make my heart feel whole again, and I don't want to waste the time we have left. I'll gladly risk anything to spend the rest of my life as your mate." She slid her hand up, over his siphon, resting it on the back of his head, and leaned forward until her lips hovered near his. "Will you join with me, Ector? As my husband?"

A rush of heat flowed through Ector. He couldn't tell where it began, but it quickly permeated his entire body, and he knew his skin had already shifted to maroon in an instinctual expression of his desire. He drew in a deep breath; it came out a moment later in a low, hungry growl.

Ector closed the distance between their mouths and claimed hers with a kiss just as powerful and consuming as the one they'd shared at the stream. Prickles of electricity sparked where they touched, quickening his hearts and breath as a rush of need blasted through him.

Kathryn pulled him closer, scraping her blunt little nails over his scalp. Her lips parted, beckoning him to deepen the kiss, to stroke his tongue against hers in a dance more intimate and intricate than any he'd ever performed. Another growl escaped him, forced out by the pleasure rippling down his spine to race to the tips of his tentacles. His cock pushed against his slit.

Without breaking the contact between their mouths, Kathryn rose from Ector's lap and turned her body toward him. The fleeting moment it took her to move was enough time for his cock to extrude fully from his slit, throbbing and hungry. She straddled him, thighs pressing to his sides, and her pelvis came down directly over his shaft.

The pressure inside Ector increased, intensifying the ache in his cock. It was torture; it was ecstasy.

Kathryn leaned forward, pressing all of her softness against him, and they moaned in unison as she rocked her hips. He dropped his hands to her backside and guided her to repeat the action, again and again. His tentacles curled around her legs, urging on her motions as his suction cups tasted her skin. His grip on her tightened, and his breaths grew more ragged with each gyration.

He'd never felt anything like this, had never imagined anything like this, had never craved anything like he craved Kathryn. The feel of her mouth and her body against his, her scent, her *taste*…

He could taste her desire in the air.

Kathryn invaded his senses, and he wanted more, needed more.

Ector broke the kiss. His chest heaved as he studied her face. Her eyes were dark with lust, her lips swollen and pink, and there was a delightful flush to her cheeks.

He plucked at her shirt with his claws. "Remove these, female."

Kathryn paused, and something flickered in her eyes. She nodded and eased off him. Ector reluctantly released her so she could stand. Looking down, she dropped her hands to the waistline of her shorts and slowly pushed them down, kicking the garment aside once it reached her ankles, granting him sight of more of her supple thighs—but her shirt still hung low enough to hide what he longed to see the most.

She moved her hands to the shirt's buttons and unfastened them one by one. Ector watched, rapt, as the cloth parted to reveal the skin beneath. But as Kathryn reached her middle, she hesitated, stilling her fingers.

Ector flicked his gaze back up to her face. She wasn't looking at him. There was a worried crease between her lowered brows, and a small frown on her lips.

He gathered his tentacles beneath him, rose, and eased closer to her. "Kathryn?"

"It's been eighteen years since anyone has seen me naked.

Since I've been intimate," she said, her eyes still downcast. "My body... It's not what it once was."

Ector reached forward and covered her hands with his. "Nor is mine. You were beautiful then, but you are at your most beautiful here and now, Kathryn."

She tilted her head back and looked up at him, her features easing as the corners of her lips turned up.

He gently guided her hands aside, released them, and moved his fingers to the uppermost of her fastened buttons. Anticipation thrummed through him, and instinct demanded he simply tear her shirt apart. He resisted the urge despite the desperate need behind it. Slowly, carefully, and with some difficulty—the buttons were not made for big, claw-tipped fingers—he unfastened her shirt the rest of the way. The gap in the fabric revealed a strip of her pale flesh; he slipped his hands beneath the sides of her shirt and swept it open farther, brushing his palms over her belly and to her sides.

He felt every line, every silvery mark, and he took his time moving his fingers over them. Each was evidence of her life, a record just as profound as those they'd watched on the little recording device only minutes before. "You have lived. You have loved. Your body has created and carried life. There is *only* beauty to be found here, Kathryn."

With two tentacles, he grasped her shirt and pulled it open, drawing it over her shoulders and down her arms to reveal her body to him in its entirety. Her skin glowed in the firelight, and her silver hair shone as it fluttered around her shoulders in the breeze. There was a small patch of darker hair between her legs. His eyes stopped on her chest, and his chest rumbled in appreciation. Her breasts were lush and full, tipped with dark pink nipples.

He smoothed his hands up her stomach until he had her breasts cradled in his palms; they were softer than he imagined.

He brushed his thumbs over their hardened peaks, and Kathryn gasped softly as a tremor swept through her.

Ector dropped her shirt onto the ground and moved a pair of tentacles to her legs, settling their tips at her ankles. Slowly, he slid both tentacles up, coiling them around her legs as they moved, sampling the taste of her flesh with his suction cups.

"You are beautiful, Kathryn," he said before dipping his head to cover one of her nipples with his mouth. He pulled the tempting little bud between his lips and sucked.

Kathryn gasped, and her hands flew to his head, but she didn't push him away. Instead, she pulled him closer, pressing her chest toward him in offering as she moaned softly. Ector sucked a little harder. Only when her breath hitched did he draw away to switch to her other breast. He licked and sucked, unable to get enough of her taste.

"Ector," she whispered.

As his tentacles reached her upper thighs, her taste changed. Her flavor became so sweet, so potent—even through his suction cups—that it startled Ector. He raised his head and slid his tentacles higher. Her inner thighs were slick with her oils. Anticipation made his breath catch in his throat as he grazed the tip of a tentacle along Kathryn's slit, eliciting a whimper from her. He slipped the tip deeper into her folds. Her hips bucked as Ector's grazed something small at the top of her sex, and a fresh gush of heat coated his flesh in her slick.

"I guess—*ah*"—she trembled, her lashes fluttering, when his suction cups pulsed against her—"you discovered what else can make me wet," she said with a breathless laugh.

His mind darted back to a conversation from the first day of their trip; he hadn't understood what she'd meant when she'd implied something other than the ocean could get her wet. Even then, days ago, she'd been teasing him, had been *wanting* him. That knowledge poured fresh heat into his blood and made his cock strain with want for her.

Withdrawing the tentacle, he lifted its tip to his mouth and slipped it between his lips. Her flavor flooded his mouth with almost overwhelming sweetness. He growled deeply and sucked every trace of her oils off the tentacle, but it wasn't enough. He could never have enough.

He locked his gaze with hers. Her eyes were wide, and her lips were parted in surprise.

"I want to kiss you," Ector said.

She nodded and tipped her face up toward him.

He released one of her breasts, cupped her sex with his hand, and carefully slipped his middle finger between her folds to stroke her slick flesh. "I want to kiss you *here*, Kathryn."

Her eyes widened again, and she pressed her hands to his shoulders to steady herself as her hips rocked against his palm. Heat emanated from her. "Oh! You want to... I've never..." Her cheeks turned a darker red.

Some of the younger male kraken—those with human mates—had spoken of using their mouths on their females' slits, but Ector had never truly considered it before. It was simply one of those strange things to which he'd had no connection; he'd seen nothing wrong with it, no reason to condemn it, but he'd been without a mate for so long that it hadn't warranted a second thought.

But now that he'd had a taste...he was helpless but to seek more.

He slid his hand up along her sex slowly, careful of his claws, his fingers delving deeper into her wet slit, before he raised his hand to his mouth and ran his tongue over his palm to lick away her oils. He couldn't prevent an appreciative hum from rumbling in his chest. "Then we will learn together, Kathryn."

She stared at his mouth, eyes darkening sensually as she watched his tongue on his webbed fingers. "Yes. I want you to... kiss me, Ector. Whatever you want. I am yours."

Those short, simple words—*I am yours*—struck him with

more power than should've been possible, blasting directly to his core, where they awoke something primal. Even in the lustful haze that blanketed his mind in those moments, the weight of what she'd said was not lost on him. She'd spoken clearly and confidently.

His. Kathryn was his. His mate.

Nothing had ever felt so *right*, so important, so certain, in all his life. And he'd never been so possessive of anyone or anything as he was of her in that instant.

He slammed his mouth over hers, demanding everything through a kiss even as he wrapped his arms around her waist. When he lifted her off her feet, she didn't resist; nor did she resist as he guided her legs up his sides with his tentacles still wrapped around them. He held the kiss all the way down as he laid her on the soft grass near the fire.

Only after nipping at her lip did he break the kiss and pull back, withdrawing his tentacles and moving his hands to her knees. He spread her thighs wider and shifted back, positioning himself between her parted legs, to stare down at her glistening sex. It bloomed like a flower, revealing its pink petals.

So beautiful.

Mine.

Lowering his head, Ector flicked his gaze up to meet Kathryn's. She watched him raptly with her bottom lip caught between her teeth. The sight of such vulnerability in her eyes, bolstered by such trust and eagerness, made his hearts stutter.

He inhaled deeply the fragrance of her desire. His eyes snapped shut, and he shuddered. The tremor ran all the way down to his shaft, and he nearly spilled his seed right then, holding back only through sheer force of will. He would savor this moment and gift his mate with pleasure before taking his own. But this… This was a gift for him, too.

Curling his fingers around her thighs, he dipped his head, pressed his mouth to her sex, and *kissed.* Conscious thought ceased at his first full taste of her on his tongue. That primal instinct that had stirred in him only moments before resurged, blasting through his body on a wave of heat and hunger, leaving him with only a want, a need, for *more*. He feasted upon her as though he'd been starved for eternity, and nothing could quench his thirst and hunger but her. He drank, licking everywhere, sucking everywhere—especially the little bud at the apex of her sex that seemed to wring more nectar from her.

Kathryn's hands, which Ector barely registered were upon his head, gripped him as she cried out and bucked her hips. He snarled against her, forcing her thighs back to the ground. That sound—which had risen from his throat involuntarily—combined with her desperate cry, brought Ector back to his senses.

Eyes wide, he lifted his head. His hearts were racing for an entirely different reason now. "Are you all—"

"No! Don't stop," Kathryn begged breathlessly. Her chest rose and fell rapidly, and her skin was flushed. Her eyes, half-lidded and gleaming, locked with his. "Please, don't stop."

For a moment, he couldn't understand how what he'd perceived as a pained reaction could possibly be an expression of pleasure, but the pleading tone in her voice cut through his doubts. It was about so much more than his need to drink from her; his mate was desperate for pleasure, and he would always do all he could to fulfill her desires.

He dropped his head at her urging, and kissed her again, using his lips and tongue—but this time, he maintained his control. He was rewarded by his mate writhing in his grasp. Her eyes closed as she tilted her head back and arched her chest, thrusting her breasts into the air. She undulated her hips as much as he'd allow, seeking his mouth and tongue with her sex, filling the night air with her moans.

"Oh God, I'm so close," Kathryn rasped. She released her

hold on him to cup her breasts, pinching and squeezing her nipples. "My clit, Ector. *Please!*"

Breathing raggedly, he lifted his mouth from her sex only far enough to ask, "Your what?"

Opening her eyes, Kathryn raised her head and met his gaze. She laughed. Releasing one of her breasts, she reached down her body toward her sex. Ector had to hold himself back from swatting her hand away. She slipped her finger into her slit and touched the small bud nestled at the top, slowly circling it.

"This is called a clitoris. A clit," she said. "It's what brings women the most pleasure. What brings *me* most pleasure."

Despite his reluctance to do so, he removed one of his hands from her leg and took hold of her wrist. He drew her hand away from her sex, pausing briefly to suck her oils from her finger, and guided it back to his head. Then he grasped her thigh again and dropped his mouth to the spot she'd shown him—her *clit*—and sucked.

Kathryn dropped back to the ground and gasped. Her nails bit into his scalp, and she thrashed beneath him, but he didn't relent. He only sucked harder, stroking his tongue over the little bud that brought her so much pleasure.

Suddenly, her body tensed, and she screamed as a rush of nectar flowed from her. She trembled as she came, her scream fading into breathy moans. It wasn't until she gently pushed his head and said his name that he released her clit, giving it a gentle kiss before he lapped the oils from her sex. Her body was languid now.

"Ector?" she repeated.

As he lifted his gaze to meet hers, he slipped his tongue out to lick her moisture from his lips, savoring every drop.

She held her arms out to him. "Join with me."

His cock pulsed in response to her invitation, reminding him of the immense discomfort that had gripped him. He removed his hands from Kathryn's legs, planting them on the ground to either side of her, and pushed himself up, sliding his body over hers. He stopped only when the tip of his cock was touching the hot, slick flesh of her sex.

Kathryn smiled, slipped her arms around his torso, and ran her palms along his back. His tentacles moved restlessly upon the ground. Two of them found her legs and twined around them, keeping them spread wide. She rocked her hips upward, and the tip of his shaft slipped inside her. A tremor ran along his spine, and he gritted his teeth.

"You are mine," Ector growled, and thrust his cock deep.

Heat, *so much heat*, surrounded him, squeezing him tight.

Kathryn gasped, tightening her hold on him, but she didn't move. He was glad for it; he knew the slightest motion on her part in that moment would've been too much, and he would've disgraced himself. He locked his elbows and leaned his weight on his arms, which threatened to tremble.

His shaft was sheathed in warm bliss. It had been so long since he'd mated, so long since he'd felt anything like this.

No. I've never felt anything like this. This is rapture.

Kathryn bit her lip against the incredible sensation. Ector's slick cock stretched her, filled her, and oh God, she wanted *more*. His shaft throbbed, and she felt his rapid pulse through their connected bodies. She felt his struggle just as clearly. Though all she wanted to do was pull him closer, undulate her pelvis, and take him deeper inside her, she held still; she didn't want this to end too soon. Her resistance was only made harder by the little tendrils around the base of his cock, which teased her sex with featherlike caresses.

Tilting her head back, Kathryn looked up at him. His eyes were squeezed shut, his jaw clenched with sharp teeth bared, and the cords of muscles in his neck stood out clearly. She glanced beside her. His fingers were rigid, claws buried in the ground. His tentacles—even the ones curled around her legs—were equally stiff, and his body trembled as though he were desperate to maintain control. She had the sense that he'd been struggling to maintain that control throughout their trip.

Ector had smiled and laughed with her, had spoken openly about a great many things, and hadn't been shy about expressing his desire for her, but he'd somehow seemed guarded through all of it. Kat guessed it had to do with the kraken culture and his former role as a leader and mentor—he'd likely trained himself to appear stoic and calm no matter the situation so his people always had someone to look to for stability.

But she didn't want him in control. She wanted him wild. She wanted that same ferocity, possessiveness, and need she'd seen in his eyes when he'd tasted her.

She wanted all of him. Nothing held back.

Lifting her head, Kathryn brushed her nose and lips across his chest. Her tongue darted out to lick his nipple. A full body shudder wracked him, and he hissed.

"And you are mine. Husband." She bit his nipple and, using the tentacles around her legs as anchors, thrust her hips upward, taking him fully inside her.

Ector bowed his back and roared; it was a guttural, bestial sound that blasted a thrill through Kathryn, making her toes curl. He shoved his hips forward, pressing her into the ground, and those delightful tendrils skimmed and stroked, vibrating over her sex and clit. Her breath hitched as her core clenched.

Within the next instant, Ector was pumping in and out of her rapidly. His thrusts were not soft, but punishing, brutal, *sublime*. Growls, grunts, and guttural sounds escaped him, mixing with her gasps and moans. Sheer pleasure rippled through her with every slam of his cock. She was hot, too hot, and her skin was overly sensitive as the sensations built.

Kathryn curled her fingers and raked her nails over his back; she needed him closer, needed him ever deeper.

He shifted her with his tentacles, pulling her legs higher up around him; it was just enough of a change to make his cock stroke her clit directly.

Kathryn broke apart. Her body tensed and spasmed as she came with a choked cry. Blistering, delicious pleasure flooded her, and she squeezed her eyes shut against the blissful torment. For that time—whether it was mere moments or an eternity— her body was weightless, insubstantial, not a physical thing but a manifestation of pure pleasure. And she was flying through the starry sky, everything around her reduced to a spectacular blur by her ecstasy. The world and all its worries were far, far below, unimportant and, for a little while, forgotten.

Ector snarled, and his ruthless thrusts stuttered. For a moment, it seemed as though every muscle in his body were stiffening around her, and the tentacles on her legs coiled tighter. Then he growled. A gush of heat exploded within Kathryn in that same moment, and Ector sagged forward, catching himself on his elbows as he filled her with his seed.

Kathryn panted beneath him, quivering as his little tendrils stroked and teased her sex. She came again with a series of gasps when one of those tendrils found her clit and remained there, vibrating against it. Her sex fluttered, gripping Ector's cock, and Kat ground against him, clawed at him; the sensation was so intense that it was almost painful. Still, she reveled in the staggering, overwhelming pleasure he wrought her—especially as he continued to pump his hips in erratic but firm motions.

"Kathryn," Ector groaned, shuddering as more of his seed filled her. "I am *yours.*"

A different kind of warmth bloomed within Kathryn, one that made her heart skip and ache with an abundance of love. She pressed her face against his chest, inhaled his sea-laced scent, and smoothed her hands up his back. She would never get enough of touching his velvety skin.

This was what she'd been missing, what she'd been craving all along. This connection, this intimacy, this feeling that no matter what, she would never be alone again.

Ector held himself over Kathryn as their bodies eased, keeping the majority of his weight off her. Eventually, her sex relinquished its grasp on his shaft, and her breathing and heartbeat steadied. Though little whispers of pleasure continued to course over her skin and tingle at her core, weariness sank into place as her euphoria diminished.

She had no idea how long they'd listened to Luke's recordings, but the moons had nearly completed their trek across the night sky; the sun would rise soon enough. Kat hadn't stayed up so late in a long, long time—not since her girls were little and one of them had been sick. Before that...well, it hadn't been since she and Colin had been young themselves.

Despite her exhaustion, she was still disappointed when Ector reluctantly withdrew from her. She immediately missed that fullness, that satisfaction, that intimate, undeniable connection. But he didn't leave her—he just rolled aside, onto his back, keeping his arms around her to pull her along with him. He lifted his torso off the ground for a few seconds as he grabbed her backpack, dragged it over, and positioned it beneath his head. Then he lay down, propping his head on the bag.

Kathryn sprawled atop him, resting her head on his chest, and listened to the strange, rhythmic beating of his hearts. Her thighs were wet and sticky, but she didn't care. She didn't want to move from this spot.

Ector's tentacles coiled around her legs and draped over her body, blanketing her, and his suction cups kissed her flesh wherever they touched. She was cocooned in warmth. A content smile stretched on her lips, and she hummed as every muscle in her body relaxed. She rubbed small circles on his chest with the tips of her fingers, relishing the feel of his skin, which had reverted to its normal drab green.

He stroked his clawed fingers through her hair, smoothing it down her back. He inhaled deeply and released it in a low rumble. "I have never felt so at peace as I do now."

Kathryn tilted her head back and looked up at Ector. He was staring down at her, his strange, beautiful, golden eyes shining in the firelight, and the depth of emotion, adoration, and awe in his gaze made her heart sing. She couldn't help but think back to something both Luke and Hera had echoed in the recordings —Ector was looking at Kathryn as though she were the most amazing, most wondrous thing in all the world.

Her smile widened as she moved her hand up to cup his jaw, stroking his lower lip and cheek with her thumb. She lifted her head and placed a light kiss on his lips. "You made me soar, Ector." She lay her head back down on his chest and closed her eyes, hugging him tight. "I flew amongst the stars tonight."

CHAPTER 11

ECTOR SPED THROUGH THE SHALLOW COASTAL WATERS, FUELED BY his eagerness to return to Kathryn—to his mate. Leaving her alone had been difficult even knowing full well that she could take care of herself. He knew the renewal of his reluctance had been sparked by what they'd shared the night before.

It had been so much more than he could ever have hoped for or dreamed. It had been…perfect.

He'd mated with many females in his younger days, but none of those experiences compared to his joining with Kathryn. Those couplings had been matters of duty and necessity, and whatever pleasure had been associated with them had always been overshadowed by the simple need to procreate and continue the existence of their species.

But with Kathryn, the underlying emotions, the connection between their minds and hearts, had elevated their joining to something euphoric beyond Ector's comprehension. Though he knew nothing about flying, her comparison seemed apt.

They'd slept away the morning with Kathryn draped over Ector, her skin warm and soft and still tasting of their lovemaking, and had mated again immediately after waking. By then, the sun had already crept past its zenith. Ector had readily agreed with Kathryn's suggestion that they maintain their current camp until the following day—they would've only had a few hours of daylight by the time the boat was loaded and in the water.

Of course, her suggestion had also sparked an internal battle between Ector's conflicting instincts—instincts that seemed to have intensified during his slumber. Kathryn had accepted his claim and made a claim of her own; she was his mate without question. His drive to protect her was stronger than ever, but so too was another primal drive—the need to provide for her. That would mean leaving the camp to hunt, and he knew full well he was not an effective hunter on land.

Ultimately, it had been her languid contentment that had driven Ector to choose the latter instinct. His female had worked hard throughout their journey, and now she'd been well loved; she deserved some rest. She'd provided their meal the day before, and he had been determined to do so today.

He tightened his hold on the pair of hefty, big-mouthed fish he'd caught. The fishermen of The Watch called these fish gapers, and always asked the kraken to scout for them—they were meaty creatures, and that meat was particularly sweet and tender, especially when cooked. Two gapers would provide plenty of meat to feed Ector and Kathryn, potentially for more than one meal—and Ector understood the value of good, fresh food. Yet the catch alone didn't seem to be quite enough to make his excursion worth the price of being separated from his mate.

The thought of staying in camp with her had been tempting. It would have been so easy to simply take her in his arms and converse for hours as the sun gradually sank toward the sea, would have been so easy to spend every moment looking at her, breathing her in, touching her, *joining* with her.

Ector had chosen the hard way, knowing that, sometimes,

they'd have to be apart to best fulfill their duties—both to one another and their community.

Fortunately, the hunt—which couldn't have taken more than a couple hours up to this point—had provided an unexpected discovery that would make up for the time lost with Kathryn. It had become more than the fish, more than a chance to feel the soothing ocean waters after nearly a full day in the warm air, more than the fulfillment of an instinctual need to provide for his mate.

Ector's views on his people's traditions had shifted significantly over the last few years. Human influence had changed everything, most of it for the better. And last night...those memories would stand as proof that those changes were good. But there was one tradition he did not want to abandon, one tradition to which he longed to adhere. Perhaps it was all out of sequence now, perhaps it would have lost much of its meaning, its power, but he would still do it.

He would dance for her—and he'd discovered the perfect place to do so while he was hunting.

Anticipation quickened his hearts and sent a faint tingle across his skin. That now familiar ache—the one only Kathryn could eliminate—sank into place, low in his belly. He'd not danced in so, so long, and he'd never had such an eagerness to do so, had never had such meaningful motivation.

Despite the little aches in his joints that his hunt had agitated, he swam a little faster. He felt stronger than he had in a long while, and glided effortlessly through the water, as though Kathryn's love were a force powerful enough to carry him anywhere. Bright afternoon sunlight spilled through the sea's surface and danced across the sandy floor in rippling waves. Tufts of sea grass and stalks of seaweed swayed in the current, their leaves and blades shifting between dark and light shades as they turned, twisted, and bent.

Kathryn had never been down here. Though she and Ector had spent so much time on the sea since leaving The Watch days before, she had yet to delve below the surface. She'd shared some of the wonder and beauty of the world she'd always known; Ector couldn't wait to share some of his. He knew that merely the look on her face would be more than enough to make this all worthwhile.

Just the thought of her potential awe and joy lifted his spirits impossibly higher. He flared his tentacles a little wider and snapped them together a little more boldly as he swam. Ector had spent so much of his life viewing most of Halora as dangerous, mysterious, and to be avoided, had always struggled to curb the curious nature of younger kraken like Jax, who yearned to venture into that frightening unknown. He'd changed his attitude on such matters in recent years, but he'd not truly begun to understand until this time with Kathryn.

There was so much beauty to be found after breaking out of what the humans called one's *comfort zone*. Sticking only to the safe, to the known, led to eventually stagnation.

Had it truly only been nine days since he'd approached Kathryn during the festival? He felt like he'd learned so much in that time—about her, yes, but also about the world, about *life*. Somehow, that time had passed with both lightning swiftness and blissful slowness. A lifetime had gone by in those nine days, and he craved a thousand more lifetimes to spend with his Kathryn.

As he neared the stretch of shoreline that was serving as a temporary home to him and Kathryn, Ector angled himself upward and lifted his head above the surface. He blew water from his siphons and filled his lungs with air. The ocean breeze was cool against his wet skin, and he couldn't help but reflect upon it. Kraken had always split their time between the sea and the Facility, including the functioning parts of the latter that were filled with recycled air, but none of that could've prepared him for the sensation of open, natural air on his skin for such long periods as he'd experienced since moving to The Watch.

The wind was not unlike the water currents to which kraken skin was so sensitive and attuned; Ector had always drawn comfort from that.

But wind and air could not long hold his attention as he swam toward the shore; Kathryn was close by, awaiting him. A wispy column of smoke rose from the camp, carried away by the breeze, and he could see Kathryn standing beside it. She was looking toward the sea, one hand over her eyes to shade them from the glaring afternoon sun. She wore only her button-down shirt, which fluttered in the wind, leaving her legs entirely bare for his perusal and offering teasing glimpses of what was hidden between them. That ache low in his belly intensified, and his shaft hardened. He willed his slit to remain tightly shut; it was a battle that he knew he would eventually lose, but they had food to prepare first.

Ector drew his torso into the air once the water was shallow enough, and Kathryn's eyes shifted to him. She waved. He lifted both arms, displaying the bounty of his hunt. Even from this distance, he saw a flash of white as she grinned.

A swelling of pride in Ector's chest increased his pace as he moved fully onto land and crossed the sandy strand. His tentacles easily traversed the rocky ground leading to their camp, which was comfortably above the high tide line. For a few moments, the camp—and his Kathryn—was blocked from his view. Then he crested the rise, and his gaze met hers.

She was still grinning, and it made her eyes sparkle; those blue orbs were more beautiful than the brightest nighttime star, more enchanting than the face of either moon. The way she looked at Ector was enough by itself to instill him with a sense of purpose, with a meaningfulness he'd been hungry for throughout his life without ever realizing it. He knew in that moment, with a confidence and certainty so strong it seemed impossible, that this was *right*. Kathryn was always meant to be his, and Ector hers. He wished he could've found her years ago, wished he'd had a full lifetime to spend alongside her, but he would gladly—and greedily—take every second with her he could have.

She was human, yes. Even when Jax had first brought Macy to the Facility, even when Arkon found his Aymee or Rhea her Randall, even when Dracchus took Larkin as his mate, Ector had never imagined himself with a human. Kathryn was small, relatively fragile, slower and weaker than a kraken—just like all her kind. But she was also stronger than most anyone he knew. She'd overcome heartbreaking tragedy and had found the courage to carry on. She'd looked at herself, her situation, and her world and said *I am not yet done*.

And Ector greatly admired her for that. It was one of the reasons he *loved* her.

His lips spread into a grin mirroring Kathryn's.

She taught me the true depth and potential of love. Something I've not truly understood for my whole life... She showed me in a few too-short days.

"I have returned with our evening meal, wife," he said as he finally entered the campsite. He enjoyed the way that word —*wife*—felt on his tongue; it had power, weight, meaning.

She ran toward him, closing the distance swiftly, and barely slowed before her body collided with his and she wrapped her arms around him.

Ector chuckled and embraced her as best he could without rubbing the slimy fish on her. "I am wet, Kathryn."

"I don't care," she said, squeezing him tighter.

His smile faded at the strange tone in her voice. He brushed his tentacles soothingly up and down her bare legs. "What is wrong?"

She shook her head and chuckled. "It's ridiculous. I just..."

Her shoulders rose and fell with a deep inhalation and a slow exhalation. Tilting her head back, she looked up at him, and it was only then that the slight sheen of tears in her eyes became visible. "You were gone for a long time, and when I saw you…I just felt this *relief*. Like my heart was going to burst out of my chest. It's stupid. You live in the sea. It won't drown you, but… I just found you, Ector." She ran her hands up his back. "There are other dangers out there, and I was scared that the sea would take away someone else that I love."

Ector frowned down at her. He passed the fish to his tentacles, laid them on the ground, and wiped his hands off thoroughly on his wet skin before covering her cheek with his palm. "It is not stupid, Kathryn. But the sea does not have me yet, and it will not for a long, long while still. I will not allow it."

Her smile returned, soft and beautiful, before she turned her head, kissed his palm, and leaned forward to press a kiss to his chest. She stepped back, and Ector withdrew his tentacles and arms from her. Her eyes rounded when she looked at the fish on the ground.

"Wow." Her features turned playful as she glanced up at him. "I suppose we did work up quite an appetite."

For a moment, Ector was forced to clench his teeth against the stirring beneath his slit; that gleam in Kathryn's eyes instilled him with heat. "We can always work to deepen that appetite further if you think this is too much food."

Kathryn laughed. "Since we're both making up for lost time, I think we might need *more* food. Let me get my knife so we can get them cleaned up."

This time, Ector helped Kathryn clean the fish, and they fell into the work as easily as though they'd been doing it together for years instead of days. Once again, he ate most of the bits she would've otherwise thrown away. When those bits were all gone, she gave him a little purplish star mint leaf to deal with what she dubbed his *fish breath*. Ector could only chuckle as he ground the leaf between his teeth. Its potent flavor burned almost as much as it had the first time he'd tried it, but it rapidly cleared away the lingering taste of raw fish parts from his tongue.

He took no insult in it; who was he to question what scents his mate found pleasant or unpleasant? There were many smells on land of which he was not fond, and it only stood to reason that there were scents Kathryn didn't care for, either. If she found those fish parts so unappealing that she would not eat them, why would she like their smell? Why would she want to taste them on his lips when they kissed?

It was a small thing to keep his mate satisfied. When Kathryn glanced up at him, Ector swallowed the mashed-up leaf and flashed her a large smile.

And as a reward, Kathryn leaned in and kissed him. It was a slow kiss; she took her time with it, and he did the same, relishing every moment. Her lips lingered against his, but it was only when her tongue teased the seam of his mouth that he reached out for her, longing to pull her against him. She withdrew before he could. The corners of her mouth curled upward in a knowing grin as she returned to her task and set the fillets to cook.

When the food was done, Kathryn piled the flakey white meat high on several large green leaves. Ector sat beside her, and they ate, enjoying one another's company as they had for days, whether in comfortable silence or conversation. During this meal, however, the air felt charged with anticipation. Ector couldn't stop his eyes from straying to his beautiful mate. She also cast him heated glances, and he knew she felt it, too.

Once they'd finished eating, Ector was unable to resist the temptation any longer. He needed to touch her, to hold her, to feel her body against his. He turned toward Kathryn, slipped his arms around her, and lifted her onto his lap. He loved the feel of her slight weight upon him.

A laugh escaped her, and she leaned back against his chest. The sea stretched about before them, darkening beneath an evening sky that was stained gold, pink, and violet, but it was still too early to head out. Ector had time to savor this moment with her.

With a contented sigh, Kathryn rested her head on his shoulder and lay her arms over his. She fit perfectly against him. Ector smiled and slid his tentacles over her legs, sampling the taste of her skin through his suction cups. She tasted of the sea, her soap, and something wholly *her*, sweet and fragrant. It was a flavor he was swiftly growing addicted to.

It was becoming difficult to understand how he'd lived without her for so long—and he knew he was well beyond the point of being able to live without her ever again. Kathryn was a part of him, now, as necessary and vital as his lungs, siphons, or hearts.

KATHRYN SMILED as she reclined against Ector. They'd enjoyed many sunsets together since leaving home, and she'd never tire of watching them. Not with Ector. He made them that much more special. She'd observed countless sunsets from her window over the years—usually sitting by herself since her daughters had moved out. Those lonely sunsets had been beautiful, but they'd also been sorrowful. They'd been a reminder that all things come to an end.

Watching them with Ector, however— protected by his big body, surrounded by his warmth—they'd taken on new beauty, new meaning. Sunset marked the end of the day, yes, but it was also the beginning of night. And she could weather those stretches of darkness secure in herself, in her future, knowing that they were always followed by dawn. There would always be light.

Her smile grew as his suction cups contracted and relaxed on the bare skin of her legs. She chuckled softly. "They feel like they're kissing me."

"Hmm? What does?" Ector asked.

"Your suction cups. It feels like they're giving me kisses." Kathryn had seen the strength his tentacles possessed, had felt it just beneath the surface of his skin. Even the smallest of his suction cups were unbelievably strong. And it amazed her still that he could be so incredibly gentle when it came to her despite the immense power held within his body.

"Like the kiss I gave you last night?"

There was a mischievous, husky note in his voice that made Kat turn her head and look at him. He was grinning; the enticing wickedness in the expression told her exactly what he meant. They'd shared a lot of kisses so far, but she knew the kiss he was referring to, and the reminder sent a shiver up her spine. Her core clenched at the memory of what *that* kiss had felt like.

Heat flooded her body and burned her cheeks. "No, these are…different. Like a gentle massage and caressing lips."

Ector's skin shifted, turning from green to maroon. Two of his tentacles slid up her legs, tickling her skin as they moved toward the apex of her thighs. Kat tore her eyes away from his to look down.

"Can that sort of different also be good?" he asked, continuing that slow trek of his tentacles. The tone of his voice suggested he'd find out by trying it himself no matter her answer. The tentacles already coiled around her legs tightened slightly, increasing the pressure of those little suction cup kisses, and spread her legs wider apart.

Kathryn's heart quickened, and she squeezed his arms, unable to pry her eyes away from his moving appendages. "I suppose it could be…"

The tip of a tentacle grazed her sex. Its touch was light as it slid through her slick, teasing her with its mere presence. Ector shifted the other tentacle higher. As it reached the small patch of hair above her sex, it curled around so its tip could settle close to her clit—keeping a couple centimeters away, heightening her anticipation, deepening her hunger.

"Ector," she breathed, her core once more contracting with a fresh flow of desire. The ache within her intensified. She tilted her pelvis, silently begging for his touch. *Needing* it.

"You are as eager to find out as me," he rumbled, voice vibrating into her through his chest. He shifted one of his arms up, bringing hers along with it, and slowly unbuttoned her shirt even as his tentacles flexed and relaxed, gifting her sensitive flesh with more of those soft kisses.

Once the top few buttons of her shirt were undone, he slipped his hands beneath the fabric and covered her breasts with his palms. Kathryn moaned, closing her eyes, and arched her chest into his hands. He cupped her breasts, kneaded them, squeezed them, and she gasped when he pinched her nipples between his fingers, which created another gush of heat between her legs.

The tip of his tentacle grazing her sex delved deeper, teasing her folds and her entrance but going no farther.

Kathryn bit her lip and undulated her hips, trying to force his touch where she needed it most. "Ector, please."

Ector released a pleased hum. "Who am I to deny my mate?"

He flatted his tentacle over the top of her sex, latching onto her clit with one of his suction cups. Kathryn sucked in a sharp breath and clasped his wrists with her hands, needing something to hold onto, something to ground her as a surge of pleasure pierced her. She bucked her hips, but his other tentacles held her thighs in place. His suction cup began moving in a rhythmic, undulating manner, sucking and releasing, massaging her clit and the sensitive flesh around it.

Kathryn panted, forcing her eyes open to look down her body and watch. The sight was more erotic than anything she'd ever seen, anything she'd ever *done*. She was splayed out, thighs spread wide, with Ector's maroon hands working her bared breasts. His claws were deadly sharp, and the tips scraped delightfully against her skin, but she trusted him completely. She rocked her hips to his rhythm, moaning as the sensation he evoked within her grew in intensity.

Ector brushed his flat nose along her temple. "I hear your pleasure. I feel it. I smell it and taste it." He released a low groan that flowed into a growl. "There is nothing sweeter in this world than you, my mate, and I *need* a deeper taste."

Keeping one tentacle on her clit, he thrust the other inside her. It pushed deep—as deep as she could take it—before he pulled it out and thrust it in again and again, matching the rhythm he'd set on her clit. The little bumps of his suction cups created a unique sensation within her, stimulating her inner walls as they kiss the flesh within. All the while, his hands continued their confident motions on her breasts, lavishing her hardened nipples with scintillating pleasure.

Kathryn's awareness narrowed down to only the places where he touched her. Her body quivered, teetering on the edge of bliss.

"Harder," she commanded breathlessly.

With another growl, he obeyed, increasing both the strength of the suction cup over her clit and the force of the tentacle thrusting into her. It was exactly what she needed.

She reached up, caught the back of Ector's head, pulled him down, and slammed her mouth against his as an orgasm roared through her. Her body trembled with a flood of heat. White-hot pleasure poured through her veins; she cried out against Ector's lips.

He took control of the kiss, and his tongue delved between her lips, moving with the same powerful certainty as his tentacle. He didn't slow, didn't relent; he continued at the same pace, prolonging her climax.

Once he had wrung everything from her, Kathryn lay limp upon Ector, with her eyes closed and a dreamy smile on her lips as he rained soft kisses over her face. His tentacles, unmoving except for the occasional pulse of his suction cups, remained upon and within her sex. His slick, hard cock had emerged from his slit, and was now pressed against the curve of her backside.

Finally, he withdrew his tentacle. Kat immediately missed it; the emptiness left in its wake was almost unbearable. She opened her eyes to watch as he brought that tentacle up and slipped its tip into his mouth.

He hummed appreciatively, lips curling into a smile. "Would that there was time for a real taste, directly from the source."

Kathryn stroked his jaw and chuckled. "We have plenty of time. And…maybe I could taste you?"

Ector groaned again; this time, it was a truly tortured sound. His cock pulsed against her. He drew in a deep breath that swelled his chest and released it in a soft huff. "I…have not experienced that."

Brows rising, Kathryn turned in his embrace until she was straddling him. They both moaned when his cock slid along her wet sex and nestled there, its little tendrils stroking her softly but insistently.

"You haven't?" she asked.

He dropped his hands to her hips and flexed his fingers, holding her still. "My people did not use their mouths in that manner until our contact with humans…and my mating days were well behind me by then." He leaned his head forward and brushed his mouth over hers. "I would very much like to experience it with you, but it will have to wait. There is something I must show you, and it is best we are in the water and on our way before it is dark."

Kathryn drew back, bracing her hands on his shoulders to steady herself. "We're going into the water? Now?"

"Yes. It is time for you to see my world."

"Isn't it dangerous to be out there when it's dark?"

"Is it not dangerous for us right here when it is dark?" he asked gently. "I will keep you safe, Kathryn. Trust me. This is one of those risks that is worth taking."

She pressed a soft kiss to his lips. "I trust you."

In a smooth, effortless motion, he rose to an upright stance, carrying her along with him. His tentacles guided her legs down until her feet were on the ground. He leaned back just enough to rake his gaze over her body, and Kat didn't miss him catching his lower lip between his teeth and furrowing his brow.

"Go grab the diving suit," he said, voice slightly strained.

Smirking, Kat curled her fingers around his cock. He shuddered and hissed, his hips jerking forward. His natural secretions made his shaft glide easily within her fist.

"Are you sure that's what you want?" she asked, tightening her grip and stroking him a couple more times.

He took in another deep, shuddering breath and said in a measured tone, "Yes. But later, after we have re—"

Kathryn dropped to her knees and took him into her mouth.

"*Kathryn!*" Ector hunched forward, his hands falling upon her head and fingers tangling in her hair. His tentacles writhed upon the ground and curled around her, circling her waist and legs.

She drew him deeper into her mouth, her lips stretching tight around his girth, and sucked, stroking him with her tongue. He tasted salty and sweet. It was a combination she loved—a combination she craved with every fiber of her being. She drew her head back and ran her tongue along his length, licking the head of his shaft and the slit at its tip before taking him deeper into her mouth again. Unable to draw him in fully, she kept her fist around the base of his cock and stroked in time with the movements of her lips.

Ector moaned low as his hips rocked with her strokes. The tendrils at his base vibrated and twisted against her hand. Using her other hand, she caressed and teased them in turn.

His claws scraped her scalp, sending shivers through her and heightening her own growing desire. Her nipples were hard, pulsing and needy for his touch, and her sex clenched. Slick coated her inner thighs. Sucking him in deep, she moaned, allowing the vibration to flow into him.

Suddenly, his grip on her hair tightened and his entire body went taut. With a snarl, he held her head trapped as he pumped his cock in and out of her mouth in short, quick bursts. Kathryn opened her eyes and looked up. Ector's eyes were squeezed shut, his brow low, and his lips were pulled back to bare his clenched teeth. He was as lost in the torturous throes of pleasure as she'd been while on his lap only moments earlier.

Kathryn took everything he had to give, sucking him with every pump, until finally his shaft expanded, and he roared his release. His seed flooded her mouth. She drank it greedily, licking every drop from his cock. Her hand continued to pump at his base as he shuddered, his breath ragged, and his palms petting her hair as though she were the more treasured thing in the universe.

Giving him one last lick, she released his cock and peeked up at him. Ector was gazing down at her with a smile on his lips and his golden irises almost fully eclipsed by his expanded pupils. He brushed the backs of his fingers down her cheeks and cupped her jaw.

"Did I hurt you?" he asked.

Kathryn grinned. "Not at all. I love how you lost control."

"I…I, uh…" He chuckled and shook his head. "For the first time, I have no words. I am utterly in awe of you, wife."

She smiled, loving the way that word—*wife*—sounded

coming from him. He said it with so much pride, adoration, respect, and *love* that it seemed unreal; she never would've believed anyone could put so much meaning into so short and simple a word.

Kathryn ran her palms up his chest as she rose, sliding them around to the back of her neck. She stood on her toes to press her mouth to his in a brief but passionate kiss. "No words need to be said"—she brushed her nose against his and stared into his eyes—"husband."

CHAPTER 12

Kathryn held the black diving suit in the air with both hands and eyed it critically. It looked as though it was made to fit a child the size of her seven-year-old grandson, Logan. When she'd first discovered the suit on the boat, she hadn't realized how small it was. She glanced at Ector, who stood next to her holding the glass mask.

"This'll fit me?" she asked incredulously.

He raked his gaze over her body again. "Every delicious curve."

Kathryn laughed and playfully swatted his shoulder. "If you plan to make it into the water, you better stop that."

Ector grinned. The hungry glint did not fade from his eyes. "The true test of whether we will make it into the water will come now. You need to remove your shirt."

Smirking, Kat kept her gaze locked with his as she unbuttoned her shirt the rest of the way. She shrugged it off her shoulders, removing her arms from the sleeves one at a time to keep hold of the suit, until the shirt fell to the ground.

Ector perused her again with those ravenous eyes, and the pure lust in those golden orbs annihilated any insecurities she might've had at her naked body being seen in the light of day. Ector made her feel beautiful. No, more than that, he'd made her accept the truth of his words—she *was* beautiful. Her body was a testament to the fact that she'd lived; she'd known joy and sorrow, had birthed children, had loved and lost and loved again. In one way or another, all that was on display now.

And he'd helped her understand that it was all worth it. All of it had combined to make her the person she was today, and she was allowed to feel good about who she was, to embrace every imperfection.

Goosebumps spread across her skin, and her sex clenched with lingering desire. Ector had gifted her with an incredible orgasm earlier, but she wasn't nearly satisfied—especially not after taking him into her mouth and watching him come undone. She craved so much more of him. But for now, she would restrain herself, as he was clearly trying to do judging by the way his skin fluctuated between green and maroon. Despite her desire, Kat thrummed with excitement to finally delve into Ector's underwater world and see whatever it was he wanted to show her.

Taking the suit between both hands again, she bent down and, one at a time, lifted her feet and slipped them into the suit's legs. The material stretched easily as she drew the suit up and over her hips. Once her arms were in the sleeves, her whole body was covered save for the opening at her upper back.

"How do you close it?" Kat asked, reaching behind her to feel along the gap in the material. Apart from smooth white parts at the suit's chest and right wrist—she couldn't tell if they were plastic or metal—she hadn't seen any other attachments. The suit had no buttons, zippers, or ties.

"I believe you slide your fingers around that chest piece." Ector pantomimed the action by raising a hand to his chest and twisting it clockwise.

Kathryn dipped her chin to look down at the circular attachment on the suit's chest. She wasn't sure how any of this worked, wasn't sure how to operate the suit, wasn't even sure how far she'd have to swim tonight, and she knew those uncertainties were contributing to her quickening heartbeat just as much as her anticipation. She settled her fingers on the attachment's edges.

She couldn't help but notice how odd it felt to touch anything with the suit covering her fingers; she retained a remarkable degree of sensitivity in her fingertips despite the material, but at the same time felt detached from that physical contact. She usually worked with her hands bare, even when she was helping in the fields—and she had the callouses as proof. She wasn't sure if a number existed to count how many times a needle had pricked her finger while she was still learning her craft as a seamstress decades ago.

Shoving those thoughts aside, she twisted her hand, moving it the same way Ector had shown. Her fingertips slid around the edge of the chest piece. An odd sensation followed—the seam on the back of the suit sealed itself, closing off her skin to the open air and tightening the suit around her body. She straightened her back and wiggled her shoulders. It had felt like someone running a finger down her back.

The suit was form fitting, just as Ector had implied it would be, but it wasn't at all uncomfortable. In fact, it was almost like being naked while having plenty of support and protection in all the places that needed a little lift.

She bent an arm back to brush her fingers over her spine. There was no trace of a seam anymore. Kathryn snickered. "I don't know what I expected, but it definitely wasn't that the opening would just...disappear."

Ector grinned and moved a little closer, once more trailing his eyes over her. Reveling in the heat of his gaze, Kathryn turned in place, glancing over her shoulder to watch as he perused her. The suit clung to her like a second skin and accented her curves, but it didn't reveal any true details.

When she faced him again, Ector lifted his gaze to hers. Though the hungry light in his eyes didn't diminish, his grin eased into a softer smile. This expression was warm instead of hot, hinting that, beneath the surface, he was just as enthusiastic about the imminent excursion as she.

"While I must admit to preferring the view I had of you a few moments ago, this looks wonderful, too," he said. "You will need to pull up the hood."

"Hood?"

Her brow furrowed; she hadn't noticed any sort of hood on the suit before. But sure enough, when she reached over her shoulders, there was a hood gathered behind her neck; it must've formed somehow when the suit sealed. She gathered her hair and swept it back before grasping the hood and drawing it over her head. Like the rest of the suit, it fit snugly without feeling restrictive.

Shifting the glass mask into one hand, Ector closed the remaining distance between himself and Kathryn. She stared up at him as he lifted his free hand to delicately sweep a few loose strands of her hair back from her face and tuck them beneath the hood. The tenderness of the gesture, the care and consideration, stoked the gentle warmth in her heart.

"Once you hold this up to your face, it will connect to the suit," he said, raising the curved piece of glass with its thin black frame.

"Okay." Kathryn lifted her hands and took hold of the mask on either side, meaning to move it closer to her face, but Ector held it in place. She arched a brow.

"We will not be able to speak to one another once we are under water."

"We won't?"

Ector shook his head. "We will keep very close to each other, and I will signal you should anything go wrong. But these coastal waters are relatively safe."

Kat shifted one of her hands to cover his, which was still holding the mask. "I trust you, Ector."

"And your trust means the world to me." He smiled, but the smile faded after a second. "Also…when the mask seals, a voice will speak to you. Do not be alarmed."

"What do you mean? What voice?"

"I think…" Ector frowned for a moment as though deep in thought. "I think *computer* is the right word. There are computers in those suits, and they talk like the computer in the Facility. I am not as knowledgeable concerning this old human technology as others like Arkon, Vasil, or Theodora."

Kathryn glanced down at the mask. There really wasn't much to it—it looked like a curved piece of glass with a frame around it, as simple in appearance as the rest of the suit. She'd never know how any of it functioned; the only person who likely understood such matters was Theodora, a trained mechanic and engineer who'd crash landed on Halora a little over a year ago. For the residents of Halora who'd descended from the original colonists, such knowledge was all but lost—and wasn't very practical these days, anyway, considering they had no means of manufacturing the complex components necessary to maintain such advanced technology.

She lifted her gaze to Ector and smiled; she wouldn't let a bit of trepidation diminish her enthusiasm. A lot of people back in town used these diving suits all the time without issue. "At least I'll have someone to talk to down there, right?"

He chuckled and nodded. "And I will be nearby regardless."

That meant more to Kathryn than she could express. She'd always had friends and neighbors to depend on, but she'd never felt right leaning too heavily on anyone no matter her situation. It was already different with Ector, even though they'd only spent several days together. She knew he'd support her no matter what, and she would support him just the same—an equal partnership built upon a freshly-bloomed love the likes of which she never would've thought possible at this point in her life.

If the situation were different, she knew she'd be a bundle of nerves, knew she'd be second guessing the idea of going into the water. It wasn't all that long ago that several young men and women had been attacked by a razorback just of the dock in The Watch, leaving several dead and one—that sweet girl from Emmiton, Eva—maimed.

But even remembering that tragedy, which had rocked The Watch to its core, couldn't deter Kathryn now. Humans had traveled to and from the kraken's underwater home dozens of times without incident. Besides, Ector was experienced, and she trusted his judgment—especially when it came to matters involving the sea. She wouldn't let the fear of what could happen prevent her from seizing this opportunity for a once-in-a-lifetime experience.

She brushed her thumb over the back of his hand. "Well, shall I, then?"

The warmth remained in his expression as he released his hold on the mask. He turned his hand beneath hers, taking it gently, and brought it to his mouth to place a gentle kiss over her knuckles. She found herself wishing her skin wasn't covered; even that brief brush of his lips against it would've been sublime.

He released her hand and eased back. Kathryn returned her attention to the mask. The excitement that had been thrumming in her intensified again, swelling in her chest. It was an eagerness she'd not felt in decades, a giddiness she'd not known since childhood, and she wouldn't allow herself another moment's hesitation. She lifted the mask to her face.

She felt a hint of movement around the mask's frame and the hem of the hood. The quality of the sounds around her—the singing sea and sighing breeze—altered subtly, seeming somehow both more immediate and more distant than an instant before. A faint hum flared across the surface of her skin, encompassing her entire body. It wasn't an uncomfortable sensation, but it was an unfamiliar one, and she wasn't sure what caused it.

"Good evening," said a voice in her ears.

Even after Ector's warning, Kathryn started, raising a hand to her chest as her heart quickened a little more.

"My apologies," the voice continued. "I don't recall cradling your naked body before, so I should have assumed you were a first-timer and adjusted the volume of my voice."

"I...um... What?" Kathryn asked with a nervous chuckle. She glanced at Ector, who was watching her with his brow knitted and a slight frown tugging down his lips.

"My name is Kane," the voice replied. "I'm here to assist you with the operation of your diving suit and provide you with riveting conversation. I do hope you'll provide me with a bit of the latter, as well—it gets rather dull lying dormant in these suit computers waiting for someone to use them."

Kathryn's brows fell low, and she pressed her lips together. *Kane.* The name sounded familiar, but she couldn't quite place it, couldn't quite remember why it'd be familiar. Maybe it was...

She sucked in a sharp breath. "The Kane that's inside Theo?"

"The very same. Though technically I am a copy of that Kane created when he interfaced with these diving suits." Kane lowered his voice to a conspiratorial whisper. "I would say I'm the more pleasant version, but we'd best keep that between the two of us. I doubt his ego could handle it."

Kathryn laughed and shook her head. "I just...didn't expect this. Not that I knew what to expect to begin with."

"I do tend to defy expectations. Do you have a name? This is a somewhat intimate situation in which we're involved, and it would be strange to refer to you as just *miss* or *ma'am.*"

"Sorry. My name's Kathryn. It's nice to meet you, Kane. Meet you again, I guess. I've spoken with you—the other you, anyway—once before, when him, Theo, and Arkon set up my house with hot water."

Kane laughed. "I have the pleasure of meeting you for the first time, and you the pleasure of meeting the best me. Seems we're both coming out ahead on this, Kathryn."

Kathryn looked at Ector, whose brow was drawn low, and smiled wide. "Ector and I are going for a swim. I've never done this before, so I'm glad you're here to guide me."

"Well, you're in good hands. I am referring to myself, of course, though I do not have hands. I mean it in a metaphorical sense. Obviously, if I were referring to your escort, I would say you're in good tentacles." A thin yellow outline appeared around Ector, making him stand out against the darkening sea and sky. "Though it would normally be outside my scope to speculate... he is your mate, isn't he?"

Something giddy and warm filled Kathryn's heart. Somehow, her grin only widened as she looked into Ector's eyes. "Yes. He is my mate."

Ector's expression softened, and he extended a tentacle to brush along her leg.

"I suspected as much, considering his brooding countenance and agitated stance," Kane said. "I'll spare you the follow up questions regarding tentacular penetration and the like. Theo made it clear that such matters are private business and that it didn't make a difference whether I was in her head or not, I was to keep my nose out of it."

Kat's brows lowered. "Tentacular...*what?*"

"Penetration. The entry of tentacles into various bodily orifices. Again, it's none of my business, so you needn't give me any details. Unless...you're willing to sh—"

"No! No, Theo's right. It's...private business." Heat flooded Kathryn. Even if Kane wasn't *exactly* a person, Kat couldn't help her embarrassment at him speaking so openly about such an intimate matter.

Kane made a sound like he was clucking his tongue. "Your body heat's rising. I must apologize—I didn't mean to embarrass you. Your boundaries have been clearly broadcast, and I will proceed accordingly. There will be no discussion of penetration, whether involving tentacles or not, going forward."

"Thank you, Kane."

Ector tilted his head. "You are turning red, Kathryn. What did he say?"

She shifted closer to Ector and reached for his hand. "He, uh… You know what? Don't worry about it."

He closed his hand around hers and frowned. "Is he causing you distress of some sort?"

Kathryn smiled. "No. Let's just say…he seems to be *very* knowledgeable about the mating practices of humans and kraken. Shall we go before it gets too dark?"

Ector glared in a way she'd never seen from him—it was a menacing look, bearing just a hint of threat. She knew it was meant not for her but Kane.

"They can be intimidating, can't they?" Kane asked, sounding entirely unconcerned. And why would he worry? It wasn't as though Ector could cause him any bodily harm.

Kathryn smoothed her other hand up Ector's chest to settle it on the side of his thick neck. "It's fine, Ector. I was just a little embarrassed. I don't usually talk about things like that with strangers."

For a few moments, Ector narrowed his eyes, and his frown deepened into something closer to a scowl. He glanced at the sky before his gaze shifted to hers. His expression eased, and he nodded. Excitement rekindled in his eyes. "You are correct, Kathryn. We should go. I will flash yellow to warn of danger if necessary, but we should be safe."

"I am well versed in kraken sign language, as well," Kane

said, his voice projecting outside the suit, "should you need to communicate anything more complicated than *look out*. And regardless, I'll monitor the surrounding waters for life at all times and warn Kathryn of anything concerning."

Ector lifted his brows. "You could have spoken aloud the whole time?"

"Yes, but my conversation with Kathryn was private. I am here to assist *her* through this process."

Kathryn laughed and shook her head. "This is going to be an interesting experience."

Smirking, Ector chuckled. "My hope was for it to be an unforgettable experience—for the best reasons."

She brushed her thumb over his jaw, again wishing she could touch him skin-to-skin. "It will be."

Ector leaned down and kissed the top of her head.

"Just consider me your *experience enhancer*," Kane said.

Shaking his head, Ector straightened and, still holding Kat's hand, led her into the surf. She felt the water flowing around her feet but couldn't feel its wetness or temperature. It was… strange. By the time the water was up to her waist, she was a bit more used to the sensation, and the reality of the situation hit her—she was about to see what lay beneath the waves. Halora was mostly covered in water, and after fifty years of life here, she was about to have her first glimpse of what comprised the majority of her homeworld.

Once the water was a little deeper, Ector submerged himself. He gently tugged on her arm to lead her under with him. Instinctively, she drew in a deep breath.

"The suit will provide you with air," Kane said. "Just breathe normally. You don't need to worry, Kathryn."

"Just habit, I guess," she said, cheeks heating a bit. And despite Kane's reassurance, it was a difficult instinct to resist as she followed Ector under the water; the most primal part of her brain demanded she take in as big a breath as she could because people *couldn't* breathe underwater.

The sound of moving water rushed in around her, undercut by the distant, rumbling thunder of crashing waves, but it wasn't overwhelming—it seemed a natural, almost comforting sound. She recalled it well from her youth, when she used to swim and play on the beach often. But that didn't stop her anxiety as they swam farther from shore. She took a few more deep, calming breaths and focused her attention on Ector, who was the one constant, truly familiar thing within this new experience.

He was also the one thing she could really see as they moved steadily deeper; the setting sun had already been touching the horizon by the time she'd donned the diving suit, and its light barely penetrated the water now. Kathryn knew she wasn't more than a few dozen meters from land, but the slowly thickening darkness and her shrinking range of view served as a reminder that the ocean was near infinite compared to her. She and Ector were as insignificant as two drops of water here. As the tide swept inland and Ector led her against it, a small part of her wanted to ride that current back to solid ground.

But she wasn't going to give in to that rogue urge. She refused to let fear dictate even one more decision in her life.

She squeezed Ector's hand a little tighter and continued onward. Before long, her awareness had expanded beyond her tight focus on her husband, and she realized just how easy it was to move through the water despite not having swum in years. Her limbs flowed without resistance—as though she were in open air—and she found that her movements were propelling her without difficulty; Ector was leading her, but he was by no means pulling her along.

"I don't feel like I'm in water at all," she said.

"Part of this suit's design," replied Kane. "It absorbs and redirects various sources of energy, including the pressure of the water around you and your own movements, to help ease your passage and propel you through the water. It's all invisible energy fields and whatnot."

"Oh. That sounds...complicated."

Kane laughed. "For anyone unfamiliar with the basic principles at work, it must be. But this is relatively basic technology. By modern standards, it's utterly primitive. I don't mean any offense, Kathryn, or to seem like I am insulting your intelligence."

"No offense—nor insult—taken, Kane. You and I are from very different worlds—just like me and Ector. Of course, we'll all have had different experiences and educations."

"I must say, Kathryn, that you're proving to be more pleasant company than I can recall ever having enjoyed. And, to be honest... I'm a damned computer and even I find all the science behind this suit woefully dry and boring. You're not missing out on much."

Kathryn chuckled. Even when she'd first encountered Kane —then as a voice emanating from a floating ball of light projected from Theo's wrist—it had been hard not to think of him as a person. He was at least as much of a person as any human or kraken she'd ever met.

She allowed herself to finally take in her surroundings and accept fully that she was really here, that she really was doing this, and that, despite some of her lingering instincts, she was *fine*.

She was okay with her vision being limited in all directions; it forced her to focus on the here and now, on the immediate. Above, the surface shimmered in brilliant, ceaseless motion, lit up by the last rays of the setting sun. The sky beyond it was already darkening toward purple. To the sides, the water was a blue that darkened rapidly with distance. It was difficult to estimate, but she guessed that she couldn't see much beyond fifteen meters—and it felt like that range was gradually diminishing.

But she could see the ocean floor below her. It was largely barren, little more than grass, sand, and chunks of bare stone at first, but that changed as she and Ector finally broke free of the waves that had threatened to sweep them back to shore.

There were living creatures in the water. Fish of various shapes and sizes swam alone and in schools; odd creatures, many with shells—some of which were segmented—scurried along the bottom; and an increasing number of plants grew from the seafloor or the rocks jutting out of it. At least she assumed they were plants—most swayed freely with the ocean current, but some seemed to have much more deliberate patterns of movement she didn't think were the result of flowing water.

Of all the creatures she saw, she recognized only a handful; she could only imagine how many more species might've been visible in the light of day.

Her wonder had soon destroyed any of her remaining misgivings. She was breathing as easily as she would've been on land, she felt fast and weightless—as though she were flying—and everything was new and wonderful.

When Ector released her hand a short while later, she didn't panic. He swam ahead of Kathryn and turned to smile back at her. She returned the smile.

Though the water and sky were still darkening, both were calm, and she had Ector and Kane—and Kane had maintained that faint but unmistakable yellow outline around Ector's body, making the kraken stand out against the encroaching darkness. Besides, Ector didn't stray too far away as he continued forward, and it provided Kathryn her first real look at him moving in his element. On land, Ector and the other kraken moved with odd gaits. They didn't walk as much as drag themselves along in a contradictory blend of awkwardness and grace she'd long suspected possible only due to their immense physical strength.

But in the water… Well, she couldn't help but stare. The tentacles that sometimes seemed erratic or uncontrolled on land were precise and fluid here. They flared out wide, revealing their paler, suction cup lined undersides and stretching the skirt-like skin between their uppermost portions. Each time they snapped together again—drawing into a neat, tight bundle that tapered toward its end—Ector surged forward. He'd let those bursts of momentum gradually decay before repeating the process, creating a hypnotic rhythm.

He kept an easy pace that allowed her to comfortably follow within a few meters of him. She knew from the times he'd left the boat to scout that he was capable of far greater speed than this; what was it like to be able to glide through the water that way?

Kathryn was in awe of him again. She'd found him plenty appealing on land, but seeing him like this increased that appeal tenfold. Yet despite her awe, she didn't miss the way he kept his head and eyes in constant motion, as though perpetually scanning their surroundings. She had no doubt that his kind could see better—and farther—than humans under water. How much did he see right now that she couldn't? How many of the ocean's secrets were hidden in plain sight, masked from Kathryn both by her dwindling field of vision and her lack of familiarity with this underwater world?

"Should you require a light—or some other enhancement to your vision—let me know," Kane said.

After swimming for so long in silence, his voice shattered Kathryn's thoughts. It took a few moments for her to register what he'd said. Once she realized it, her eyes flared, and her heart sped. "Are you…are you in my mind, Kane?"

"What? No, Kathryn. That's not how these suits operate."

The tightness that had gripped her chest eased just a bit. "So how'd you know I was thinking about vision?"

"I didn't," he replied. "It's getting dark, and human eyes are rubbish at night, especially under water. I just wanted you to know there are options, should you feel the need to explore them."

Kathryn couldn't help but shake her head and chuckle at herself. "Sorry. I just…I'm not used to all this, and it spooked me how relevant your offer was to what I was thinking."

"Coincidence, I assure you," Kane said pleasantly. "For the record, the only one to have the coveted privilege of Kane on the brain is Theodora."

Poor Theo.

Kathryn couldn't imagine having someone in her head all the time, especially during those *private* moments.

"What about when she is…intimate?" Kat asked.

"She tells my…progenitor to piss off. And please forgive my vulgarity, but that *is* the watered-down version of how she might say it. She has full control when she desires privacy, but she and I—the other I—are quite close."

Kat took a few moments to consider the situation. While the thought of having an independently thinking voice in her head was initially unsettling, there was the potential for a degree of comfort in the idea. Having something—some*one*—like Kane meant never truly being alone. She didn't know much about Theodora or the woman's past, but the way Theo and Kane had talked to each other while they worked on Kathryn's house had implied a very deep, meaningful friendship—one of the strongest bonds two people could make.

That path of thought led her to reflect upon something she might not otherwise have noted—the hint of sadness that had been in Kane's voice.

"You miss her, don't you?" Kat asked.

"Me? Miss *her*?" Kane scoffed, but it was clearly bluster. "I'm glad to have some time to myself. Why, there were times when she'd just talk and talk on and on, and she'd insult me and I'd insult her, and then she'd get in a really good one and we'd both laugh and… Damn it, you're right, Kathryn. I do miss her."

Her heart broke for him. "I'll be returning to The Watch soon. Maybe…I can bring this suit to her?"

"I would like that, Kathryn. Thank you."

She continued swimming, only taking her eyes off Ector to look at her surroundings. Every minute the world around her darkened further.

"I'll have some light now, Kane," she said.

"My pleasure, Kathryn," Kane replied.

A light flashed on from somewhere along the upper edge of the mask, intensely bright but somehow not blinding despite its closeness to her eyes. It projected a strong cone of illumination ahead of her that followed wherever she turned her face and cast that little slice of the ocean in stunning clarity—including Ector.

He flared out his tentacles, slowing himself to a stop, and let them go limp as he spun to face her. The light cast hard shadows on his body, accenting his musculature, and his eyes gleamed with twin reflections—like each held a tiny, silvery moon. He shook his head.

Kathryn knitted her brows and gestured questioningly toward the light.

Ector nodded and proceeded through a quick series of hand and tentacle gestures.

"No light," Kane said. "Almost there."

Kat frowned. "No light? But it's almost full dark."

"Would you like me to comply with him?"

The thought of floating through endless, impenetrable darkness was a terrifying one, but Kathryn didn't waste time considering it. "Yes. He knows what he's doing."

The light vanished as abruptly as it had appeared. For a few moments, her vision was blanketed by solid black that was broken only by an indistinct silhouette—an afterimage of Ector that quickly faded. Even when her eyes had adjusted, the water seemed significantly darker than it had a few moments before. Ector was a dark blue shape, discernable only because of that persistent yellow outline from Kane, as he moved closer to her. He closed a hand around hers, covering it completely, and led her forward.

Only the barest hint of light remained on the surface—the final glow of a sun that had already been devoured by this dark, hungry sea. Were it not for Ector, whose features were almost entirely masked by the gloom, Kat would've have felt utterly, desperately alone, like she'd been tossed into a starless night sky to drift aimlessly.

But as they swam—their pace slower now—she realized that it wasn't all darkness. There were faint lights scattered around the seafloor and its rocky outcroppings. Some of them were even recognizable in shape—plants she'd seen while the sunlight was stronger, fish that had been swimming around her during this journey. Each source gave off its own gentle blue glow, all of which were surrounded by black. To Kathryn, those little sources of light were beacons, sparse but unmistakable stars against the backdrop of infinite space.

She'd seen glowing plants many times in the nighttime jungle. She'd found them fascinating as a girl, had found them magical. That wonder translated well to seeing them in the sea; they were even more ethereal down here, surrounded by their own bluish auras in the otherwise consuming shadows.

Ector slowed as they neared something huge looming in the water ahead. The object nearly filled her entire field of view, blending in with the blackness that had come to dominate her vision to the left, right, and below. The only contrast was from the surface, which still possessed a hint of its own now gray light.

"What is that?" Kathryn asked.

"Stone," Kane replied. "A rather large formation rising from the sea floor. It extends quite a way to either side."

Ector drew to a stop at the base of the formation, which gained a few details as she stared at it—primarily due to the deeper shadows in its recesses and crevices. It had a gradual upward slope, reaching toward the surface but coming at least a few meters short.

Ector turned to face Kathryn, and his skin suddenly lit up.

Her eyes widened as she swept them over his body, which was now cast in a gentle blue glow emitted by countless points of light along his stripes. That light made his normally drab green skin a deep, muted blue.

For the first time, she had the sense that she was looking upon a truly alien being, a creature of allure beyond human capability; he was otherworldly. But that body, that face, those eyes—they all belonged to Ector. *Her* Ector. Her mate, her husband.

Ector released her hand and backed away slightly. He pointed a finger at Kat before turning that finger toward the seafloor.

"He wants you to stay here," said Kane.

Kathryn chuckled. "Yeah, I think I understood that one."

"Sorry. I don't have hands—or a body at all, really—so it's not always natural for me to discern between full-blown sign language and universally recognized gestures."

"It's all right, Kane." Kat smiled at Ector and nodded.

He smiled back at her. Turning back toward the rocky hill, he pressed his hands to it and pulled himself up, swiftly and silently, to the top. He paused there, a ghostly figure with his tentacles fluidly moving around him like they were part of the water.

Kathryn's curiosity grew. What was he looking at? What was he looking *for*? She knew he had something specific he wanted to show her, but what would she possibly be able to see without a light in this darkness?

Ector is my light.

The thought—the realization—warmed Kathryn's heart and softened her smile. It was the truth; she didn't know how it had happened so fast, but it was the *absolute* truth.

She wasn't sure how long he remained in place. It couldn't have been more than a minute or two, but she would've been content to watch him, admiring his otherworldly glow, for hours. Still, she wasn't disappointed when he drifted back down to her. That the eager smile hadn't left his face was an encouraging bonus. He made several quick gestures with his hands.

A few seconds passed in silence after Ector's hands had stilled. He stared at Kat expectantly, and all she could do was stare back.

"Uh…Kane?" she prompted gently.

"Hmm? Oh, right!" Kane made a throat-clearing sound. "He says he will take you over soon."

She nodded to Ector to indicate her understanding. "Thank you, Kane."

"You are welcome, Kathryn. I must confess that the only translations I've had any real experience with have been translating technical specifications into practical applications."

"Don't worry about it," she said distractedly as her eyes roamed over Ector's body again. She'd had no idea that the kraken could make themselves glow like this. She had so many questions, but she probably wouldn't have asked them then even had she been able to speak with Ector—the answers weren't important right now.

She and Ector were on the cusp of something amazing. She could feel it pulsing off him, sensed it in every cell of her body. Even if they were to turn back now and head to camp, this swim was the most memorable of her life. She'd never forget this look she'd had at Ector's underwater world. But it wasn't done, and her anticipation of what was next made her heart thump and her stomach flutter in the most delightful ways.

She kept her eyes on him as the blackness beyond his glow reached its fullness and the last shred of sunlight, which had been merely an echo, a stubborn memory, vanished. She'd been a fool to think of the water as dark before; it was nothing compared to this, and only Ector's glow—as simultaneously strong and gentle as the kraken himself—held it at bay.

Kathryn reached for him then, and he readily took her hands in his, twining their fingers together as much as his webbing allowed. His smile stretched wider. If she'd harbored any lingering doubts, they would've vanished in that instant—he would not let that hungry maw of darkness harm her.

Ector rose, spinning to turn her back to the rock wall as he drew her along with him. Their ascent was smooth and slow. She wondered if this was how it felt for those little paper lanterns the children of The Watch sometimes released into the air; given Ector's glow, the comparison felt particularly apt.

For that little while, Ector was the only thing in her world, existing in defiance of the void behind him, and that suited Kathryn just fine. Staring into his eyes, she hardly noticed when their upward motion ceased.

Ector dipped his head forward, shifting his gaze to some point over Kat's shoulder, and lifted one of her hands to twirl her around.

Kathryn's eyes flared, and her breath caught in her throat. She barely registered the movement as Ector crossed his arms around her and drew her back against his powerful chest.

The rocky hill ran in an irregular oval along the seafloor, but rather than form an underwater plateau, it was cut through by a bowl-like depression. Distance was difficult to determine in the water, but the depression looked at least thirty meters across and nearly twice as wide—visible in its entirety because of its contents.

The bowl was filled with life—lush plants, clumps of coral, and creatures of more species than she could ever hope to count —and almost all of it was glowing as brightly as Ector. She couldn't have described most of it if she was asked to. The beauty was surreal, and the quality of the bioluminescence gave everything the same ghostly glow that shrouded Ector. But it was all so *alive* despite that ghostly aspect, all so wondrous.

"It's so…beautiful," she whispered.

"It is," Kane replied. "I think it's best if I go into a standby mode, Kathryn."

"You're going?" She couldn't keep a hint of alarm from her voice.

"I'll be right here. All you need to do is call if you need me. But this moment is for the two of you, not me."

His words coaxed her smile back into place. "Thank you, Kane. I'll talk to you soon."

"Enjoy, Kathryn."

Kathryn twisted in Ector's arms to look up at him, raising her eyebrows in question. Ector nodded and released his hold on her. He positioned himself at her side, took her hand, and guided her past the ridge.

The light from all the plants and creatures below gave her diving suit a blue tint, completely altering its look, but she didn't waste any time studying that; there was so much else to see. Clusters of plants with thick stalks and heavy, bulbous growths at their ends—from which their glow emitted—rose from crevices in the rocky downslope like mountainside copses of trees presented on a much smaller scale. Plants—though some might've been creatures, she couldn't have been sure—that were comprised of dozens of tentacle-like appendages were gathered in patches along the bottom. There seemed to be several variations of them. Some had more or fewer tentacles, some had tuft-like growths on their appendages, some had longer or shorter tentacles, but almost all of them glowed from their cores, making their appendages seem darker in comparison.

There were several tube-like formations rising from the bare stone in different locations. Some of these appeared empty, but long, translucent, hair-like tendrils extended from others, each lit up by tiny pinpoints of blue light. Clumps of seaweed grew in other places, their leaves varying in size and shape. Most had a deep violet hue in the current light, and some bore glowing growths that resembled large seed pods. There were flashes of bright red, purple, and green throughout from a variety of strange underwater plants and creatures, including things that looked like large-petaled flowers growing directly from the coral.

And the fish...there were so many kinds, most of which possessed uniquely vibrant coloration in this light. Some were so vibrant that part of Kathryn's mind insisted they couldn't possibly be real.

When they were over the center of the underwater garden, Ector brought them to a stop. He swung around to Kathryn's front and raised her hand to his mouth. Once again, he brushed a kiss over her knuckles, and once again, she was saddened that their skin was separated by the suit. In that moment, she wanted more than anything to run her hands over him, to *feel* him.

He let go of her hand and eased back, putting a couple meters of distance between them. She moved her arms and legs in slow, easy motions to maintain her position; it didn't take much effort thanks to the suit. His tentacles slowly spread to the sides, many of them curling up at their ends, and his chest swelled as though with a deep breath. She had the sense that he was presenting himself.

For me.

Ector's eyes locked with hers. The joy his gaze had held moments before had receded to the background, overpowered by fiery intensity, and his smile had faded. She recognized that expression, that smolder. Before her eyes, his skin changed. Though it was made much darker by the predominant blue light, she'd have known that color anywhere—it was the same maroon he often took on when he was particularly...*amorous*.

She had no idea what he was about to do, and she couldn't look away from him.

Maintaining that eye contact, Ector moved his body. He began slowly, but there was an underlying rhythm to it, like he heard music that she could not. His muscles stretched and contracted, pulling his skin taut over them. His every motion conveyed strength, control, and an undeniable sensuality.

He gradually increased his speed and expanded his range of motion. Kathryn's wonder regarding their surroundings fell away, forgotten; Ector alone commanded her full attention now. And she was impossibly more enrapt when he spun for the first time and a ripple of color pulsed over his body from top to bottom. Those color-changing ripples grew faster and more varied as he spun again and again, gaining speed with each rotation. His arms and tentacles stretched and curled, and his body tilted from side to side, and all those colors combined with his spinning to create scintillating patterns on his skin. He was a living work of art.

And every time he turned toward Kathryn—no matter how fast he was moving—his eyes snapped to hers.

Kathryn was his focal point, his anchor, and she fully understood that this wasn't some show, wasn't meant as entertainment. This was a declaration. He was dancing *for* her.

Heat built rapidly at her core. It flared and spread each time Ector's gaze met hers, and soon had suffused her entire body. His intensity, his prowess, his devotion...it was so much, so strong. She wanted it all. Needed it all; needed him.

His spinning slowed, and the colors that had been pulsing over his skin gave way to that maroon that was so much darker in this light. He finally spread his tentacles and splayed his webbed fingers, bringing himself to a halt as he came to face her again. She released a breath made shaky by anticipation when he eased closer. His tentacles grazed her legs, and a tingling sensation coursed over her skin. She longed to feel him flesh to flesh, to be free of the barrier created by the suit.

She could only stare at him, heart pounding, as he took one of her hands in his and looped his arm around her lower back. He drew her against him. Even through the suit, she felt the delicious velvet-over-steel that was his body. Kathryn instinctively placed her free hand on his shoulder.

She suddenly realized that this was the stance many couples in The Watch assumed when they danced together—and just as that realization struck, Ector swept her into the most memorable dance of her life.

There was still no music to be heard, but she felt the song in his heart as he twirled, sank, and glided, moving Kat through the water with a gracefulness she'd never imagined possible. They flowed together to that silent, all-encompassing rhythm. Kathryn giggled and laughed as her stomach fluttered. The glowing underwater garden spun all around her, its many sources of light reduced to streaks of color that added another layer of surrealness to the entire situation.

She knew then that he'd been right—swimming was like flying. She felt like she was dancing across an endless, clear blue sky, staring into eyes more brilliant than the sun. But even without this experience...

Ector made her heart soar.

CHAPTER 13

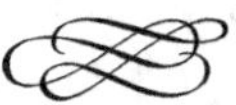

"THIS IS BEAUTIFUL," KATHRYN SAID AS SHE TOOK HER FIRST STEP onto the sandy shore. Though nothing could compare to the underwater paradise Ector had shown her the night before, this new location was still breathtaking.

It had been the waterfalls that had drawn Kat and Ector to this spot. There were several of them along jungle-topped seaside cliffs, their waters crystal blue and white, flowing into the ocean below. Kathryn and Ector had followed those falls until the cliffs opened to reveal paradise—a sheltered lagoon with bare rocks on both sides and a cliff face at its back. The vibrant turquoise water connected to the sea through a sandy gap in that ring of stone and was fed from the land by another waterfall—though Kathryn couldn't rightly consider it a singular waterfall.

It was dozens of streams flowing from the top of the cliff and tumbling down over the uneven stone to create an erratic curtain of water that stretched across at least thirty or forty meters. Green and violet vegetation sprouted from the rocks and dirt all around, accented by flowers of at least a dozen colors.

The break in the cliffs continued beyond the lagoon, which had left plenty of beach and a gradual enough incline for Ector to push the boat above the tideline. After taking a few moments to enjoy the scenery, Kathryn led Ector on a hike to find a suitable spot for camp. Fortunately, they discovered it in short order—a wide shelf partway up the cliffside that was partially covered in that long, soft grass so common along the coast and which overlooked the lagoon. It was far enough away from the falling water to keep dry, but close enough to still pick up that strange but soothing blend of saltwater and freshwater smells.

They unloaded the necessary supplies from the boat and carried them up to the spot. Kathryn turned toward Ector, watching the play of muscle beneath his skin as he set down her backpack, and was once again struck by a deep sense of belonging, of happiness. Of *love*.

And, not for the first time since they'd woken this morning and packed up their camp, she wondered, *Why aren't we going home?*

She was happy. Happier than she'd been in a long time. She was enjoying herself, enjoying the freedom, enjoying the sights, but most of all, she was loving every moment she spent with Ector.

But she also missed her family. She missed her daughters and grandchildren, all of whom were likely worried sick about Kat and eager for her return.

I'm ready to go home.

Kathryn smiled. She'd left the comforts and safety of The Watch to discover who she was, but she'd known the answer all along. She was a huntress, a wife, a mother, a widow, and a mate. She was all those things and more. She was Kathryn Russell, and that had always been—and would always be—exactly enough. But she'd needed this, this break from her daily routine, this time to just enjoy being alive, to remember all that.

And this trip had given her Ector, a result she'd not expected but for which she'd always be grateful.

As Ector straightened, Kat reached out, brushed her fingers along his jaw, and turned his face toward her. She stepped closer and pressed her mouth to his. He enfolded her in his arms, pulling her against his body as he tilted his head to deepen the kiss. His tentacles slipped behind her thighs and knees and held her securely. She looped her arms around his neck and licked the salt from his lips; she immediately wanted more.

He's mine.

The happiness brimming in her heart overflowed, filling her with warmth, and she chuckled against his mouth.

Ector broke the kiss and drew his head back. "Is my kiss amusing?"

Kathryn shook her head and laughed again. "No. No, not at all." Her lips eased into a tender smile and she caressed the back of his neck and shoulders. "I was just thinking…about how you're mine, and how happy I am right now."

"Oh?" He grinned. "I am quite happy myself, because *you* are *mine.*"

Her heart quickened, and her sex clenched. She knew she was his, but hearing it out loud instilled a thrill in her that she could not deny—a thrill she'd already come to crave.

"I think we should go home," she said.

Brow furrowing, he glanced at the supplies he'd just hauled to the campsite.

Kathryn chuckled. "Not *now.* I'd love to spend the night here with you." She pulled a hand back and ran her fingers over his siphon and jaw. "I mean tomorrow. We could start heading back in the morning."

He settled a hand over her cheek and brushed the pad of his thumb over her cheekbone. "So long as I am with you, I will go anywhere."

Kathryn blinked back the tears that suddenly threatened to

fill her eyes. "Thank you for pressing to join me on this trip. For pursuing me…despite myself. I didn't know what I needed—what I *wanted*—until you."

Ector's thumb slid up to wipe away a tear that had escaped, and his smile softened. "I can say the same of you, Kathryn. Thank you for being…you. For becoming mine."

Kathryn kissed him again. Their lips caressed each other in gentle strokes, but before the kiss could escalate and plunge her into a passionate haze, she drew back and grinned at Ector. "Shall we make the most of our last day of exploration and climb to the top to get a better view?"

For a few moments, he kept his eyes closed and his lips parted. Then his tongue slipped out briefly, as though sampling a taste from his lips, and he opened his eyes to meet her gaze. He gritted his teeth, and his hands flexed upon her. The tips of his claws pressed against her skin, separated from it only by her clothing, and Kathryn wondered if he was about to tear her clothes off—just like he'd practically torn the diving suit off her the moment they'd reached land after his dance last night. The memory of his worshipful hands and mouth on her, of finally feeling him, hard and thick, pumping into her, forced her to clench her thighs against a surge of arousal.

Ector's pupils, dark and dilated, slowly reverted to their normal oblong shape, and the maroon that had begun to creep over his skin receded. He took in a deep breath and slowly released it in a low groan that made Kathryn wet. She was almost tempted to tear her own clothes off.

Almost.

"Yes," he said, tucking a loose strand of hair that had escaped Kat's braid behind her ear. "There is no sense in being all the way out here if we do not take advantage of the unique landscape."

Kathryn pecked another kiss on his lips and extracted herself from his embrace, skimming her fingers along one of his withdrawing tentacles before bending down to grab her rifle. She flashed him a playful grin and began the trek to the top of the cliff.

ECTOR FOLLOWED Kathryn as she picked her way up the rocky incline. Though the urgency of his desire had ebbed, he still felt its hold. He smiled to himself as he glanced up and fixed his gaze on his mate's shapely backside.

Later. The day is for exploring to my mate's content, but at night, she *will be mine to explore.*

He forced his attention toward other things; there was plenty here to occupy his focus, plenty to offer distraction. The cloying scents of vegetation, earth, and stone mixed with those of brine and mist. He could taste the former group through his suction cups as he moved in Kathryn's wake. Yet the one scent that truly stood out was hers—there was only a hint of it on the air, but that was more than enough for him.

You are doing it again, Ector.

His nostrils flared with a quiet but prolonged sigh. As much as he wanted to join with her right here, right now, his duty at the moment was to keep her safe. That meant he could not place his focus solely upon her. And it wasn't like having to keep a close eye on his surroundings was torture—she was right in saying this place was beautiful. This was a perfect spot to stop.

She'd called the body of water below a lagoon, and it was the most intimate mingling of land and sea Ector had ever seen— more so than the stream they'd been camped near the last couple days, more so than any stretch of beach they'd passed during the entire trip. At the base of these cliffs—themselves an imposing, powerful symbol of land—fresh water and sea water mixed freely. The plants growing amidst the rocks surrounding the lagoon were like the jungle's fingers, stretching out for a feel of the ocean.

It reminded Ector of himself and Kathryn; what was their relationship at heart if not a mingling of land and sea? Like the other kraken and human couples before them, they were a blending of two worlds—two worlds that were very different but not incompatible. He could think of no better a place for her to have made the choice to head home.

And that was the right choice. As much as he wanted Kathryn to himself, they both had people they cared for waiting in The Watch. However lost Ector and Kathryn had felt, they'd found direction in each other, and that had only solidified a simple fact—though he'd spent almost six decades under water, living in the Facility, The Watch had become Ector's home. *Kathryn* had become his home.

Ector smiled as he looked at Kathryn, who'd stopped next to a thick bush with bright red flowers. She bent down and smelled one of the large blossoms. The loose hair that had escaped her braid fell forward to brush her cheek. Ector's hearts ached at the vision before him.

My Kathryn.

He finally had a female to call his own, one who'd claimed him in return, and he could not have been happier.

She turned her face toward him, and her lips stretched into a wide smile. That smile was for him and him alone. Her eyes shone with so much love that Ector felt it like a physical thing, and it flowed straight to his core. The ache in his chest intensified. He brought a hand to his chest, rubbing at its center, but the ache would not be soothed. He felt so *full*. Kathryn was... everything to Ector.

She straightened and stepped toward him until the slope placed her face on level with his. She planted the butt of her rifle on the ground, leaned forward, and pecked a kiss on his lips. When she pulled back, her smile shifted into something mischievous. "Come on, old man. We're nearly to the top."

Ector's smile widened even as he narrowed his eyes at her. "*Old?* I am not that much older than you, female."

"I guess you'll have to prove it," she said as she proceeded up the rise.

Some primal part of him recognized the challenge in her voice, but he knew she was being playful, and he adored her all the more for it. Even her teasing was infused with warmth and love—that sort of interaction had been unknown to the kraken before humans, and Ector might've taken some degree of offense to it only a few years ago. But things had changed since then.

He hurried along after her.

When they reached the top of the cliff, they found themselves at the base of a slope that rose as it moved inland, climbing toward much larger rock formations. The only word he had for that distant formation was *mountain*, but he'd always had the sense during his conversations with humans that mountains were much larger than this.

The surrounding vegetation was much thicker up here—even the relatively short grass—and blanketed the incline until it became too steep for anything to grow but the occasional wiry tree or stunted bush. The patch of land directly ahead was dominated by grass and other plants that were lower to the ground, but it was flanked on both sides by tall trees and hanging vines.

This was the cusp of the jungle; even Ector could not mistake it for anything else.

Kathryn paused, lifted a hand to shade her eyes, and turned to survey their new surroundings. "Let's see if we can get toward the end of that promontory." She pointed to a large section of land that jutted back out toward the sea, overgrown with plants and trees. "We should be able to see everything from there."

Ector nodded and gestured for her to lead. It went against the habits he'd learned as something of a leader to his people, and in some ways, it violated the strongest of his protective instincts, which demanded he place himself between her and danger. At the same time, it would allow him to keep her in sight at all times. He couldn't do that if she was behind him. And he had to acknowledge the truth of the situation—Kathryn was better equipped to navigate such terrain both in terms of anatomy and experience.

Kathryn swung her rifle into both hands and walked in the direction she'd indicated. Ector dragged himself along behind her, suction cups picking up at least half a dozen new tastes and smells from the vegetation beneath them. Fortunately, all those flavors came together in a relatively neutral amalgamation he could largely ignore.

Her pace slowed as the plants became larger, thicker, and more obstructive. She used the barrel of her rifle to brush aside leaves, branches, and stalks, picking her way into the jungle a little at a time. Soon, Kathryn and Ector were moving through the lush trees and plants. In the more open patches of land, the grass barely reached past her thighs; here, much of it was over her head. Were she to step into one of the many thick clumps, she'd be totally swallowed, completely hidden from Ector's view.

Ector found his attention divided as they pressed onward. Part of his focus was on avoiding scratches from the many branches around and beneath him; part was on his surroundings, which were so choked by greenery that he couldn't discern much of anything beyond a body length's distance; and part, as always, remained on Kathryn.

She walked with confidence she'd not displayed a week before, her gaze in constant motion, her steps deliberate and almost silent. She was Ector's stalking huntress. He had no doubt that the path she was carefully selecting was forged with consideration for his comfort—she seemed to avoid fallen branches and trees as much as possible even though she could've easily stepped over them, and gave as wide a berth as she could to thorns and sticks that would've harmlessly brushed over her clothing while potentially cutting his skin.

The leaves overhead rustled softly in the breeze, and distant animals made their calls, which echoed faintly across the sky. The air was fragrant and alive, though here it was underlaid by an odor of must and rot. Ector could only assume it was from the fallen wood and leaves decaying across the jungle floor.

Kathryn came to a halt and tilted her head, angling it to the left. Ector stopped behind her and watched as she took a large step forward, two steps back, and finally eased herself down onto one knee, all while looking in that same direction.

"What is it?" he asked, a crease forming between his brows.

"Animal trail," she replied. "Looks old, but it runs in the direction we want to go."

Ector's lips fell into a frown as he moved forward to join her. He saw no indication of a trail, only more of the thick, tangled jungle. But as he drew up beside her, everything became clear— the path was suddenly visible. It was like a tunnel cutting through the vegetation, with wild branches and leaves reaching into its otherwise clear space. It was relatively narrow, but the arched boughs over its top were at least as high as Kathryn was tall. When he shifted forward or backward, even just half an arm's length, the path vanished from his perception amidst unbroken jungle foliage.

"You have keen eyes, my wife," Ector said, embracing the swelling of pride in his chest.

Kathryn chuckled and glanced at him. "Not as keen as they used to be. I almost walked right past it."

Ector smiled. "But you did not. Lead onward. I will be right behind you."

She gifted him with a smile in return just before she stepped onto the trail and resumed their trek. Ector adjusted his tentacles to lower his torso, dropping his head below the ceiling of the tunnel like path. He noticed an immediate difference; though the ground was blanketed in plants life everywhere else in this jungle, it was relatively clear of debris, and Kathryn brushed aside most of the fallen branches she came across with her boot before they presented any issue for Ector. It was thus far the easiest travel he'd experienced within jungle so thick—not that he'd been anywhere like this more than a handful of times.

As they proceeded, the vegetation on either side of the trail grew increasingly thicker, especially on the right; before long, it was a solid looking wall of green and violet that didn't even allow light through.

"It opens up farther ahead," Kathryn said over her shoulder.

Ector flicked his gaze down the trail. He couldn't guess the distance in these tight confines, but there was golden, glaring sunlight concentrated ahead, a sure sign that they'd soon emerge from the jungle—hopefully close to the spot Kathryn had intended.

A faint rustling in the foliage to the left of the trail was their only warning before something shot out of the greenery.

Kathryn cried out and leapt aside, stumbling and falling backward into the thick vegetation on the right. Ector darted forward without thought to intercept the attack. Instinct and reflex were all that drove him; his hand snapped out and closed around the long, thin, fleshy creature's neck. It thrashed and curled its body—which was like a single tentacle with no other appendages to be seen—around his arm, coiling in a stunningly strong grip.

Leaves, grass, and branches shook and snapped to Ector's right.

Kathryn screamed. The sound prickled Ector's skin and sent a rush of fear through him.

The creature opened its jaws—they opened side-to-side—and several long, glistening fangs sprung out.

There was a large splash from somewhere beyond the right-hand vegetation.

Growling, Ector squeezed as tightly as he could. Bone crunched and flesh burst within his fist. Warm blood trickled from between his fingers. With a fading hiss, the creature stilled and went limp. Ector tossed it aside without second thought and thrust himself into the broken greenery that Kathryn had fallen through. He found himself moving down a steep decline.

His hearts raced with speed and force enough that they were likely to shatter his ribs, and it had nothing to do with the creature's sudden attack. He could not reconcile the sounds he'd heard—breaking vegetation, snapping branches, a scream, and a splash.

"Kathryn!"

Just as he was about to shout her name again, his eyes flared, and his hearts stopped. He thrust his tentacles out to the sides and behind him, latching onto anything he could grab, and only barely caught himself before he could plummet directly off the edge of a sudden drop.

There was a huge hole in the ground in front of him, at least fifteen or twenty meters across by human measure. It was ringed by thick vegetation all around, with roots, vines, and flowering branches dangling from it in many places. Beneath the vegetation was bare, smooth stone. The stone face led down another twenty meters or so—as high as the cliff they'd climbed to get here, he guessed—to blue, still water.

And in the center of that pool was a single wide-eyed human with strands of wet hair stuck to her skin, looking small and lost.

Ector's hearts resumed their frantic beating.

"Kathryn," he called again, lowering his torso and placing his hands on the edge of the drop. "Are you all right?"

She spun in the water and tilted her head back, looking up at him. "I-I'm fine. Just a few bumps and bruises, but nothing's broken." Bits of debris rained down from beneath Ector's hands to fall into the water near her. "Don't get too close!"

Powerful instincts tore through Ector's mind, vying for dominance; most insisted he leap down to her. He drew in a deep breath through his nostrils, growled, and tossed those instincts aside. Rash action would not help this situation. He needed to *think*.

That moment of clarity was enough for him to understand the wisdom of her words; he could *feel* the precariousness of his position. The vegetation around and beneath him was serving as anchor enough for now, but he could not rely on any of these fragile plants to hold him. The smallest slip could provide enough momentum, given his weight, to send him over the edge.

And from where he was currently positioned, he couldn't see any part of the smooth-walled hole that would provide adequate holds to climb.

"Are you safe?" he asked, trying to keep his panic from entering his voice.

She turned her head from side to side, studying the water. Ector couldn't see anything in it beside Kathryn and the numerous leaves, sticks, and flower petals floating on the surface, but that didn't offer him any comfort; *anything* could be lurking below, where the water was dark.

She looked back up at him. "I think so."

Carefully, he turned his head and glanced behind him. There was a tree not far away. He eased a pair of tentacles toward it, leaning his torso away from the edge, and wrapped them securely around the trunk. He gave the tree a tentative tug. It held solid.

With that anchor established, he leaned closer to the edge. Sunlight hit part of the water, but it wouldn't be long before the sun had moved far enough toward the sea that the hole would be completely shadowed. And even with that sunlight, he could not see the bottom of the water. He couldn't guess how deep it was.

"Do you see any way out or up?" he called.

"No, I don't." There was a slight tremor in her otherwise calm voice.

Ector's mate had been shaken, but she wasn't letting it control her. Not yet. He needed to find a way to get her out of there before she began panicking.

Before he gave in to his own panic.

But this wasn't the sort of situation he had experience dealing with. Nothing like this would've happened to his people; in the sea, she could've simply swum up.

This is a simple problem. It must have a simple solution.

She couldn't swim up, couldn't climb up, so he needed to pull her up.

Ector ran his gaze around the interior of the hole again, studying every detail without focusing on any one in particular until his eyes stopped on one of the long, dangling roots hanging over the edge of the stone.

He understood in that moment what he needed to do, and it simultaneously filled him with a burst of hope and wrapped cold dread around his hearts. "There is rope in the boat, is there not?" he asked.

Kathryn smiled, and hope—the same hope he felt—shone upon her face. "Yes!"

The last thing Ector wanted to do was leave her here alone, but he didn't have a choice. Even if he managed to piece together enough of the long roots and vines to reach her, he didn't trust them to hold her securely, and she'd already been fortunate not to have been injured during the fall. He couldn't risk her falling again.

"Will you be all right while I get it, Kathryn?" This time, he was unable to keep his voice steady; it was rough, raw, and strained.

"I'll be fine. And I don't plan on going anywhere until you get back."

Ector admired her effort to keep her tone light; it was a display of that inner strength he'd come to admire so much.

"I will return as swiftly as possible." He longed to say *I love you*, but it seemed too much like an admission that this could go wrong, that he would somehow fail. That was unacceptable.

"I know," Kathryn called.

He let his eyes linger on her for a second before he forced himself to turn away. He didn't allow the urgency blazing through his veins to hasten his ascent of the slope that led back to the path; speed was his enemy in that endeavor. But once he'd hauled himself up and was back on that trail, he hurried along it, uncaring for how much noise he made in his passage. Branches and thorns tore at his flesh, but he was beyond pain.

Ector crashed through the jungle with only one thought in mind—*save Kathryn*.

By the time he reached the boat, his breath was ragged, and his lungs and throat were burning. But he did not allow himself to slow; he snatched up the coiled rope stowed beneath the bench, turned away, and raced back the way he'd come. His path through the jungle was easy to retrace—his passage had flattened enough vegetation for even Ector, inexperienced as he was at tracking on land, to follow it exactly.

By the time he was making his way down the little decline to the edge of the hole, the only sound he could hear was the thundering of his own hearts and the sawing of his breath. He anchored himself on the same tree as before and leaned forward, peering down into the water.

Kathryn was still in the same spot, sunlight brightening her silver hair. She looked up at him, and despite the distance, he saw the vulnerability and fear in her eyes before she could hide it.

"I am going to lower the rope," he called. He took one end of the rope and wrapped it around his hand securely before tossing the still-coiled bundle over the edge. Once it was uncoiled, he grasped it with is other hand as well.

She swam toward the dangling end of the rope and stopped directly beneath it. "It's too high, Ector. Two meters short, at least."

"*No*," he rasped. Tightening his tentacles around the tree trunk, he leaned his torso forward—past the edge. He found himself looking directly down at her, and Kathryn's eyes were wider than ever. He extended his arms, stretching every part of his body toward her, making his joints ache and his muscles burn. Forced to accept more and more of his weight, his tentacles screamed in protest.

"It's still too high," she said. Debris and bits of rock rained down around her as the ground crumbled beneath Ector's tentacles. "Ector, get back!"

Gritting his teeth, he strained farther out over the edge. It didn't matter if his other tentacles were losing purchase; he had his anchor, and the rope *had* to reach her.

But when the tree trunk he was holding creaked and produced a muted crack, Ector knew he was being a fool. The cords on his neck stood out as he flexed his abdominal muscles and lifted his torso away from the edge, shifting his center of gravity backward and gradually easing the strain on his tentacles—and the tree. He forced himself to breath slowly and evenly.

On top of the other aches and pains that he'd awoken in his body, his jaw throbbed from clenching his teeth so tightly.

Panic danced along the edges of his mind, threatening to

push him toward acting in desperation, toward doing something stupid. Kathryn was his *mate*. And he'd failed her. His tentacles writhed around him, his breathing quickened, and his hearts pounded in fear for her.

"Ector?"

Ector closed his eyes. "I am here, Kathryn."

And my presence is doing you no good.

"You can take down the rigging on the boat for more rope. If you tie it to this one, it should be more than enough to reach."

That flicker of hope rekindled in his chest, and a tiny smile tugged up the corners of his mouth. He'd faced the infinite dark of the sea and the terrifying creatures that dwelled within it for all his life, but he'd never allowed himself to be so overwhelmed by emotion, to be so gripped by fear, as he had here and now. It was only further proof of how immensely important Kathryn was to him—she really was *everything*.

And despite her apparent fear, she was still thinking clearly.

Ector opened his eyes and glanced down at her. "I will go and—"

A large, dark shape stirred beneath the surface of the water, moving from the shadowed portion of the hole to the sunny side. He glimpsed a long, powerful, pale body with three sets of fins jutting from along its length, its finer details blurred by the water.

His hearts seized again, and the ache it produced in his chest was almost crippling. For a second, his body felt impossibly weak, and his head spun; he seemed on the verge of pitching forward.

This is not done. She needs me now more than ever.

He willed strength through his veins, forced it into his muscles, clenching his fists and jaw with newfound resolve.

"Be as still as possible," he called. "There is something in the water with you."

Her face paled. There was a hesitance in the way she drew her eyes away from him to look down into the water around her.

Ector leaned forward to get a better view of the pool in its entirety, spreading his tentacles as he did so to anchor himself more solidly. One of his tentacles bumped something hard and loose. The greenery around him rustled as the object—a rock—rolled down the remaining slope. It clacked hard on the bare stone around the edge and bounced out into open air.

His eyes widened and his hearts thundered as he watched the stone fall. It landed with a heavy splash with a body's length of Kathryn.

The creature under the water darted toward the splash with frightening speed and angled itself up, breaching the surface with its blunt snout. It opened a huge, toothy, circular maw and snapped it shut as though to swallow whatever had made the splash. The fleeting instant during which its head was out of water was enough for Ector to see that the pale-skinned beast didn't seem to have any eyes.

Eyes rounded in fear, Kathryn swam backward, moving away from the creature as it sank back into the water and its form was again obscured.

"Don't move, Kathryn!" Ector shouted. There was no time to go back to the boat, no time to carefully tie together bits of rope. He needed another solution, and quickly.

Below, the creature neared the surface again, its pale back briefly rising above the water to brush aside a few floating branches and leaves before it dipped under again. Ector forced himself to reassess his surroundings; there had to be something, had to be some way.

The answer came as he raked his gaze around the crest of the hole. On the far side, almost directly across from him, the ground dipped significantly; it was at least a meter and half lower than where he was now. It was a small gain, but it was likely their only chance.

He'd just have to prevent himself from falling off the edge as he rushed through the tangled vegetation and across uneven, sloping ground—and he'd have to get there before his Kathryn was taken from him forever.

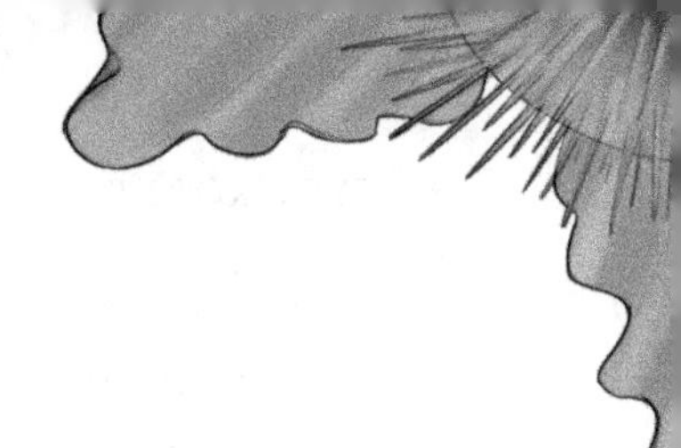

CHAPTER 14

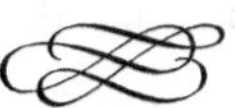

WITH HER STRAINED BREATHS BURNING HER LUNGS AND THROAT, Kathryn treaded water as gently as possible. Fear constricted her airway, tightened her muscles, and quickened her heart. The current shifted beneath her as the beast swam near, and she stilled her arms and legs. She sucked in a breath just before her head sank below the surface.

The muffled sound of moving water filled her ears, making everything seem suddenly closer and more immediate. She held as still as possible as she watched the creature swim by. It was larger than she'd thought upon that brief glimpse of it when it had broken the surface. It was pale, its flesh almost pure white where it was touched by sunlight, and had several sets of fins jutting from its long, serpentine body. The creature moved slow and steady, turning its blunt head from side to side as though searching blindly for prey.

She realized suddenly that something was missing from this huge, terrifying creature—it didn't have eyes.

When the creature was finally far enough away, Kathryn carefully kicked her legs and swung her arms. She resisted the urge to desperately gulp air as her head broke the surface, forcing herself to breathe slow and quiet despite the intensified burning in her chest. It took even more willpower to resist swimming to the rock face nearest her. But Ector had told her to stop moving, and she trusted him.

"Are you all right?" Ector asked tightly.

Kathryn looked up at him. His skin was yellow—a color she'd never seen on him before, but she knew in her heart what it meant. He was afraid.

She nodded, unable to force any words out of her constricted throat.

He nodded, too, and seemed to steel himself. He pointed to the other side of the hole, and his deep voice—calmer now than a moment before—echoed off the walls as he said, "We need to move to the far side."

Kathryn wished she could wrap herself in that voice, that it could shield her and make all this go away. She followed his gesture with her gaze. He was indicating a spot along the cliff that was lower than the rest, but it was a treacherous looking section of clifftop that was so overgrown with plants that it would be difficult even for him to find solid footing—or tentacle hold—if he was even able to get there to begin with.

It was too dangerous for him to risk it.

"Ector, I don't want you to fall! It's too—"

"Quiet!" The firmness and alarm in his voice made her snap her mouth shut.

But it was too late. The creature was heading straight for her, its body close enough to the surface to create a visible wake.

Something hit the water with a splash to the creature's left. It turned sharply, bending its long body, and darted to attack, thrashing and splashing before plunging under again. For a few seconds, Kathryn's chest was so tight that she couldn't draw breath.

She looked up at Ector. Even from this distance, she could see his shoulders and chest heaving with desperate, ragged breaths. The yellow of his skin seemed even more intense than a few seconds before.

"Do not speak," he said. "I will distract it as I go. When it attacks—and *only* then—you must move. Do you understand?"

She nodded. As hard as it was to remain calm and keep still, she had no choice if she wanted to make it out of this hole alive.

Ector hurriedly coiled the rope around his arm. As soon as he was done, he bent out of her sight, only to rise a moment later with a branch in hand. He threw it. She watched it fall, mentally bracing herself, until it hit the water's surface. The creature attacked almost immediately; she forced herself to move for a frantic instant.

She froze when the creature went under again. Despite the exertion her brief but desperate bit of movement had required, Kat's destination seemed impossibly far away, and she felt like she'd covered almost no distance.

Moving one centimeter at a time with a sea monster right next to me. What a vacation.

Leaves and branches rustled above. She pried her eyes away from the water to see Ector on the move, starting his trek around the ring. He paused to tear up more vegetation and throw it over the side.

She forced herself to wait a second after it hit the water before moving. The creature broke the surface, baring its inward-pointed teeth, and she swung her arms and kicked her legs to push herself a little closer to her goal.

Ector continued to toss objects into the water. The creature, despite getting mouthfuls of leaves and branches, attacked every time something hit the water. Kathryn crept a little closer to her destination every time the creature surfaced. Her whole body ached, and the frantic beating of her heart had become an all-encompassing throbbing. Soon, the water was in constant motion, churning and rolling just like waves on the ocean.

Her heart seized, filling with jagged shards of ice, when something big, slick, and smooth brushed against her leg. Kathryn squeezed her eyes shut. Her body trembled uncontrollably, finally submitting to the cold fear slithering through her veins.

There was a roar from above, followed by another splash and a surge of movement beneath her as the monster sped away.

"Not the sea nor this creature—not *anything*—will take you," Ector growled. "Only *me!*"

Kathryn opened her eyes and looked up, meeting Ector's gaze. His expression was fierce, hard, and resolute, and his skin had gone from yellow to crimson. Any fear he'd displayed before was gone, replaced by a determined rage the likes of which she'd never seen.

And she knew then that if there were some other way out of this hole, he'd have leapt into the water to fight this creature with his bare hands and tentacles.

The thought that had in some ways set this whole trip into motion struck her again in that moment—*I'm not dead yet.* And there was even *more* for her to live for now than before she'd left. She still had her friends, her daughters and sons-in-law, and her grandchildren back in The Watch. But she had Ector now, too. She had Ector here, fighting alongside her. Fighting for her. She refused to give up, refused to allow this situation to arrive at that last, terrible resort—Ector joining her in this hole to kill the creature.

Kat clenched her teeth. She wasn't going to let this creature have her; she was going to get out of this damned hole.

This time when Ector tossed debris into the water, Kathryn pushed herself onward, swimming as fast and as far as she could while the creature was distracted. She finally reached the spot he'd indicated; she couldn't have moved more than fifteen meters, but it felt like she'd traveled a thousand kilometers to get there. The bare stone loomed ahead of and over her, its mostly smooth surface rising from the water and curving very slightly inward toward its top, creating a lip from which leaves, roots, and branches dangled.

If the distance she'd had to cross to reach that spot had seemed insurmountable, this was something else entirely. For a moment, the top of the hole might as well have been on one of the moons for how impossibly high it looked now. But Kathryn seized hold of that thought and cast it out.

From her new position, she could no longer see Ector—but she could follow his progress based on the amount of noise he was making, the shaking of the plants around him, and the objects that he threw down every few seconds.

If he keeps at it like that, the debris will eventually get so high I'll just be able to climb out.

Despite everything—including the barely controlled terror still flowing through her veins—she couldn't help but smirk.

She swam to the rock face, seeking some sort of handhold by which to at least hold herself up, but there was nothing. The wall was as smooth below the water as it was above the surface.

The vegetation directly overhead thrashed and rustled, and loose leaves and twigs rained down into the water. Even through all the noise, it was Ector's grunts—desperate, tired, but determined sounds—that stood out more than anything.

The rope suddenly tumbled down to dangle ahead of her, just out of arm's reach. Its end was still almost a meter above the water's surface.

Kathryn swept her gaze across the pool, but the churning water and increased amount of debris on the surface made it difficult to spot anything—even a creature as large as the one stalking her. As much as the vegetation Ector tossed in had helped, it was suddenly a hindrance.

It won't matter in a few moments.

She gently pushed herself away from the wall and, keeping her movements as slow and minimal as possible, placed herself beneath the rope. Ector was leaning over the edge of the hole, the rope wrapped around one arm.

Kat reached up, stretching out one hand. Her fingertips brushed the end of the rope. It swayed, but it wasn't close enough.

There was no time to despair.

She took a deep breath, pressed her lips together, and let herself sink under the water. Her heart skipped a beat when she spotted the creature swimming only a few meters away, its motions erratic and jerky, as though it were being led in conflicting directions. If it was only responding to sound and movement—which she was almost certain of by now—she guessed it was being overly stimulated by the churning water and the debris floating atop it.

Tilting her head back to set her focus on the rope, which was blurred and barely visible through the rippling surface, Kathryn kicked her feet and swept her arms down, launching herself up into the open air. She thrust her hand up again. The rope brushed her palm, and she closed her fingers around it.

Gravity pulled her back down. For an instant, the rope went taut, and she felt the strain on her shoulder and elbow as the rope took her weight. Then the rope slipped out of her wet hand.

Her heart stopped for an instant as she dropped back into the water, plunging deeper than before. Her hair obscured her view; she swept it aside as she desperately attempted to orient herself. True terror pierced Kathryn's heart the instant her vision was clear.

The beast, with its big, tooth-ringed mouth opened wide, was speeding directly toward her.

Kathryn refused to let fear freeze her in place. She called

upon all her strength to swim out of its path, swinging her arms and legs desperately. The creature's mouth passed within a few centimeters of her back. But she didn't have any such clearance from its fins, which struck her hard, powered by the creature's size and momentum.

She spun around, and her world became a chaotic blur of bubbles and roiling water. Effectively blind in those moments, she kicked her legs, forcing herself toward what she hoped was the surface.

When her head broke into open air, she threw it back and sucked in a burning breath.

"Kathryn!" Ector desperately called out. "The rope!"

Kat turned and nearly cried out in relief when she spotted the rope nearby—half a meter of which was now floating on the surface of the water. Behind her, the creature thrashed, sending out waves that threatened to push her away from her lifeline, from her salvation. She gritted her teeth and swam harder than ever to cover that last bit of distance.

She stretched out an arm to grasp the free-floating rope and quickly wrapped it around her wrist, pulling herself to it. "Now," she shouted as she latched onto it with her other hand.

The force suddenly exerted on that line was immense. The rope bit into her wrist and threatened to pull her shoulder and elbow out of their sockets, but she would not let go. Her torso emerged from the water. Another yank tugged her legs out to the knees.

The creature whipped its snake like body toward her and lunged again, lifting its toothy maw partway out of the water.

Ector roared.

Just before the creature could strike, Kathryn was pulled out of the water completely. Her boots brushed the monster's back. She clutched the rope and, limbs trembling, lifted her legs away from the thing. The creature dipped under the surface again, becoming a pale, blurred shape in the deep blue.

Another tug on the rope lifted her another meter over the water. Kathryn released a rough, ragged breath, relaxed her legs, and finally looked up. Her eyes widened all over again.

Ector wasn't just *leaned* over the edge—almost his entire body was beyond it, his torso angled down toward her. The end of the rope was wrapped around his right arm, and he was using both it and his left hand to haul her up a little at a time. His muscles were strained, defined harshly by his exertion, and she could see the bulging veins under his skin even from this distance. At least four of his tentacles were on the rock face below him; she imagined his suction cups had taken whatever desperate purchase they could on the bare stone.

She felt twice as heavy as normal, especially given her wet clothing, but Ector barely swayed as he pulled her up. She knew in the logical part of her mind that she should still be terrified; his position looked so dangerous, so precarious, that he could've fallen at any moment. But her relief was too immense, and it was difficult to focus on any logical thoughts while her skin was impossibly hot, and her heart was racing.

As soon as she was within reach, Ector wrapped an arm around her and drew her against his hard chest. As hot as Kat was, the heat radiating from Ector was far greater—but it was welcoming, soothing, comforting. His crushing embrace was the best thing she'd ever felt. Closing her eyes, she threw her arms around his neck, wrapped her legs around his waist, and held on tight despite the aches and pains in her limbs.

Ector buried his face against her hair and rasped, "Kathryn."

For a few moments, they just held each other, and everything else was forgotten. It wasn't until he began to slowly raise his torso that she opened her eyes and allowed herself to recall their current position.

Ector's body was well beyond the edge of the hole, anchored by those tentacles on the cliff face—and his other four tentacles, which were spread wide behind them, each tangled in huge clusters of vines and vegetation that were all pulled taut.

Somehow, she found it in her to tighten her hold on him. The vegetation he was using to keep himself in place shook as he continued his smooth but slow movement. Kathryn did the only thing she could do to help—she bent all her willpower toward the plants, silently begging them to hold, to remain strong.

Though it felt as though an eternity had passed, Ector was upright and easing back from the edge within seconds, maintaining his solid embrace on her.

They said nothing as he carried her back to camp. Ector refused to relinquish his hold on her, and Kathryn was fine with that. She needed his solidness, his closeness. She needed *him*. His hearts pounded, his body shivered around her, and his grip only seemed to tighten as he moved.

It wasn't until they were in the center of their camp—which they'd not even set up yet—that everything crashed down upon Kathryn. They were alive. *She* was alive. The relief was so powerful it brought tears to her eyes. They spilled down her cheeks and onto Ector's skin. She released one shuddering breath after another, her shoulders shaking with her cries.

Ector slid one hand up along her spine and buried it in her hair, cradling the back of her head. His entire body was wracked by shivers.

Kat lifted her head and drew her arms back to cup his jaw. Expression strained, he searched her face as though memorizing every minute detail. Within those golden eyes, she saw all the same fear, relief, love, and need that was brimming within her.

"Ector," she whispered, brushing her thumbs over his cheeks.

He pulled her head down and slammed his mouth against hers. She opened to him without hesitation. His kiss was wild, feral, and unguarded, empowered by the depth of the emotions roiling within him. He consumed her with his lips and tongue.

She clung to him as lust sparked swift and urgent at her core, amplifying her need nearly to the point of pain. His demanding lips bruised her mouth, but she eagerly returned the kiss. His cock, hard and insistent, extruded to press against her belly.

He crushed her to him with possessive hands, as though afraid she might disappear. The tips of his claws pricked her flesh, but Kathryn didn't care. She was *alive*.

Ector broke the kiss and touched his forehead to hers. Their ragged breaths mingled. His taut body continued shivering.

"I need you," he said hoarsely.

"Yes." Kathryn feathered her lips over his mouth, nose, and cheeks before returning to his mouth. "You have me. Always."

Her answer was all Ector needed to release that last bit of control he'd somehow maintained; he let it snap without a second thought, allowing his hunger, his need, to consume him. And Kathryn's clothing was the final barrier keeping him from taking her.

He laid her down on the grassy ground, propped himself up with his tentacles to either side, and tore at her clothing, shredding the fabric with his claws. He was desperate to feel her skin, to feel her heat, her vitality.

As soon as her delectable body was bare, he shoved her thighs wide. His eyes fell to the dewy, pink petals of her slit. The sight made his cock throb and ache, and the tendrils at its base, as desperate and needful as Ector himself, reached toward her. He leaned his body over hers and braced himself on trembling arms. With a growl, he thrust his hips forward, burying himself in her heat.

Kathryn tilted her head back as she released a choked cry.

She dragged her fingers over Ector's shoulders and down his back, raking her blunt nails across his skin, and tugged him closer even as her sex hungrily clenched around his shaft. A ripple of pleasure ran along his spine. Her heat enveloped him, and her scent flooded his senses.

He coiled his tentacles around her calves and guided her legs up, cinching them around his waist and pulling her tighter against him. He needed to feel all of her, his lover, his mate, his wife, his Kathryn. His *everything*.

And I nearly lost her.

The same dread that had suffused him at the hole threatened to overcome him again in that moment, as though it were dissatisfied with being a memory. It knew the truth as well as he —one crisis had been narrowly averted, but there was always more danger looming in the murky waters of the future. Either Kathryn or Ector could meet their end at any moment.

But we are still here, and she will always *be mine.*

He growled again, forcing back that heavy, nauseating sensation that had been paired with his terror. Because what was here in his arms, against his skin—what he felt in his hearts— was stronger than anything that might have happened or might yet happen. Kathryn was real, and she was his here and now.

A shudder rippled through Ector as he drew his pelvis back and slammed forward, pushing himself deeper into Kathryn's loving heat. He tasted her through his suction cups and tendrils and longed to have her flavor on his tongue again.

Spreading his back tentacles wide to create a solid base for himself, Ector gathered Kathryn in his arms, drew her flush against his chest, and lifted his torso upright without breaking the connection between their bodies. Her thighs flexed around his hips, and her nails dug wickedly into his skin. He bent his middle slightly, leaned his torso back, and pivoted his hips forward, entering a position that allowed Kathryn to lean over him with her head level with his.

Her cheeks were flushed, and her breath ragged as she met his gaze. For a moment, they stared at one another, her eyes gleaming with as much lust as burned inside Ector. He moved a hand to the back of her head and pulled her face down into a kiss, again claiming her mouth as his.

He dropped his hands, spanning them around her hips, and ground her against him. A moan tore from her throat, and he swallowed the sound, deepening the kiss as he lifted her and pulled her back down upon him. He set a frantic, ruthless pace. Kathryn clutched his shoulders and matched that pace with every movement of her legs and hips.

Pleasure built in him rapidly, radiating outward from his core to chase away the lingering shakiness and fear that had so tightly gripped him earlier. That pleasure was just as desperate as the emotions it replaced, but it was even more powerful, and Ector *wanted* it to consume him.

Kathryn broke the kiss, flattened her hands on his chest, and pushed herself up. Her drying hair bounced around her naked shoulders as she moved upon Ector. Soft gasps escaped her parted lips with every driving thrust. Her delicate brows angled down, and her eyes met his, their blue as endless as the sea.

Ector slid two tentacles around her chest, positioning them to take her nipples into his suction cups, which pulsated around the hard nubs as he circled her breasts. Kathryn moaned and curled her fingers against his chest. She dominated all his senses; her feel, taste, sound, scent, and appearance were his entire world, all delightfully, maddening sweet and sensual, pushing his pleasure to impossible heights.

He was on the verge of an explosion, of being torn asunder by everything she made him feel. He wanted nothing more than to throw himself over that edge.

Baring his teeth, he dropped his hands to her backside, squeezing the yielding flesh, and slammed her down faster, harder. Her rhythm staggered, and her inner walls fluttered with her oncoming release. Lifting her again, he brought her down savagely, and her sex constricted around his cock. One of his tendrils found her clit and latched on. She gasped and cried out his name as she spasmed and doubled over, leaning against him, her body winding tighter and tighter as sweet nectar flowed from her.

Clutching her backside, Ector ground himself against her, pushing as deep as he could go. The pressure within him finally burst. He clenched his teeth and snarled as his seed poured into her. She writhed atop him, and he curled his tentacles around her body, holding her captive, unwilling to relinquish her as thrumming, overwhelming ecstasy coursed through him.

Ector cupped his hand around the back of her head and turned her face toward him. He captured her lips with his, swallowing her cries of pleasure and mixing them with his own groans.

Even when the maelstrom of their passion had ebbed and their kiss had become a gentle, caressing exploration of lips and tongues, his tendrils continued stroking her sex—and Kathryn shivered in response.

Pleasure pulsed from the points at which their bodies were connected, and Ector refused to break that contact. He eased down onto the ground, turning to lay on his back, and let her weight settle atop him as he closed his eyes. The grass was soft, and the fragrance of their mating was fresh and alluring. His hands and tentacles roamed her body—along her spine, over the curve of her backside, up and down her arms and legs. Before long, it was impossible for him to know where he ended and Kathryn began. They were one.

The breeze swept over their bodies, caressing them with pleasantly warm air, and the sounds of the sea and the nearby waterfalls were constant and soothing, but none of it meant anything without Kathryn. She was the reason Ector felt so full, so fulfilled. So loved. He'd seen several relationships like this form over the last few years, had known there was something special involved, something precious. Something the kraken had never really been able to have. He'd recognized that even from the outside.

But now he understood it fully. This connection, this emotion, this *love*. What he couldn't fully understand was how he'd lived so long without even a taste of it—how he'd lived so long without his Kathryn.

EPILOGUE

366 Years After Landing

"THEY FOLLOWED THE SUNRISE," Ector said, changing his skin to a lovely shade of golden orange as he gestured vaguely inland, "until they finally reached the shore. With wonder and a little fear, she moved onto the beach with Luke. It was the first time Hera had ever seen the land, the first time she had felt the sand beneath her. All the plants and trees were alien to her, all the animals, all the sounds and smells. The air was different than any she'd breathed. But she had Luke with her; she had been brave in helping him escape the Facility, and now she drew strength from him, her mate. She placed her fear aside, and together they went off to make a new home for themselves. They knew survival would not be easy, but their love would make it possible."

As he said that last part—the bit about love—Ector's gaze met Kathryn's. The warmth in her chest, which was stronger than ever now, a year after their unforgettable trip, intensified. All it took was the simplest of looks from him to make her heart flutter and her cheeks heat. Though he was telling a story about two people who'd lived a long, long time ago, the truth of his thoughts was clear in his golden eyes—when he spoke of love, he was thinking only of Kathryn.

"What happened next, Grandpa?" asked Megan, who was sitting on Kathryn's lap. The little girl—Kathryn's youngest grandchild at six years old—had insisted that Grandma Kat come listen to Ector's story.

Kathryn hadn't needed any convincing; she'd come to love these times when Ector regaled the town's children, human and kraken alike, with tales made larger than life. There was a crowd gathered around Ector now, sitting in the sand—children and some parents, too.

Ector smiled and sank down in front of Megan and Kathryn, shifting his attention to the little girl he'd come to call his granddaughter. "They *lived*, little one. Just like your grandmother says sometimes—happily ever after."

"Like you and Grandma?"

That bright gleam was in his eyes as he looked to Kathryn again. "Yes. Like me and Grandma."

"Tell us another story," one of the nearby children said.

"The one about the lady who fell from the sky," shouted another.

"I want to hear about the monster in the hole," declared a third.

The children broke into chatter as they argued for their favorite stories—nearly all of which were based on very real events that had occurred right here on Halora.

Kathryn grinned at Ector, who chuckled and shook his head helplessly. Were there time to do so, she knew he'd spend hours more telling the children all manner of exciting tales; when he ran out of stories about Halora, he'd just turn to telling the old myths he'd been studying, with Kathryn's help, in The Watch's remaining computer systems.

"No more stories," said Kronus firmly, setting his little daughter, Phoebe, on the sand as he rose. She shifted closer and clung to her father, curling a tentacle around one of his. He frowned down at her; the expression was so tender, so gentle, that it melted Kathryn's heart. He quickly bent down to scoop Phoebe into his arms. "It is time for the race."

An almost deafening chorus of cheers rose from the children as they scrambled onto feet and tentacles to hurry away, Ector and his stories forgotten for now. Kronus, still carrying little Phoebe, herded them toward the race's start point farther down the beach while the adults who'd been listening to the stories straggled behind the children. Even Megan leapt out of Kathryn's lap to follow the others—though she skidded to a halt after a few steps and rushed back to give Ector and Kathryn quick, tight hugs.

Megan beckoned them. "Grandma, Grandpa, come watch!"

Kat pushed herself to her feet and brushed the sand from her backside and legs. "Go ahead. We'll be there soon."

"Okay!" Megan darted off, kicking up sand as she ran to catch up with the others.

Ector rose to his full height beside Kathryn, and she stepped closer, slipping her arms around him. He embraced her in return. She rested her chin on his chest, meeting his gaze as he tilted his head down to look at her.

"You are not allowed to leave the festival early this year, Kathryn," he said with a smirk.

Kat grinned. "Oh? But I thought I'd slip away after the relay race...and this time, I thought I might take you with me."

He hummed thoughtfully, the sound making his chest rumble. "Well, I suppose I can allow it...so long as you do bring me along."

They moved toward the race, his arm around her shoulders and one of hers around his middle, taking their time to cross the soft, warm sand. The crowd ahead was the biggest she'd ever seen. So many people had come to the Dryfall Festival last year, but there were even more now. Some of the humans who'd been reluctant to mingle so freely with kraken had taken a chance, and a number of kraken who still lived at the Facility had made the trip to join the celebration.

Knowing all she did now, this festival meant so much more than it ever could have. She was glad that Luke and Hera had forged a happy life for themselves despite everything even as Kat wished they could've had the opportunity to live in the world as it was now—that they'd been able to love openly without giving up everything either of them had ever known. Perhaps they never could have imagined things being this way— humans and kraken together in peace and friendship—but they'd been the first to achieve it. They'd been the first to prove it could be real.

Kathryn looked up at Ector and smiled. "Of all the stories I've heard you tell, I think that one is my favorite."

He glanced at her and returned the smile. "Is it?"

"It is. I really enjoy when you tell stories about love, because that love shines so bright in your eyes. And that one... Well, it's about love being possible no matter the situation, isn't it? That it's never too late. That means a lot to me."

Ector nodded. "It means a lot to me, as well, but...it is not my favorite story."

"Which is your favorite?"

He came to a stop and turned her to face him, lifting one hand to cradle her cheek within his big palm. He brushed the pad of his thumb over her cheekbone and stared into her eyes. As always, Ector looked at her like she was the most wondrous, most precious treasure in all the world. "Ours."

Before she could reply, his mouth captured hers in a kiss that conveyed his love more powerfully than words ever could.

The Delver

The Hunter

THE CURSED ONES

His Darkest Craving

His Darkest Desire

ALIENS AMONG US

Taken by the Alien Next Door

Stalked by the Alien Assassin

Claimed by the Alien Bodyguard

Saved by the Alien Crime Boss

STANDALONE TITLES

Claimed by an Alien Warrior

Dustwalker

Escaping Wonderland

Yearning For Her

The Warlock's Kiss

Ice Bound: Short Story

ISLE OF THE FORGOTTEN

Make Me Burn

Make Me Hunger

Make Me Whole

Make Me Yours

VALOS OF SONHADRA COLLABORATION

Tiffany Roberts - Undying

Tiffany Roberts - Unleashed

VENYS NEEDS MEN COLLABORATION

Tiffany Roberts - To Tame a Dragon

Tiffany Roberts – To Love a Dragon

ABOUT THE AUTHOR

Tiffany Roberts is the pseudonym for Tiffany and Robert Freund, a husband and wife writing duo. The two have always shared a passion for reading and writing, and it was their dream to combine their mighty powers to create the sorts of books they want to read. They write character driven sci-fi and fantasy romance, creating happily-ever-afters for the alien and unknown.

Sign up for our Newsletter!
Check out our social media sites and more!
http://www.authortiffanyroberts.com

www.ingramcontent.com/pod-product-compliance
Lightning Source LLC
Chambersburg PA
CBHW071426200726
48294CB00002B/536

* 9 7 8 1 9 6 1 3 7 6 0 7 6 *